Ron Ellis was studying at Liverpool Polytechnic when he became involved in the Merseybeat phenomenon. He imported records from America for The Beatles, ran an entertainment agency and finally took to the stage himself as a DJ, eventually becoming Promotions Manager for Warner Bros Records. In 1979, he made the New Wave charts with a self-penned song, 'Boys on the Dole', an ironic title when the *Sun* acclaimed him as the man with the most jobs in Britain in 1992. The eleven jobs included that of librarian, lecturer, salesman, landlord, DJ, actor (he frequently appears in *Coronation Street* and *Brookside*), broadcaster, photographer, journalist – and author!

Ron still lives on Merseyside with his wife and two teenage daughters. He broadcasts regularly on local radio and reports on Southport FC matches for the press. He also owns a property company in London's Docklands near the Millennium Dome.

'Ellis's speciality is a gritty rendering of Merseyside crime. Here we have the most exuberant outing yet for his wisecracking protagonist, the radio DJ Johnny Ace, whose knowledge of rhythm'n'blues is matched only by his sleuthing skills on Liverpool's mean streets'

The Times

Also by Ron Ellis, featuring Johnny Ace,
and available from Headline:

Ears of the City
Mean Streets

Framed

A Johnny Ace Mystery

Ron Ellis

HEADLINE

First published in 1999
by HEADLINE BOOK PUBLISHING

First published in paperback in 2000
by HEADLINE BOOK PUBLISHING

10 9 8 7 6 5 4 3 2 1

ISBN 0 7472 6220 9

Printed and bound in Great Britain by
Clays Ltd, St Ives plc

HEADLINE BOOK PUBLISHING
A division of the Hodder Headline Group
338 Euston Road
London NW1 3BH

www.headline.co.uk
www.hodderheadline.com

To Andi, for all your help and support, Lucy, for the brilliant publicity, and Joan who has eagle-eyes!

Prologue

The body of the woman sometimes known as Michelle Lunt was found on a Thursday evening in July, hanging from a light fitting in a flat off Liverpool's Sefton Park. It gave a hideous new meaning to the phrase 'swinging from the chandeliers'.

I had every reason to be concerned about the event because the flat in question happened to be mine.

At the time the news reached me, I was sitting in a marquee in Sefton Park.

So far, it had been a lousy summer. All the world seemed to be enjoying sunshine and heatwaves whilst we'd been battered by gales and non-stop rain, with temperatures more suited to March. On the other hand, we hadn't had droughts, forest fires or tornadoes so I suppose there were compensations.

Apart from the weather, it had been a good year for Liverpool. The dock strike and the rail strike were both long over. The new four-star Swallow Hotel was almost completed in Williamson Square, the Crown Plaza was going up at the Pier Head, Ford were building their exciting 'baby Jag' at Halewood and several million pounds of lottery money had gone to improve the city's museums.

Even Everton's fortunes looked to be on the upturn, with ex-Rangers supremo Walter Smith taking over as manager to the approval of most fans, although some of us remembered the wretched track records of the last five incumbents of the position and were keeping the champagne corked for the time being.

I was in the park for one of the Summer Pops Concerts put on by the Royal Liverpool Philharmonic Orchestra. Tonight's had been a Spanish event featuring guitarists, flamenco dancers and Ravel's *Bolero* with Carl Davis conducting as usual.

Afterwards, I joined a few showbiz liggers in the adjoining tent, where we were entertained by a local gospel group from Toxteth – which I enjoyed more than the flamenco.

We put a few drinks away and talked about rock'n'roll, ending up in an argument about which had been the definitive record of the Flower Power era. Spencer Leigh said it had to be Scott McKenzie's *San Francisco*, Billy Butler plumped for *Reach Out in the Darkness* by Friends and Lovers whilst I put my money on The Mamas and the Papas' *Creeque Alley*.

Eventually the conversation moved on to weightier topics, like the need for a new tram service in Liverpool and a motorway that didn't stop three miles short of the city centre.

Truth to tell, I was at a bit of a loose end. Hilary, my girlfriend, was away on holiday. Hilary and I have an understanding. We're what I call loving best friends. Neither of us wants to be tied down and we reserve the right to see other people, but we've lasted over twenty years together which must say something.

For the past few months, I'd also been seeing a librarian called Maria. Maria is divorced with a son at university, and there is nothing she would like better than to settle down again – but that, as I've made perfectly clear, is not on my schedule.

Oddly enough, it was Maria who had helped me with the detective work I'd done recently, and I'd grown fond of her company – but not enough to exclude all others, and certainly not Hilary.

On the other hand, I didn't know how I'd react if

Maria found her Mr Right; it wasn't something I liked to think about.

Maria, too, was away – at some book convention at Hay-on-Wye, which was another reason why I was kicking my heels.

I was thinking about moving on to the Masquerade Club for a last couple of drinks when my pager started bleeping.

I'd only recently bought the pager. There'd been a lot of talk in the medical journals about radioactive rays from mobile phones but, before that, I'd already decided it was a bad idea to be forced into private conversations that could be overheard, or to have to make important on-the-spot decisions at moments when I couldn't give the matter my full attention.

Now, people can still get in touch with me but I call them back in my own time, which puts me in control.

Also, you don't get brain cancer from a pager.

The message on the screen read: *Ring Badger – Urgent* and it gave a Lark Lane number.

I excused myself from the others, who were still arguing, and walked to a call box down the road. My caller Badger – otherwise known as Neville Mountbatten – was a tenant in my house in Livingstone Drive.

Over the years since I stopped being a Merseybeat drummer with The Cruzads, I've invested my money buying up old Victorian houses round Toxteth and Liverpool 17, the student area, and converting them to self-contained flats which I've then rented out.

It's sometimes a lot of hassle but it's a good living and gives me plenty of time to do my weekday 'Johnny Ace Radio Show', not to mention starting a new 'career' as a private eye.

I'd not had a case since the Bradley Hope affair in the spring of this year, but I'd been giving some thought to renting an office and setting up officially in the investigation business.

I reached the phone box and dialled Badger's number.

Something serious must have happened because Badger had never rung me at midnight like this before. I had wild visions of the roof being blown off and the house burning to the ground after a gas explosion.

It was much worse than that.

'Hey man, we need you down here pronto. We got big trouble. That lady in No. Three – you know, the fancy piece?' Badger sounded panicked.

'Mrs Lunt – what about her?'

'You'd better get down here quick.' His voice was bordering on hysteria. 'She's dead.'

'She's *what*?' I stared at the phone in shock.

'She's dead, man. Swinging from the flippin' ceiling.'

'Is this a wind-up?' I was angry. I don't like practical jokes.

'A wind-up? Christ, what do you take me for?' He was right. Badger was not given to frivolity.

'Have you phoned the police?'

'And the ambulance, but it's too late for them. She ain't breathing none.' I could almost see him shudder.

'OK, Badger. I'll come down. Give me ten minutes.'

Flat Three was on the ground floor; it was let to a couple called Lunt. They'd rented it for twelve months while Mr Lunt, Wilbur, was on secondment in the UK from some American bank.

He was in his late forties and, by all accounts, seemed to spend most of his life in the business section of executive jets, leaving his young trophy wife on her own at home.

I'd left my car keys and stuff in my holdall back in the tent so, by the time I'd gone back for them, made my excuses and picked up the RAV4, it was more like fifteen minutes, by which time the police and ambulance people were out in force in Livingstone Drive, together with half the neighbourhood.

I explained who I was to the Constable at the door and was ushered into the Lunts' flat, where a plainclothes officer was talking to Badger.

I didn't know the detective. I put him in his late thirties, one of the new breed of college policemen. Probably he had a degree in Social Sciences and was doing his bit for society. Either that or he'd been turned down on the Marks & Spencer management trainee scheme.

Since they invented all these new universities, graduates don't walk into jobs any more. There's far too many of them. These days, the girl selling you a Big Mac probably has a PhD in Classics.

'Excuse me, sir,' interrupted the PC, 'this gentleman's the landlord, Mr Johnny Ace. This is Detective Sergeant Leary,' he said to me.

Leary eschewed the handshake but Badger and I exchanged nods. All the time, everyone's eyes kept darting to the grotesque figure dangling from a rope attached to the light fitting in the middle of the ceiling.

'I knew I should have stuck with the paper lanterns,' I said.

'I beg your pardon?' Leary gave me a cold look.

'The chandeliers; they're strong and screwed into the joists. A paper lantern wouldn't have supported her weight.'

'Ah. I see what you mean.' Leary showed no sense of either irony or humour but Badger gave a sickly grin. Truth to tell, I felt a bit queasy myself.

'When did this happen? Who found her?' I asked.

'Their door was slightly open when I came in half an hour ago,' ventured Badger. 'I thought it seemed a bit dodgy, so I peered through to check it out and saw her hanging there. I ran straight upstairs to dial 999 and get hold of you.'

'I shall need some details from you, sir, concerning the identity of this lady,' said the Sergeant, asserting his position as investigator in charge, 'plus her next-of-kin and so forth. Mr Mountbatten here tells me she was the occupant of the flat.'

I took a longer look at my erstwhile tenant. Michelle was wearing a pair of Armani denim jeans, platform trainers and a print top. She'd been very attractive but now her tongue poked out of her distorted mouth and her face was purple and swollen.

'That's right. Her name was Michelle Lunt. She lived here with her husband but he travels a lot on business.'

'He's an international financier,' explained Badger.

'Is that right?'

'I think he's with Citibank,' I said. 'I can check his references for you in the morning.'

'Is he away at the moment?'

'I wouldn't know, but it's very likely.'

'I believe he is,' intercepted Badger. 'He drives a green Mercedes and I ain't seen it all week.'

'You wouldn't have any idea how we could get in touch with him then?'

'No, but you'll be able to trace him through his company, I would imagine.'

'Then, if you could get that information for me as soon as possible, sir. You can ring me on this number.' He handed me a card.

I looked at him closely for the first time. Leary had a pockmarked face and yellowing teeth. I wondered how his wife or girlfriend felt about kissing him without a mask on. 'First thing in the morning,' I promised. 'I take it that she did kill herself?'

'It appears to be suicide but we'll have to wait for the postmortem to confirm it.'

'Did she not leave a note?'

'If she did, we haven't found it yet.' He looked around the room. 'Does this furniture belong to them or is it yours?'

'Just the carpets and curtains are mine, the rest is theirs.'

'Mm. It looks quality stuff. None of your flatpack rubbish.'

I had to agree. The leather three-piece suite must have set them back a couple of grand, the TV was a large widescreen model and the mahogany dining table and chairs were from MultiYork rather than MFI. Even the ghetto-blaster boasted a recordable mini-disc player.

'Do all your tenants live like this?' Leary asked me.

'Not all of them.' Most of them were students for whom I provided budget or saleroom gear although, lately, more people wanted unfurnished flats.

Pat Lake and her mother, who lived in No. Five directly above this on the first floor, had brought most of the old lady's antiques with them when they moved in, whilst Badger's flat, No. Seven, above *them*, resembled a cross between Kew Gardens and an IKEA showroom.

Leary grunted, not completely satisfied. 'A lot to fork out when you're only renting.'

'I think the bank might have reimbursed him. After all, it's cheaper than putting him in the Adelphi.'

'I suppose so,' he conceded. 'Right, I shall want a list of all the people living in the house – those who are not here at the moment, that is. Some of the tenants are in Miss Lake's flat and I shall be interviewing each of them shortly.'

'I wonder why she did it? They were well-off, seemed happy together.'

'Did you see much of them then?'

'Well, no. I haven't spoken to them since they moved in but I didn't notice any tension between them when I let them the flat.'

'Mr Mountbatten here tells me Mr Lunt was a lot older than his wife.'

'Late forties, I would guess.' I looked across at the body. 'And Mrs Lunt was about twenty-nine. He was American, of course.'

'And she wasn't?'

I thought. 'No, I don't think she was. I only actually spoke to her on the one occasion but, as I remember, she had quite a posh English accent.'

'You don't know how long they'd been married?'

'Sorry, no.' Indeed, I didn't know whether they were married at all. Who was nowadays? But Leary had referred to her as Lunt's wife and I'd no reason to doubt him. The days were long gone when people had to pretend to be joined in holy matrimony in order to rent a room. 'Living over the brush' as my grandmother would have called it.

Leary seemed to have run out of questions. 'The forensic team will be here any minute. I'm afraid I shall have to seal off this room for the time being.'

I felt dismissed, like an errant schoolboy, when he suddenly wheeled round. 'By the way,' he snapped, 'I believe you've been known to fancy yourself as a bit of a private eye, Mr Ace. Well, as far as this case goes, although the matter has taken place on your property, I must remind you that it has nothing to do with you.'

I didn't like his tone but restrained myself from making any smart comment. 'Did I say it was?'

'I'm just warning you. *Stay out of it.* It's not your problem.'

I'd heard those words before and they were as inappropriate now as they had been on previous occasions. Like it or not, it was very much my problem.

Michelle Lunt's death was to set in motion a series of events that would cost me my freedom – and very nearly my life.

Chapter One

'Come upstairs,' said Badger. 'Everyone else is up there.'

Pat Lake opened the door to us. 'Almost a full house,' she said. 'Would you like a cup of tea or maybe something stronger?'

Pat looks like the archetypal spinster but she has a tattoo on her left arm and I've seen her bopping away to heavy metal music at the Masquerade so I reckon she has a secret agenda going on somewhere.

'Tea will be fine,' I told her. Badger elected for a brandy and Pat went off to the kitchen. I looked around the room. Miss Barrie from No. Four, the ground-floor flat, smiled across at me in her usual superior manner.

Serina Barrie was a student at Liverpool University – nineteen, blonde and sensationally pretty.

When she'd first approached me for accommodation, I'd had misgivings. Nothing specific, just a gut feeling that something wasn't quite right, but her rent had always been paid on time and, nearly two years down the line, there hadn't been any trouble. So far. I nodded back at her.

The new lady from one of the two basement flats was drinking tea in a corner, accompanied by her seven-year-old kid – an undernourished-looking brat who was bawling noisily. Every few minutes she cuffed him across the head and shouted, 'Be quiet, Ashley!' – an action which only made him cry louder.

'Shouldn't he be in bed at this time?' I asked.

'He's hyperactive,' she explained. 'It's to do with the

colouring in his orange juice.' Right. To me he just looked plain hungry; no wonder the poor little bleeder couldn't sleep.

The two male students who occupied the other basement flat knocked on the door to find out what was going on. Like many other students, they stayed on in their flats during the vacations, studying, partying or going out to work to earn their rent. These lads had been out for a drink at the Philharmonic pub. Badger explained to them about the death.

'It'll be the husband who's done it,' said one of them who was studying Law. 'It always is.'

'Actually,' I said, 'it seems it was suicide.'

'He probably drove her to it then.'

'Don't you believe it, it'll be murder all right,' persisted his friend, 'disguised as suicide. We might all be in danger. I think we should have mortice locks fitted on our doors. One of us could be next.'

That's the worst of being a landlord. You can't spend five minutes chatting sociably to the tenants without they either ask for, or complain about something.

'Their front door wasn't damaged,' pointed out Badger, 'just open. I don't think it was a break-in.'

'Perhaps she was on the game,' suggested the youngest boy, who was doing a music course at LIPA, Paul McCartney's institution. 'And they were acting out some sexual scenario that went wrong, like that MP with the orange up his arse.'

'I think you'll find it was in his mouth,' I pointed out 'otherwise a grape would have been more likely. Anyway, Mrs Lunt was hardly on the game. They were loaded.'

'She could have done it for fun. You know the sort of thing: "Bored housewife with 40 DD bust seeks lively playmate for mutual pleasure and games".' He giggled insensitively as he said it and I could see they'd both been at the lager.

Serina Barrie's mouth curled in disgust and she moved to the other side of the room. She wore a black Morgan top, which exposed her midriff with its jewelled belly button, and a leather mini-skirt. I felt that rich businessmen would have been more her scene than students her own age.

The other lad bawled, 'She was on her own, you prat. That's why they call it *auto*-eroticism.'

Pat Lake saved further argument by appearing with the drinks. She handed me a steaming mug. 'No sugar and a tiny bit of milk, is that it?'

'You've got it.' I took a sip. It was hot and strong, the way I like it.

She smiled. '"Colour of an African woman", you used to say.'

'I can see you've had tea here before, man,' observed Badger, gracefully accepting a large glass of Pat's best cognac.

'Isn't it terrible about Mrs Lunt,' said Pat soberly. 'She seemed such a nice girl, too. I mean, I only ever saw her to say hello to at the front door, but she always had a smile. I thought she looked rather lonely, stuck in that flat on her own every day – he was never there.'

'I saw her on my landing once,' said Badger, surprisingly.

'On the top floor? What was she doing up there?'

'Perhaps she'd been to see Mr Lloyd.' A mature student in his early thirties, Mr Lloyd had lived in the second-floor flat opposite Badger's for nearly a year now. He told me he was at John Moores University but nobody had seen him in the company of other students. 'He's a weirdo and no mistake,' Badger snorted. 'Never speaks to anyone and there's been a few strange characters visiting.'

This was a bit rich coming from Badger, whose own activities would, I felt, if ever revealed, warrant a special edition of the *News of the World*.

'He's hardly Mrs Lunt's type,' Pat objected. 'He always

looks so unkempt. Mind you, I never trust anyone with a goatee beard. Perhaps she was up there just wanting to borrow some sugar.'

'Is he in tonight?' I asked, but nobody knew. Lloyd, it seemed, kept a low profile in the house. One of the students said he'd never seen him in the twelve months since he moved in.

I looked out of the window. Downstairs, the forensic team had arrived, accompanied by photographers, and despite the late hour, a policewoman was restraining a growing crowd of onlookers as the entrance to the house was cordoned off. I noticed members of the press amongst them and wondered how long it would be before the TV cameras arrived.

I could see the house being featured on a City Ghost Walk by the end of the year and idly wondered about possible ticket sales.

I thought about what I knew of the Lunt couple. They'd answered my advert in the *Echo* back in April. Mr Lunt had turned up on his own to view the flat. He told me he expected to be in England for six months but, if it stretched any further, he would be able to inform me well before the final day.

I said he could stay on as long as he liked, on a month-to-month basis, after the initial six-month period.

He then brought his wife to see it the following day. She was a lot younger and I wondered if it was the second time around for him. Michelle could have given him a good fifteen years. She looked around and announced that she loved the flat.

'That's it then,' he said. 'The lady likes it so if it's OK with you, we'll take it.' He seemed besotted with her.

The references checked out and they moved in within the week. Since then, I'd heard nothing from them and never seen them. The rent had been paid on time by bank standing order. They were the ideal tenants. Until now.

Pat glanced round the room. 'Everyone's here except for The Spice Girls.'

This was the name she gave to Maggie and Chauve, two art students who rented No. Six adjoining hers and who led wild social lives which seemed to centre around Cream, the city's world-famous disco.

'It's not one o'clock yet. They won't be in for another three hours.'

I finished my tea and decided to leave before Leary came up to start his interviews, but I stopped off at the Lunts' flat to have a word with him on the way out.

Michelle Lunt's body had now been laid out on the floor and a man I took to be the police doctor was leaning over it. Other forensic experts were busying themselves round the room, measuring up, taking photos, making sketches and dusting surfaces.

'There's two flats on each floor,' I explained to Leary, 'and all the tenants are upstairs except for a Mr Lloyd at the top and the two girls on the first floor.' I gave him Maggie and Chauve's names.

'These girls been out all evening, have they?'

'I don't know. I wasn't here, was I? You'll have to ask them when they get back.'

'Don't worry, I will. What about Lloyd?'

'No idea. You could try knocking on his door but I would have thought all the noise would have brought him out before now.'

Leary grunted. 'Don't forget to let me have Mr Lunt's company details in the morning.'

I assured him I would.

I drove back to the flat feeling puzzled. I could see no motive for Michelle Lunt killing herself, but if it wasn't suicide, who could have killed her? And why?

Chapter Two

First thing next morning I drove down to my office in Aigburth Road.

'Couldn't you sleep?' Geoffrey greeted me. Geoffrey is my office manager-cum-troubleshooter-cum-repairman. He's a Corgi-registered plumber, a qualified electrician and he's also been known to act as my minder on occasions.

I told him about Michelle Lunt.

'So you've got a new case to investigate, then?'

'Oh no, nothing like that,' I assured him. 'This is strictly a police job. Nothing to do with me other than she lived in one of my flats.'

'Mm.' Geoffrey didn't sound convinced. 'So what do they want from you?'

'Simply to know where the husband works.' I pulled open the appropriate drawer of the filing cabinet and took out his papers. 'And here we are. I was right – it *was* Citibank.' I noted down the phone number and address of his office and the name of the person whom he'd given as a reference. 'That should do it.'

I rang Detective Sergeant Leary and passed on the information. 'Did you find a suicide note?' I asked him.

He seemed reluctant to share any information, but: 'We did, as a matter of fact,' he admitted, although he was not prepared to reveal its message.

'So she definitely killed herself?'

'Shall we say we're not looking for anyone else in connection with the death.' He'd learnt the college police-speak well. 'The postmortem has confirmed strangulation as cause of death.'

'How long had she been dead?'

'Some time in the afternoon,' he replied shortly.

'A shock for the husband when he finds out,' I offered.

'Indeed. Anyway, I'm sure that when we've appraised him of the situation, Mr Lunt will contact you to discuss his tenancy and make the necessary arrangements to collect his wife's effects. In the meantime, the room must remain sealed.'

'Does this mean we've got another flat to let?' asked Geoffrey after I'd replaced the phone.

'Not yet,' I replied. 'For all we know, Wilbur Lunt might want to stay on. Anyway, the standing order's gone through, so he's paid up to the end of the month.'

The police did not take long to trace the missing husband because I heard from him the very next day. He rang me from Vienna where he was about to catch a flight into Manchester.

I told him I was sorry about his wife and he said the news had still not sunk in. He'd arranged to see the officer in charge, whom I assumed was Leary, the following day and he would ring me to sort everything out regarding the flat.

We finally got together on the Monday. I met him at Livingstone Drive late afternoon. By this time, the room had been unsealed and we went into the lounge where his wife had ended her life.

Wilbur Lunt didn't have the look of a man consumed with grief. His skin had a grey tinge and he looked tired, but that could have been down to the travelling. Otherwise, he gave the impression of being in full control of his emotions. Maybe that's what it takes to be a successful businessman.

'I can't understand it,' he said. 'She had everything to live for.' He seemed almost angry, as if the suicide was a reflection on him. As well it might have been.

'How long had you been together?' I asked him.

He sat down on one of the armchairs and took out a packet of Marlboro Lights. 'About a year.' He lit the cigarette with a silver Zippo lighter bearing an engraving of Marilyn Monroe. Very American. He proffered the open packet but I shook my head. 'We met last August when I was in London at a bankers' convention. Michelle was working for a PR firm and staying at the same place – the Grosvenor House Hotel.'

'Love at first sight, eh?' I said gently.

He half-grinned. 'Something like that. I asked her to dinner one night and we sort of took it from there.'

They had taken it at a pretty fast rate. Within a month, she'd been over to meet his folks in Connecticut and they were married eight weeks later in New York.

For a few months, they rented an apartment in Manhattan then Wilbur was posted to Europe on a six-month assignment. I was curious as to why they'd chosen Liverpool as a base.

'Partly because Michelle's family live in the North of England and the airport's down the road. Also, I've always had a fascination with the city since I was a kid. The Beatles and all that.'

Michelle's family had never been mentioned before. I wondered if DS Leary knew about them.

'Where do her family live?'

'A place called Colne in Lancashire. Do you know it? I've never been there myself. In fact, I must confess I haven't met Michelle's folks. Since I came to England, I've been travelling round the Continent a fair bit.'

'I take it they know about her death?'

'God, yes. Her mother came to Liverpool yesterday, I believe.'

'You believe?'

'I didn't actually see her myself, but Officer Leary said she was due to visit the funeral parlour, what do you people call it, the chapel of something?'

'Of Rest.' I studied the man. Something didn't add up. His wife kills herself, he flies all the way home from Vienna and he doesn't even speak with the mother-in-law he's never met. 'So when do you expect to see her?'

'I don't. I'm flying back to New York tomorrow.' He gestured at the two large suitcases that stood neatly by the door.

'You're going back to America?' I was astonished. 'What about the flat?'

'Oh, of course, you'll be wanting the keys, won't you?'

'You mean, you're not keeping it on? But what about your work over here?'

'It's been terminated: I've been recalled to the States. Michelle's family is taking care of all her things and they'll be handling the funeral arrangements. I've left word that her mother can have all the furniture. She will doubtless be in touch with you to arrange a time to collect it.'

I must have looked uncertain at this last statement because he went on to assure me it was all paid for. 'Citibank look after their employees.'

I started to remind him that the tenancy agreement was for six months but he forestalled me. 'Obviously I've cancelled the standing order for the rent, but here's a cheque for the remaining two and a half months of the contract, which I think makes us straight.'

There wasn't a lot more to say. Ordinarily, I'd have offered to refund him if I re-let the flat in the next two months, but if Citibank were paying, why bother?

I looked around the room and wondered if Michelle's mother had called at Livingstone Drive. The police would have let her in. It was hard to remember that a young woman, her daughter, had been hanging from that ceiling just a few days ago.

'We had some good times in your city,' Wilbur Lunt said reflectively, 'but this room is not a memory I shall want to carry with me, not after what has happened.'

'And you've no idea why Michelle killed herself?' I asked him directly.

'None in the slightest. We were very happy.' He drew deeply on his cigarette.

If that was true, I thought, why did she end it all?

'She'd given up her job but she said she enjoyed being at home.' He laughed, it was a hollow sound. 'She'd started to write a novel, something she'd always promised herself she'd do. They say every person has a book in them, don't they?'

'Apparently.' Except that in real life, most of us are too busy or lazy or illiterate to write it.

'Perhaps we all have a song in us as well, or a great painting, I don't know.'

I said nothing. Maybe we all had the answers to Quantum Physics hidden somewhere deep in our psyche but not too many of us would be digging around searching for them.

Lunt stood up, looked once more round the room. 'Well, I mustn't take up any more of your time, Mr Ace. Thank you for all your help. I'm only sorry it had to end like this.'

I walked with him to the gate. He was driving the green Mercedes, which was parked behind my RAV4.

'Just one thing,' he said, stopping suddenly. 'Would you mind terribly if I took a photo of the house?' He took out one of those fun cameras you pick up at most stores. 'The last place Michelle and I lived together,' he explained, stepping back to get the angle. 'I think I ought to have some memento, although I can hardly pretend it will be a pleasant one.' He pressed the shutter.

'No,' he said quietly to himself, putting the camera back in his pocket, 'in the circumstances, I shan't be sorry to leave.' He held out his hand. 'Once again, thanks for all your help, Mr Ace. I don't expect I shall be seeing you again.'

'What about the funeral?'

'Oh yes, of course, I'd forgotten about that. Yes, I'll see you at the funeral then.'

'Right.'

But I knew as he said it that, whoever else attended Michelle Lunt's funeral, her husband would not be present. What I didn't know was why?

Chapter Three

I drove to the radio station just in time for my evening show at six.

'Only just made it again,' Ken, my producer, greeted me.

'One of my tenants left,' I explained shortly. 'I had a few things to sort out.'

'Owed you rent, did he?'

'It was a she. Luckily no. She's dead.'

'The lengths people will go to,' Ken tutted, 'to leave your flats.' I think he thought I was joking. Ken never knows when to believe me. He's only just turned thirty but any day now I expect him to sew leather patches on the elbows of his sports jackets and join the local bowls club.

I started the show with a couple of Dale Watson records. Dale's a honky-tonk singer who plays small bars and rodeos around Texas and Alabama.

The old country singers like Hank Williams, Willie Nelson and the likes of Dale Watson were po' boys who came from the same background as their fans, but that's all gone now that money and big business have taken over.

The stars of 'New Country' play large stadiums with million-dollar light shows, date movie actors and have never been to a rodeo in their lives: they wouldn't recognise a steer if it shat all over them.

There's a moral there somewhere. I think it means that Dale Watson's going to be stuck on the rodeo circuit for a mighty long time.

After the show, I handed over to Godfrey Withers, probably the oldest DJ in the world, who plays forgotten hits of
the 1930s for a dwindling band of retirees. 'Seven o'clock,
Godders,' I said. 'Your listeners will just be making their
cocoa!'

I stopped off for a pizza at the Casa Bella then went down
to the Masquerade Club. Monday used to be a quiet night, but
in an effort to draw in a few more punters, Tommy McKale
had recently hired a drag queen DJ called Gloria.

He/she had obviously done the trick as the place was
heaving.

'Full of brown-hatters,' commented Tommy as he walked
with me to the bar. 'I've latched on to the pink pound.
They buy expensive soft drinks and cocktails which is the
important thing, so what's a bit of buggery amongst friends?
Your usual is it, Johnny?'

I nodded. 'I bet Vince is loving it.' Vince the barman
came over at that moment to take our order. He wore a big
smile and a David Beckham dress.

'Hello, Johnny,' he said. 'Not quite your scene, dear.' He
pulled me a pint of Scrumpy Jack.

'Actually, there's some nice-looking women here as well.'
I looked across to the dance floor. The music was 1970s
disco, currently enjoying a revival since *Boogie Nights*
cleaned up in the cinema. Gloria was playing Tavares'
'Heaven Must Be Missing An Angel'.

'Wrong again, dear. Dykes with dicks, that's what they
are. The only woman you'd be a hundred per cent safe
with in here is Dolly.' Dolly is Tommy's grandmother –
she looks after the door. 'And she's eighty-four.' Vince
handed Tommy an orange juice and we walked to the back
of the club where the music was quieter.

'Where's your lady tonight?'

'Hilary? On holiday. She's gone to Thassos for a fortnight
with one of her chums from work. She's due back at the
weekend.'

'You didn't get the trip this time then?'

'The week we had in Majorca in June was enough for me. I'm not keen on foreign holidays, Tommy – all that sunshine and sand. Give me winter in New Brighton.'

'You're not a day person, Johnny. You belong to the vampire club. You come out at night.'

I told him about Michelle Lunt.

'This won't be the end of the matter,' he said, when I'd finished the story. 'There'll be more to come.'

'Well, I won't know about it.'

'I wouldn't bet on that, Johnny. You have a habit of getting involved in things.'

'There's nothing to get involved in. The husband's gone back to the States, and once the family have been to take away her things, I'll be letting the flat to someone else.'

'End of a chapter, eh?'

'Precisely.'

He looked at me darkly. 'Not for the girl's family though. There are bound to be repercussions somewhere along the line, and sooner rather than later.'

'Thanks, Tommy. Just what I needed.'

'Well, I'd like to wager that you'll be tied up in some sort of business with those people before the week's over, and I'm not a betting man. And now, Johnny, you must excuse me. Work to be done.'

I downed a couple more Scrumpy Jacks and had a few dances with one of the ageing hookers.

'Not much trade in here for you tonight, Evie, with this lot.'

She stroked my cheek with her wrinkled hands and I noticed her pink nail varnish was peeling at the edges. 'Where do they all come from, Johnny? What happened to old-fashioned masculine Englishmen like Jack Hawkins and Kenneth More?'

I didn't like to tell her that if she could remember Jack

Hawkins and Kenneth More, she'd be better off looking for a job modelling elastic hosiery.

'Modern-day women, Evie. Men are scared to death of them so they turn to other blokes in desperation.'

'It hasn't happened to you, Johnny.'

'I stick to old-fashioned women.' And I gave her a comradely pinch on the backside.

At around one-thirty I left the Masquerade and walked back to my flat in the Waterloo Dock.

There was just the one message waiting for me on my ansaphone. Would I ring Linda Roberts?

I didn't know the name and I didn't recognise the voice but she sounded young and strangely nervous. She didn't say what she wanted either, but she did say it was urgent and she left her number, which had an 01282 dialling code.

A shiver ran down my spine. That code was a Colne exchange, and Michelle Lunt's family lived in Colne. Too much of a coincidence.

I set the alarm for eight and rang her when I woke.

'Linda Roberts? Johnny Ace. You rang me.'

'Thanks for calling,' she said. 'You are the landlord aren't you, from Livingstone Drive?'

I admitted I was.

'I'm Michelle's sister.' Her voice quivered.

'Oh. I'm so sorry about Michelle,' I said. 'It must have been a terrible shock for you.'

'It was. I only found out last night when I got this phone call.'

'Last *night*? But Wilbur gave me to understand you'd all been told last Saturday. Look, I'm sorry, I would have telephoned you myself but I'd no idea Michelle had a sister. Wilbur's was the only contact number I had.'

'Oh, I wasn't reproaching you. I didn't even know Shelley was back in England.'

'Oh yes. They returned from America last April.'

'America?'

'You knew they got married over there?'

'I beg your pardon?'

'Michelle and Wilbur.'

There was a slight hesitation at the other end of the line then Linda Roberts said quietly, 'I'm sorry, I don't understand. I've never heard of anyone called Wilbur.'

Chapter Four

The wedding wasn't the only thing Michelle Lunt had kept from her sister. Linda had last heard from her eighteen months ago when Shelley rang her and announced she was going to France to work for a fashion house as a private secretary.

'But she was in America, not France.'

'So it seems.'

'What exactly was her occupation?' I asked curiously. 'Wilbur told me that when he met her, she was working for a public relations firm.'

'She'd done lots of things in her time. I suppose nothing she did would surprise me, although I never heard her mention public relations. But, look, I want to hear about this Wilbur.'

I told her the story as I knew it. 'His name is Wilbur Lunt. He works for Citibank. She met him in a London hotel and went across to the States with him. They got married then he was posted to Europe and they came to live in Liverpool. According to Wilbur, Michelle said she wanted to live in the North of England to be near her family in Colne.'

'That's a laugh. She hasn't been near us for years.' Linda sounded more sad than bitter.

'So why would she say it?'

'I don't understand. I know nothing of all this.'

'But Wilbur said he'd spoken to your mother on the phone a couple of days ago. She was supposed to be coming over to collect Michelle's furniture. In fact, he said she's already been once to the flat, on Sunday.'

There was a silence at the other end, then, 'Mr Ace. Our mother died thirteen years ago.'

I didn't know what to say. 'But . . .'

'Look, this isn't something we can talk about on the phone. I have to go to Liverpool later today to see Shelley's solicitor.' She named a respectable firm of lawyers in Lord Street. 'Could I perhaps meet you somewhere?'

'What time's your appointment?'

'Half-past three with a Mr Martin, Ted Martin. Do you know him?'

'I've heard of him. He's quite reputable.' I looked at my watch. 'It won't take you more than a couple of hours to drive over from Colne. How about if we have lunch?'

'That would be nice.'

We agreed to meet at the Moat House Hotel in Paradise Street at one. When she put the phone down, I immediately rang Detective Sergeant Leary.

'Have you had any contact with Michelle Lunt's family?' I asked him.

'Mr Lunt came to see me, yes. You gave me his number yourself.'

'Apart from her husband, I mean. Did he not mention her mother coming over from Colne? Or her sister?'

'Mr Lunt told us his wife had no family. He was her only relative.'

'That's very odd. He told *me* that it was you who'd informed him his mother-in-law had visited the funeral parlour.'

'Me?'

'But I've just spoken to Mrs Lunt's sister and apparently their mother has been dead for years.'

'Why would he lie about a thing like that?'

'Precisely.'

'You say you've spoken with the sister?'

'She's coming to see me this afternoon. She lives in Colne.'

There was a pause. Leary was presumably taking in all this new information. 'Well, it doesn't make any difference to the verdict. According to the pathologist, Mrs Lunt hung herself and I'm sure the inquest will confirm it.'

'It might affect her will, though. Did she leave one, do you know?'

'There wasn't one in the room, put it that way, not that it's any of your business. I've already warned you about interfering with police matters.'

I didn't argue. It seemed that, as far as the police were concerned, the case was closed. Never mind about the inquest. They'd already decided it was suicide, a nice, neat verdict. All the loose ends tidied up. Leary certainly didn't give the impression that he would act on the information I'd given him.

I was at the Moat House a few minutes before one. I gave the receptionist my name and told her a lady would be asking for me. I then took a seat in the foyer.

A few minutes after one, a young woman came in, looked around, and then went to the desk where the girl pointed me out to her. She came over.

'Mr Ace? I'm Linda Roberts.'

She couldn't have been less like her sister. She was tiny, barely five two. Her hair was mousy brown and held in a ponytail by a brown elastic band. She was dressed in a shaggy sweater and faded denims, which had an Oxfam look about them, and a pair of once-white trainers.

She wore no make-up but when she smiled, her hazel eyes lit up with an almost religious glow. I could see her going down a storm on the Billy Graham circuit.

'Hello.' She took my hand and held it for a moment as if she needed something or someone to hold on to.

I escorted her through to the bar and found a table in a quiet corner. 'Let me get you a drink.'

The waitress came over and Linda ordered a lemonade shandy. I chose my usual cider. We spent the next five minutes checking out the menu. 'I'll just have a toasted sandwich,' she said. 'I don't eat much at lunchtime.'

'Make that two,' I told the waitress when she brought the drinks, then I turned back to Linda.

'So, tell me about your sister.'

She looked me in the eye. 'It seems you know more about her than I do.' She sighed. 'She's always been the wild one of the family. Mum died when Shelley was sixteen. She'd just finished her GCSEs and she'd done really well – got eight grade As. She wanted to study Law at university, but our Shelley didn't just want to be an ordinary solicitor, oh no. She wanted to study Criminal Law and become a barrister.'

'What went wrong?'

'It was after Mum died – she seemed to lose all interest in things. It was so sudden with Mum, you see, Mr Ace. A brain haemorrhage.' Linda gulped. 'She was making breakfast one morning, gave a sudden cry and fell to the floor. She was in a coma for a couple of days and never woke up. She was only forty-four.'

'How old were you when it happened?' I asked.

'Thirteen. Three years younger than Shelley. I'm twenty-six now.'

I imagined the effect this would have on two teenage girls.

'Shelley quit school and never got to do her A levels. Instead, she took a typing job in a local solicitor's office.'

'What about your father?'

'Dad was devastated when Mum died but he eventually met this woman and they got married and went to live in Irthlingborough.'

'Leaving you and Shelley on your own?'

'No. When Dad put our house on the market I'd already started at college so I'd virtually left anyway. When Dad said he was moving, Shelley immediately packed her job in and went off to London.'

'Did you see much of her after that?'

'I've not seen her from that day to this. She rings from time to time but she's never been back to Colne again.' She'd lost the accent, too, I thought. Michelle had had quite a cultured voice but Linda spoke with a distinct Lancashire twang. 'Come to that, I haven't seen Dad for a long time either. We used to exchange Christmas cards but he's got a new family now.'

'What about you?'

'I carried on with my course and got my qualifications.'

'So you're a teacher now?'

'That's right – at a primary school in Nelson. Eight-year-olds and they're monsters.' It was the first time she'd smiled in the conversation and I guessed she was rather fond of the monsters.

'No boyfriend?' I'd noticed she had no ring on her finger but that meant nothing.

She shook her head. 'Just me and my cat,' she said. 'Emily.' She'd bought a little terraced house in Nelson, not far from the school. A male teacher kept asking her out but so far she'd resisted. 'Doesn't do to get involved with people you work with.' Most of her evenings were spent on school projects or working on her hobby, tapestry.

'It's the school holidays now,' she explained. 'That's how I'm able to come over today.'

'I can't tell you much more about Shelley,' I said.

'The inquest's on Friday, I believe. I don't know about the funeral. I suppose it will be up to me to arrange it, but if you're right about her having a husband . . .'

'Wilbur told me your mother was arranging it. Anyway, he's gone back to America so I guess it will be down to you.'

'Oh dear, I've never organised a funeral before. What do I do?'

'The people at the funeral parlour will handle it all for you, so I'd let them make the arrangements. Do you want her to be buried in Colne with your mother?'

'Mum was cremated so I suppose Shelley will be too.'

'In which case, will you want it here in Liverpool or back home?'

'I don't suppose many people in Colne remember her now. We might as well have it here.'

'That'll be the Springwood Avenue Crematorium then, I would imagine.'

'When should I have it?'

'You'll have to wait until after the inquest but, assuming everything goes all right, then any time the week after that to suit you. Providing they're not booked up, of course.'

That was unlikely. July wasn't a popular month for dying. It was in the cold months of January and February that old people were dropping like flies and the council had to bring out the refrigerated vans to cope with the mortuary overflow.

'I take it her husband won't be there at all if he's gone back to America?' she said.

'He told me he'd come but I wouldn't count on it.'

Linda leaned back on her chair. 'I just don't understand it. Why should he pretend he'd spoken to our mother? I can't see the point of it.'

Neither did I. He wasn't under suspicion regarding his wife's death yet he seemed in a mighty hurry to leave the country.

'Unless it was to reassure me that someone else was taking care of things so he could slip away quietly,' I suggested, 'but you're right, it doesn't make sense. And another thing; who was it who phoned you to tell you Shelley had died? And who gave you my number?'

'The solicitors. There was a message from them on my ansaphone. Said they wanted to discuss the effects of my deceased sister. It gave me a terrible shock.'

'I can imagine. How did they find out she'd died?'

'Apparently the police found some letter addressed to them.'

'Ah.' That had not been mentioned when I was at Livingstone Drive. Obviously Detective Sergeant Leary was playing his cards very close to his chest.

'Anyway, I arranged to see them this afternoon.' Linda bit her lip. 'I don't suppose you would come with me? I'm rather nervous about it. I could do with a bit of support.'

'Of course I will.' I wasn't just being chivalrous. I was most interested to find out more about the enigmatic Mrs Lunt. 'But first of all, I'll take you to see your sister's flat. That's if you want to. There's all the furniture and her things to sort out.'

Linda looked a little hesitant. 'If it's not too much trouble? I would like to see where she died.'

'Of course. Providing you can give me a lift back to town.' I explained that I'd left my car at home and walked into town.

We finished our snack and I followed her to the Paradise Street multi-storey where she'd parked her car. She was in a blue P-reg. Fiesta. I sat in the passenger seat and we set off for Livingstone Drive.

Linda drove like a Sunday driver, slowly and with great care. I wouldn't have given much for her chances round Hyde Park Corner. I reckoned I'd have done the journey quicker in a wheelchair.

'Here we are,' I said, at last. 'There's a space up on the left to park.'

She glided in at the third attempt.

'There's eight flats,' I explained. 'Two on each floor. Your sister lived in the ground-floor left one, Flat Three. Come on, let's go inside.'

I ushered her through the front door into the communal hallway and opened the door to Michelle Lunt's flat where, less than a week ago, her sister had ended her life.

We entered the lounge and she gazed about her. 'Is this . . . the room?' she faltered. I nodded and she walked round silently as if by absorbing the vibrations she could somehow reach out to the dead.

A copy of *The Times* dated the day of Michelle's death still lay on the table and a silk scarf I'd seen her wearing the first day I met her was draped over the back of one of the chairs. It looked like one of those Hermès things the Queen wears.

'Let me get you a coffee.' I sensed Linda wanted to be left alone. I went into the kitchen, boiled a kettle of water and opened a jar of Gold Blend that her sister wouldn't be using any more.

In the cupboard, I found a couple of bone china mugs with coloured drawings of pigs on them and spooned coffee into one of them. Into the other I put a teabag from a pile in an unmarked glass jar.

'Sorry there's no milk.'

'That's all right.' Linda took a long sip from the mug. 'I needed that. I don't usually drive much further than Blackburn.'

She sat down on the three-seater settee and I took a place alongside her.

'According to your sister's husband, all the stuff in here is paid for, and as he said your mother could have it, I imagine it's all yours.'

'Perhaps we should wait for the will before I take anything. Just to be on the safe side.'

'OK – no problem.'

'You see, I like to have things done properly and know what's mine,' she explained. 'I don't suppose my sister had much to leave. Shelley was never good with money, she liked to spend it too much.'

It was a big surprise to both of us, therefore, when we

were seated in the lawyer's wood-panelled office an hour later, opposite a short, pleasant man in his late fifties with a grey moustache and sandy hair, to be told . . .

'You are the sole beneficiary of the estate, Miss Roberts, and it is not inconsiderable. Your sister left nearly three hundred and fifty thousand pounds.'

Chapter Five

Linda put her hand to her head and looked as if she was going to faint. I knew how she felt. I was pretty gobsmacked myself.

'I never met Mrs Lunt myself, you understand,' he told us.

'Then how did you come to act for her?' I asked. Linda seemed incapable of speech.

Mr Martin pulled out a well-worn pipe and prodded the inside of the bowl with a smoker's penknife. 'We received a letter from her some weeks ago containing a copy of her will which she had drawn up at a London solicitor's a few days previously. Apparently, she had earlier telephoned our senior partner and arranged for our firm to act as executors in the event of anything happening to her.'

'But she was only in her twenties. What was she doing, making all these arrangements? It's almost as if she was planning her death.'

Mr Martin shrugged his shoulders and took out a pouch of tobacco.

'It is genuine, I take it?' I asked.

'Oh yes, no reason to doubt it. One of the paragraphs in the letter instructed us to contact Miss Roberts immediately in the event of her demise.'

'And, according to Miss Roberts here, Mrs Lunt herself sent you notice of her death.'

'A letter addressed to us was left beside the body. The police passed it on to us.'

'What did it say?'

'Merely that Miss Michelle Roberts had died and would we carry out earlier instructions.'

'How bizarre,' I said.

Linda was still recovering from the shock of her inheritance. 'How much did you say?' she stammered.

'Three hundred and fifty thousand,' repeated the solicitor, 'give or take a few hundred for costs and expenses.'

'But there must be some mistake. She never had a proper job, that is . . .'

Mr Martin sighed patiently. 'Miss Roberts, how long is it since you last saw your sister?'

'It must be nearly ten years. But we've spoken on the phone,' she added defiantly, 'and she never mentioned coming into a fortune.'

'Hardly a fortune,' said the solicitor. 'You couldn't retire on a million pounds these days, not unless you were already a pensioner – and I can see you're not in that category yet.' He chuckled at his outburst of whimsy and proceeded to fill his pipe with St Bruno flake.

'But what about her husband?' I said. 'Doesn't he automatically inherit?'

'There's no mention of a husband in this will, Mr Ace.'

'But they were married over six months ago, in America.'

Ted Martin looked at me closely. 'You know that for a fact, do you?'

'I met her husband, if that's what you mean.'

'Interesting.' Mr Martin struck a Swan Vesta and applied it to the tobacco. A couple of puffs and he was away. 'Have a look at this.' He pushed a letter across the desk. I picked it up and held it for Linda to read as well. 'You'll see the deceased signs herself Michelle Roberts.'

I scanned the rest of the letter. There was a paragraph instructing the firm to pass on to Linda Roberts the telephone number of her landlord.

'I don't understand it.' I said, handing back the letter.

'She was certainly living in my flat as Mrs Michelle Lunt on the date that was written.'

'Have you no idea how she came to have all that money?' asked Linda.

'Oh yes,' said Ted Martin surprisingly, from behind a cloud of smoke. 'It was a life insurance policy payable on her death.'

'I thought insurance companies didn't pay out on suicides,' I said.

'Sometimes they do, sometimes they don't. Quite often they have a suicide clause in the policy whereby they won't pay out if the person kills himself or herself within a certain time, usually about two years. Otherwise, it depends on their circumstances. In this case, I've no reason to believe they will withhold the money but, of course, the settlement will be dependent on the inquest verdict and subsequent probate.'

'Why would Shelley insure herself for that amount?' Linda looked bewildered.

'From what I can gather, the policy was taken out on her behalf by her employers.'

'Hang on,' I said. 'There must be some mistake there. Mrs Lunt or Miss Roberts, whatever you call her, wasn't working. Her husband worked, he was with Citibank, he travelled all over the Continent, but she stayed at home.'

'She may well have stayed at home, Mr Ace, but Miss Roberts was certainly working. She was a civil servant, attached to a police department.'

'What!'

'Which is why I asked you how long it was since you saw your sister, Miss Roberts. I take it you had no idea that she was connected with the law?'

'None at all.'

'Or rather, to be exact, she was engaged on an operation as an undercover agent for the Drug Squad.' The solicitor tipped his chair on its back legs and hung his thumbs under his waistcoat. 'According, that is, to the brief information she gave us. I don't have any details other than that but it would certainly explain why she was, shall we say, aware of her mortality.'

Linda Roberts and I looked at each other in amazement. 'But what about Wilbur Lunt?' I asked at last.

'I'm afraid I can't help you there. I've never heard of the man.'

'Perhaps he was with the Drug Squad too and they pretended to be married.'

'Or perhaps,' ventured Mr Martin ominously, 'he was her quarry.'

There was a silence as we considered that possibility.

'If that was the case, and he found out she was tailing him, that would make the suicide verdict look shaky. It would seem more likely to have been murder.'

'That is for the coroner to decide.'

'But the death certificate, if she really was married – that will have her name on it as Michelle Lunt.'

'Quite probably it will, if Mr Lunt was the one to identify the body and confirm it was his wife.'

'I identified the body, Mr Martin, but as Michelle Lunt, so that will be the name on the certificate.'

'Ah well, that will only be an interim death certificate. Further investigations might prove her real identity to be otherwise, in which case the final certificate will carry Miss Roberts' official name.'

'But it could still be Mrs Lunt, couldn't it? You don't know she didn't marry?'

'I think it unlikely but I will concede it is possible. And now you must both excuse me, I have another appointment at four o'clock.'

'Well, I'm completely baffled,' admitted Linda as we stood on the steps outside the office. 'It's like a dream. Or a nightmare – I don't know which. Everything's so complicated.'

It seemed pretty simple to me. Her sister was brown

bread and she was worth nearly half a million quid; the
rest was incidental. But I didn't think she'd want to hear
that so instead I suggested we went for a drink while we
assimilated everything we'd been told.

'Come on,' I said, 'I'll take you to the spiritual home of
The Beatles.' So off we went to the Grapes in Mathew Street
where The Fab Four used to drink with their old manager
Allan Williams and Cavern disc jockey, Bob Wooler.

'I never realised the Beatles thing was as big as this,'
she said, as she read the names of the bars on the way –
Rubber Soul, Abbey Road, Lennon's Bar – all alluding to
The Beatles and their songs.

'A hundred years from now, Liverpool will have become
another Stratford or Haworth, a place of pilgrimage for
Beatles followers.'

'Haworth's not so far from Nelson,' said Linda, 'and
you're right – it's full of Brontë teashops, galleries and
gift shops.'

'There's money in history, which means it's in the interest
of a lot of people to keep the legends going.'

'I don't think I'll have to worry about money any more,'
sighed Linda.

'Don't you believe it. You heard what that solicitor
said. Even a million pounds won't last long these days.'
He was right too. It would hardly buy one foot of an
Everton midfielder. Mind you, most of them only seem
to use one foot.

In the pub, she asked for a brandy. 'Not my usual tipple,'
she gave a nervous giggle, 'but I feel I need something to
jolt me into reality.'

I got her a double Courvoisier and myself a cider and we
sat at a corner table.

'What are your plans?' I asked. She'd taken two firm sips
from her glass and it appeared to have had the desired effect.
Her cheeks had reddened from her neck upwards.

'I want to go and see Shelley in the Chapel of Rest,' she

replied without hesitation. 'I haven't seen her since she was barely more than a teenager and I want to know what she looked like. In some ways, she's a stranger to me now, the life she's led and the length of time that's passed.' She looked me in the eye. 'I want to see the woman she'd become, Mr Ace.'

It was the longest sentence she'd spoken. I think she'd been saving it up.

'You can call me Johnny,' I told her. 'Yes, I'm sure that can be arranged. Do you know where they're keeping her body?'

'I've got it written down somewhere.' She delved in her handbag and brought out a screwed-up piece of paper. 'The firm is at a place called Wavertree.'

'Three miles down the road. I'll give them a ring and fix a time.' I checked my watch. 'It's going to be too late to go today. What about tomorrow?'

She looked discomfited. 'I don't know. It'll mean I'll have to go home and then drive all the way back to Liverpool again tomorrow.'

'You could stay overnight.'

'Who'll look after my cat?'

'Isn't there a neighbour you can ring?'

She looked doubtful. 'My friend Nicola has a key; she teaches at my school. But I've not booked a hotel. It'll cost a fortune to stay here.'

'You've got a fortune,' I pointed out, 'but there's no need for a hotel. You can stay with me if you like. Your virtue will be quite safe,' I added, as her face dropped even further.

'But I've no nightclothes or anything.'

'No problem.' When we'd finished our drinks, I walked her to Church Street Market where I bought her a large Everton T-shirt from one of the stalls. 'There we are. It's not Janet Reger but it'll keep you warm for one night. And I've got ample supplies of shampoo and bath oils.' Hilary had seen to that.

She stood examining Duncan Ferguson's picture on the shirt without a hint of recognition. 'He's the centre forward,' I explained, but she knew nothing about football.

'I don't know what to say, Johnny. You're very kind.'

'Goes with the job,' I said. 'Landlords are really social workers in disguise. Now, I'd better get you back, I've got a radio show to do at six.'

Linda was suitably amazed when she saw my flat. I think it was the white Steinway in the lounge that made her flip. 'Do you play?' she asked.

'Very badly. The drums were my instrument but now I just play records. It's a lot easier.' I told her about life with The Cruzads in the Merseybeat days.

She smiled. 'You're not your average landlord, are you?'

'Not your average DJ either.' I didn't want to be an average anything. 'I'm going to be a private eye next.' I explained to her about my forays in the world of investigation.

'Sounds terribly exciting. And me stuck all day in a cold stone building with unruly children.'

'What could be more worthwhile.' And I wasn't being patronising. If we had more good teachers in the classrooms, many of our social ills would be cured. Providing they were allowed to hit the pupils back, of course.

I showed her the kitchen and told her to help herself to whatever she wanted. 'Have a bath if you like, make yourself at home. I'll be back at half seven and I'll take you out for something to eat.'

'You don't have to.'

'I don't but I will.'

'Put the radio on and I'll listen to your show.'

Knowing she was listening, I played 'Linda' by The Beach Boys for her and The Beatles' 'Michelle' in memory of her sister.

After the show, I picked her up and we went back into town to eat. I took her to the Rat and Parrot in Bold Street.

Linda wore the same sweater and jeans but she'd taken the elastic band from her hair, letting her brown curls hang round her shoulders, transforming her appearance.

We'd finished the meal and were polishing off our bottle of wine when she said, 'What do you think the police will do about Shelley's death?'

'Very little, I should think.'

'Why do you say that?'

'Well, they're satisfied it's suicide, aren't they? As far as they're concerned, they've got a result. They've done their bit and it's all over.'

'For them it might be. Not for me though.'

Tommy McKale's words echoed in my head. 'Maybe,' I said carefully, 'but does that matter anyway? Nothing's going to bring her back.'

'It matters to me.' Linda's chin quivered. 'Look, Johnny, you say you want to be a private eye. Well, I'll hire you. I can afford it now. I want you to find out exactly what happened to my sister. I want to know WHY she took her life.'

Chapter Six

We were back at the flat. It was coming up to midnight. A Reba McEntire album was on the CD player, and we were sitting cosily side by side on the settee.

'I want to know everything about her,' Linda told me. 'What she's been doing for the past few years. Who she's lived with – was she really married? What work did she really do, and how did she come to die the way she did?'

'It could be a nasty can of worms you're opening,' I warned her. 'You may learn things you'd rather not know.'

'It's the *not* knowing that I can't cope with.' She sipped the hot milk and nutmeg I'd made her. Linda Roberts was not a late-night drinker. 'So will you do it?'

Was there any doubt? I was as curious as she was to find out the truth about my erstwhile tenants. This gave me every reason for investigating and, as a bonus, I would be getting paid for it. After my last two cases, that was a novelty in itself.

'OK. Yes, I'll have a go for you.'

'How much will you charge me?'

I hadn't thought about that. I really had no yardstick to measure it by. I didn't know any other private investigators, although there were a few in the *Yellow Pages*. Maybe I should have gone round their offices picking up price lists. My old policeman friend, Jim Burroughs, might have been able to advise. I should have asked him before.

'Well, I get fifty pounds a night for doing my radio

show, so does fifty pounds a day sound reasonable, plus expenses?' I was probably doing myself. Car mechanics get fifty pounds an hour at some garages. Good job detecting was only a hobby.

'Your radio show only lasts an hour. I should give you a hundred.'

'I might only be on the air an hour, but there's all the preparation, letters to answer, interviews to set up, which means fifty's about right.'

'Seventy-five then and not a penny less.'

You don't argue with an heiress. 'Done.' We shook hands solemnly. She looked small and vulnerable like a kitten and very cuddly. I reminded myself of the golden rule, never do it with the tenants, and I figured clients came into the same category. 'And now I'd better get your bed ready, you've had a long day.'

She followed me into the bedroom where she'd already laid out the T-shirt on my king-size bed. 'Where are you going to sleep?'

'On the settee. Don't worry,' I assured her, seeing the dismay on her face, 'it's not the first time and it's very comfortable.'

I wasn't lying. I slept through to eight o'clock and was making breakfast when Linda emerged from the bedroom. 'Cereal and toast OK?' I asked her.

In her Everton nightshirt, she could have passed for twelve, were it not for the worry lines around her eyes. 'Fine. I'll just have a shower if it's OK?'

I made a pot of tea for two and had it all on the table for her when she reappeared, fifteen minutes later, in her sweater and jeans. 'I'm afraid I've only got these clothes with me.'

'Look, if you want to stay a couple of days while you sort everything out here, you're more than welcome. You could buy some clothes and toiletries with the money you'd save on the petrol.'

'But I'm imposing on you.'

'I'm glad of the company, honestly. You've got all Michelle's stuff to sort out and the Chapel of Rest to go to, not to mention the inquest on Friday.'

'Well, if you're sure you don't mind. It's really kind of you. If I stay just tonight and tomorrow,' she said, 'and go home on Friday after the inquest, would that be all right?'

'That'll be fine.'

She smiled and her hazel eyes shone. 'I'll go to the bank and draw some money out for you.' She paused. 'Johnny, I don't suppose you'd come with me to see Shelley, would you? I've never seen a dead person before, you see.'

I'd seen plenty and not always in the best circumstances. 'Sure.'

She made a couple of phone calls, to her friend Nicola to organise her cat, and to fix an appointment at the Chapel of Rest.

'I can go and see Shelley at half-past two this afternoon,' she said.

'Right. I'm going up to my office now so I'll drop you off at the shops on the way and meet you at one o'clock outside your solicitors.'

I drove along past the Pier Head and dropped off Linda at the end of James Street on the way, pointing her in the direction of the city centre.

'Just a day late,' Geoffrey greeted me. Tuesday was my usual day for the office.

'Something came up yesterday.'

'No more stiffs?'

'The stiffs seem to be dropping off,' I said. 'We've not had any for nearly a week.'

'Are we ready to let the Lunts' flat yet? I've had an accountant looking for a place – he left his number, a quiet lad. He's got a decent job with Macfarlanes in Cunard Buildings. He should be a good tenant.'

'I should have it sorted by the end of the week. Mrs

Lunt's sister has come over to collect her things.' I didn't mention that she was staying with me. Geoffrey reads things into situations. No sense in giving him the wrong idea.

'I've finished the central heating up at Princes Avenue for your friend Shirley.' He emphasised the word 'friend' unnecessarily. Geoffrey knew I had spent the occasional night there but that had been in the days before I was her landlord and before I met her large boyfriend, Rodney. 'She says you've not been round lately.'

'Tell her I'm busy trying to control an outbreak of suicides in the flats.' It hadn't been easy staying away. Shirley looks like Mary Wilson of The Supremes and is very sexy. 'Now, can you get the paperwork of the Lunts out for me?'

'Is there a problem?'

'No, but I want to check up on a couple of things.'

'I thought he'd paid up.'

'He has but I need to get hold of him.' I didn't explain and Geoffrey didn't ask again but put the papers on my desk.

I went through all the documents one by one. The only number I could find was the Citibank number. I dialled it. Surely somebody there would know his current whereabouts.

The number came up unobtainable.

I dialled the operator to check it and was told it was out of service. I rang the local branch of Citibank to find the number of their head office.

'I thought this wasn't a case,' commented Geoffrey.

'It wasn't but suddenly I'm beginning to think it might be.'

I got through to Head Office and explained to the receptionist who I was and what I wanted. She connected me to Personnel.

Nobody had heard of Wilbur Lunt. 'We have a Susan

Lunt,' said a lady with a deep voice and heavy Essex overtones, 'but no Wilbur.'

'He was working on the Continent but originally he was based in the States. Would you be able to trace him from the American office?'

'Leave it with me and I'll have a go.' I gave her the office number to ring back and turned my attention to Wilbur Lunt's references. They were signed by an S. Tomlinson. I'd presumed at the time that this person was Wilbur Lunt's boss as the letter was written on Citibank notepaper with the same phone number as the contact number.

The personnel assistant phoned back a few minutes later. 'I'm sorry. There's no trace of anyone of that name.'

'I've got here a reference from an S. Tomlinson on your bank's notepaper.' I read her the address and phone number. There was a slight pause.

'Just hold on a moment.' I held on. She was more than a moment. 'Sorry to keep you,' she said, just as I was tiring of the tinny digital Mozart offering in my ear, 'but I've checked up on this S. Tomlinson and I'm afraid he doesn't work for us either.'

'Could be a she.'

'No. No Tomlinsons. And that address you gave me . . .'

'Yes?'

'Well, we don't have a branch there. Are you sure you've read it correctly?'

'I've got the letter in front of me.' I read it out again. 'And, furthermore, the police rang that telephone number just a couple of days ago and spoke to somebody from Citibank.' They must have done, otherwise how could Leary have informed Wilbur Lunt about his wife's death?

'I can't help you there. I don't do mysteries, I'm afraid.' She gave a little giggle. 'Seems like this Mr Lunt has been having you on, Mr Ace.'

'Well, thanks for all your help.' I put the phone down and let out a long sigh.

'Trouble, boss?' enquired Geoffrey.

'You could say that, Geoff.'

It seemed as if Wilbur Lunt had disappeared off the face of the earth.

Chapter Seven

I met Linda at one o'clock as arranged. She was wearing a long navy jacket over a matching knee-length skirt. Her new high-heeled shoes lifted her a few inches and only her soft features and lack of make-up stopped her looking like a company executive.

'I put my old things in here,' she explained, indicating one of several bags she was carrying.

'I'm going to take you somewhere different for lunch,' I said. 'Food you won't get in Colne.'

I took her to San Francisco Wraps in North John Street. We gave in our order at the front counter and sat on stools by the window waiting for our number to be called.

All the food comes inside a soft tortilla wrapped in foil, and the fillings are different from anything you can get at any other fast food bar; they range from smoked duck to avocado guacamole with chili tomato salsa.

'You're right,' said Linda. She was enjoying a Fruity Orgasm, a drink of crushed strawberries and other fruits mixed with honey. 'You don't get food like this in Colne – or in Nelson either, come to that.'

I smiled. 'Sorry, I was forgetting you live in Nelson now. I once played with The Cruzads at the Imperial Ballroom in Nelson in the Sixties.'

'They've knocked it down now, the Imperial.'

'Scandalous.' They should put preservation orders on these old dance halls. Some of them were glorious, almost like palaces. Take Wigan Casino, for example. It could have been a massive tourist attraction for the town, a shrine to Northern Soul. Instead it's a car park.

We chatted about music as we set off for Wavertree. Linda, having grown up in the 1980s, was into electronic stuff like Human League and Gary Numan. She'd probably get on well with Geoffrey. I should scoff; there'd been a bit of an Eighties' revival this summer, as borne out by my postbag at the station. More people these days ask for Simply Red rather than Gene Vincent or The Four Seasons.

The drive to the Chapel of Rest didn't take long. An undertaker led us to the room where Michelle Lunt lay in a carved pinewood coffin.

She looked very different from when she was hanging on the end of at rope in Livingstone Drive. The once-contorted purple cheeks were now soft and white and she looked peaceful in death, but that didn't make it any easier for her sister.

'Oh God.' Tears welled up in Linda's eyes. 'She looks so old.' She didn't look old to me, but I could imagine that after a gap of ten years, her changed appearance must have been almost as much a shock to Linda as the fact that she was dead.

Her hand tentatively reached out to touch the cold face. I pulled up a chair. 'Why don't you sit with her for a little while. I'll be in the office if you want me,' and I slipped quietly out of the room. I knew Linda would need some time for reflection alone with her sister. 'I'll have a word with them about the funeral.'

It was a good fifteen minutes before she reappeared. 'Are you OK?' I asked her.

She nodded without much conviction. 'It was like touching a waxwork that's been in a fridge,' she said slowly, 'yet I felt as if she was there somehow. Not in her body but in the room itself, no specific place, just . . . there.'

I read a theory about the afterlife once. It said that the

dead are all around us; they exist like radio waves on a different wavelength but we haven't got the receivers to be able to tune in to them. Somehow, the brain blocks out the signals, otherwise, I suppose, we'd be overwhelmed by messages from the other side.

It seemed as good an explanation as anything else I'd heard and I outlined it to Linda. It didn't contradict anything she'd told me and, more to the point, she felt happy with it, which was what mattered in the end.

'What next?' she asked, as we walked back to the car. 'Have you got hold of Shelley's husband yet?'

'There's a bit of a problem there.' I recounted my efforts of the morning.

'What do you think it means?'

'I don't know. It could be nothing worse than he hadn't got a job so faked his reference to get the flat.'

'Or . . . ?'

Or what? He wasn't called Wilbur Lunt at all? He wasn't married to Michelle Roberts? He was a drug dealer? Or was he a cop? 'That's what I'm going to find out.' It was what she was paying me for.

As if reading my thoughts, Linda reached into her purse and brought out a cheque for £300. 'Will this do for starters? You can bill me for any expenses at the end.'

I put it in my back pocket. I was half inclined to frame it – my first paid assignment – but at £300 it would have been an expensive picture.

I took her back to the flat.

'Tomorrow, I'll drive over to Shelley's and sort out her things,' she said.

'I'll come with you. You might need a hand. What are you going to do about the furniture?'

She looked flustered. 'I don't know. Most of it's too big to fit in my little house. Besides, I've got my own bed and three-piece suite and furniture already.'

'Tell you what then.' I took out the cheque she'd given

me. 'Take this back and I'll keep what you don't want in the flat as my payment.'

'Oh, would you? That would be such a relief for me. But are you sure that it will be enough?'

'It's a fair price.' In fact, I was getting a good deal. The stuff was worth three times that amount new, but if she tried to sell it herself, by the time she'd paid auction fees and transport costs, she'd probably be no better off. Why bring in middlemen?

'Do you really need it all though?'

'It'll do for the next tenant.'

She gazed at me with a look approaching adoration. It embarrassed me and I turned away. 'Look, I've got a few things to deal with before I do my programme,' I said. 'How about if I come back for you at about half-past seven and we can go out for a meal?'

She smiled impishly. 'Only if you let me pay. You took me out last night – and I am your employer, remember?' It was the first time she'd really laughed since she'd arrived and it did wonders for her.

I drove over to the office. I wanted to make a phone call and I didn't feel comfortable doing it with Linda around. I also wanted to check through Wilbur Lunt's papers again.

'As far as I see it,' I said to Geoffrey, 'he gets a mailbox in London and prints up some headed notepaper with Citibank on it and giving that address. Then, he receives my letter there asking for references, writes them himself and sends them to me, all on the headed paper.'

'What about the contact phone number?'

'The telephone doesn't have to be at that address. He could be anywhere in the 0171 area saying "Hello, Citibank London, can I help you?"'

'Or anywhere in the world with modern technology the way it is.'

'Quite possibly, but now he's flown the nest leaving no trace.'

'Why would he do that?'

'Why indeed? That's the number one question.'

'Ah, so it *is* another case then.' Geoffrey looked triumphant. 'You'll be needing my help, I suppose?'

'If you mean as a minder, I hope not.'

I rang the police station and spoke to Detective Sergeant Leary. 'I'm trying to get hold of Wilbur Lunt,' I told him. 'Who did you speak to at that number I gave you?'

'How do you mean?'

'Lunt was in Vienna when he heard of his wife's death. The number I gave you was a London one so, presumably, someone must have relayed your message.'

'Actually, it was an ansaphone. I left a message and Mr Lunt contacted me the next day.'

'From Vienna?'

'That's right.'

It was feasible. He could have activated the phone by remote control from Vienna – if, indeed, he was in Vienna. He could have been anywhere.

'Why are you so interested in Mr Lunt?'

'I'm just sorting out his deposit on the flat but he's unavailable on that number,' I lied. 'Did he leave no address with you?'

'No, but he'll be at the inquest on Friday.'

'I wouldn't bank on that. When I saw him on Monday, he told me he was flying back to America.' There was a silence at the other end of the phone. 'And that address he gave me, purporting to be a branch of Citibank? It wasn't.'

More silence, then: 'I'm afraid I can't help you, Mr Ace. I'm sorry.' And the line went dead.

Chapter Eight

There was only one thing for it. I needed to see what I could find out from Michelle Lunt's belongings, preferably before anyone else got to them. I still had the keys to the flat so I drove down to Livingstone Drive and let myself in.

Nothing seemed to have been moved since my visit with Linda the day before. I looked through the drawers in the mahogany desk and found a sheaf of bank statements in the name of Michelle Lunt. The last one, dated the week before, had a balance of £212.

I flicked through the pages but couldn't spot any unusual or sinister transactions. Similarly, a file of Visa statements showed that Mrs Lunt had been very circumspect with her finances, paying off the full amounts each month and never incurring interest. None of the items were for substantial sums and her money had been spent mainly in stores such as Safeway, Marks & Spencer and Boots. Hardly questionable locations.

I was hoping to find a diary or address book, even an electronic organiser, but there was no sign of anything like that. Had they been removed already?

A half-used paying-in book and chequebook and a leather folder of credit and debit cards were in another drawer, together with her passport.

The passport was in the name of Michelle Lesley Roberts!

It appeared Ted Martin could have been right about her unmarried status. If so, why had they both found it necessary to lie about it, and who was Wilbur Lunt?

Nothing else I found in the room gave me an answer. I put everything away and went back into the hall, shutting the door behind me. As I looked up the stairs, I remembered what Badger had said about seeing Michelle in Mr Lloyd's room so I ran up to the top floor and banged on his door.

There was no reply. I took out my keys again and let myself in. Technically this is breaking and entering, as landlords are supposed to give written notice before entering anyone's home. On the other hand, in an emergency such as smoke under the door, a leak into the flat below, etc, then entry is permitted.

'Hello, anyone in?' I raised my voice. 'A smell of gas has been reported.' Cover my back. Silence. I walked through to the kitchen. A pile of dirty dishes stood in the sink, interesting formations of stale, crusted food adhering to them.

I moved on to the lounge. Judging by the half-empty glasses, cans and bottles and empty pizza cartons, Mr Lloyd had recently held a party. The carpet was covered with crisps, cigarette ash and stale beer and smelt like a Monday morning at the Masquerade Club. Only the odour of cat pee was missing.

In the bedroom, the curtains were still drawn but I could see the bed was unmade.

What I could also see, on the dresser, was a half open packet of a white powder that could not be mistaken for sugar or salt.

On TV, the detective usually dips his finger in, presses it to his lips and triumphantly pronounces what it is. I knew better than to try that. If it was cyanide, one speck on the tongue could kill you. Besides, I'd seen something like it before and I had a pretty good idea what it was. Heroin.

My philosophy on drugs is pretty straightforward. I would never take cocaine, heroin, cannabis or speed for the same reasons I wouldn't touch aspirin, Brufen, Viagra or Prozac.

I won't risk any adverse side effects to my mind or body, especially my mind.

However, I have no objection to anyone else swallowing, snorting or injecting themselves with whatever they want, even if they kill themselves in the process, providing they don't do it in any of my houses. Because then I can be prosecuted for it.

Hence I was not happy with this situation.

I knew very little about Nathan Lloyd, other than he claimed to be at John Moores University doing media studies, a course that could mean anything.

As I recalled, his last landlord had given him a reference – but maybe he was anxious to get rid of him. There's no loyalty between landlords.

I touched nothing and went back into the hallway, closing the bedroom door after me, which is when I heard footsteps coming up the stairs. They were too light to be Badger's.

Someone knocked on the door. I stayed still. They knocked once more and I remained silent. A few seconds later, the person went back down the stairs. I stepped cautiously out into the corridor and caught a whiff of perfume. Obviously the caller was female.

I ran quietly after her but there was no sign of anyone when I reached the bottom. I opened the front door but saw nobody in the street and it was then I heard the soft click of a door catch behind me. It came from Serina Barrie's flat.

I knocked on her door but she didn't answer and I wasn't going to risk letting myself in. I started to wonder. Was she a regular caller on the mysterious Mr Lloyd and, if so, was there an innocent reason for these visits?

It was getting late. I went straight from Livingstone Drive to the radio station to go through my mail and present the show. I had a phone-in on euthanasia, always a popular topic and one that had been in the news again recently.

One man rang in to say he would prefer death to having motor neurone disease; when he'd be unable to communicate in any way at all, even though his mind was working perfectly. 'Imagine,' he said, 'being unable to tell anyone "the new will is hidden in the back of the family Bible".'

A woman rang to say her father had Alzheimer's disease and didn't recognise people from one day to the next.

'Never mind,' I reassured her. 'One good thing about Alzheimer's is that you make new friends every day.'

'Really!' The woman rang off and behind the screen I could see Ken squirm with embarrassment as he braced himself for the complaints. Some people just don't have a sense of humour.

'You could have upset her,' Ken said afterwards. 'And fancy playing *Memories are Made of This* for your next record.'

'At least it was The Drifters' version.' I have to preserve some musical credibility.

Before I left the station, I recorded a message on the office ansaphone, asking Geoffrey to ring me first thing in the morning regarding an eviction. That would stir his curiosity.

I was back at the flat for just after seven-thirty to pick up Linda. This time, she was wearing a short, clingy black dress. The shopping trip had obviously been successful and I noticed she had make-up on for the first time since I'd met her.

'You look wonderful,' I said.

'Don't get too excited. I've got bad news for you.'

'What?'

'Do you know somebody called Maria?'

I did a quick calculation. Maria wasn't due back from her book trip until Friday and, whilst she knew about, and just about accepted, Hilary, I didn't think she'd be overjoyed to hear another woman answer my telephone at home.

'She phoned?'

'Worse. She called.'

'How did she get in?' There's an entryphone system in the block.

'She must know the security man, I don't know. Anyway, she knocked on the door and I opened it thinking it was you.'

'I'll say you were a neighbour feeding my plants.'

Linda looked at the floor. 'Er, it was while I was getting changed. I only had your dressing-gown on at the time.'

I groaned. 'How long ago was this?'

'About twenty minutes. After you were finished on the radio. I enjoyed the show, by the way.'

'What did you tell her? What did she do?'

A guilty look crept over Linda's face. 'I said you'd be back later but to call before eight as we were going out.'

I've noticed this about women. However nice they are as people, they are essentially in competition with other women and will use every device they can think of to put one over on each other. Don't talk to me about 'sisters'.

'You didn't tell her I was working for you on a case, or that your sister had died in one of my flats? Nothing like that?'

She shook her head. 'I'm sorry, Johnny.' Her lower lip pouted slightly. She had full lips, coloured lilac to match her eye shadow, and she'd been to the hairdressers. Her curly brown hair was streaked with golden highlights now and it gleamed silkily. 'Is she your girlfriend then?' she asked timidly.

'She was,' I said grimly. 'She may not be now.'

'She was very pretty. I thought she looked rather like Cher, with that long black hair.'

'Yes.'

'Look, Johnny, if you want I'll go home tonight,' Linda said, looking rather hurt. 'I can pack my things and be out of here in ten minutes.'

Significantly, she didn't make any move as she said it. What do they say about the quiet ones? 'Don't be silly,'

I sighed, 'I'll sort it tomorrow. Now let's go and eat, I'm starving. Besides, you're paying, remember?'

'That's right.'

We went back to Mathew Street and I took her to the Metz Bar. Their Manchester branch had won the Gay Bar of the Year award but the clientèle here was young, lively and not especially camp. Eighties music boomed from the speakers and the place was buzzing.

Afterwards, I took us on a detour round the Albert Dock and stopped the car to show her the Liver Buildings and Pier Head by moonlight.

'It's a very romantic city, isn't it?' she said. 'Just imagine all those liners sailing off to America years ago.'

'You've seen *Titanic* too?'

She blushed. 'Yes. All films reach Nelson eventually.'

'Don't knock Nelson. The people there are really nice. I used to go there to watch Burnley play football back in the Seventies, when Leighton James played for them, and the fans there were the friendliest I've met on any football ground.'

We made small talk as we drove back to the flat. 'Thanks for a lovely evening,' we said together as we walked into the lounge, and we both laughed.

'Are you sure you want me to stay after, you know . . .'

I tried to push Maria out of my mind. 'Yes, of course. Tell you what, let's open a bottle of wine and we can talk some more about your sister. Like, for instance, what sort of a person was she?'

'Probably very different from how she was when she lived at home.'

I fetched the wine from the kitchen and poured us each a glass. We settled on the couch.

'Even so, people's basic personalities don't change,' I said. 'Could you ever see her committing suicide?'

She answered without hesitation. 'Never. It wasn't how she reacted to things. If Shelley got knocked down, she'd jump straight back up more determined than ever. Not like me. I was always the nervous one.'

Nonetheless, I thought, Linda had a quiet persistence of her own, which would probably get her most things she wanted, and without upsetting anyone in the process. They probably wouldn't even realise she'd got her own way.

'Perhaps there was some terrible problem in her life we don't know about.'

'You mean, she might have had cancer or something? Or AIDS?'

'Not necessarily as dramatic as that. Maybe a broken relationship, or perhaps she was mixed up in some trouble she couldn't see a way out of – something to do with her job.'

'I can't imagine my sister as a policewoman.'

'Why not? You said she wanted to be a barrister. It's not too far removed.'

'I suppose not, except it's a bit physical, isn't it? Shelley was more, how can I put it, cerebral.'

'She must have been quite high-ranking.' One of the first things I needed to discover was which organisation Michelle Lunt had been working for. 'How about stress in the workplace – that's a popular affliction nowadays?'

Even as I said it, I knew it seemed unlikely from what Linda had told me of her sister's character. We drank silently for a while and then she put her hand on mine.

'I'd just like to thank you, Johnny, for being so nice to me about everything.'

She put down her drink and started to stroke the back of my hair with her fingertips until my neck tingled like an electric shock running through me.

Slowly, she kissed me on the lips then started to massage my shoulders. Her touch was almost geisha-like in its erotic tenderness and I felt myself responding until I remembered what she had said to Maria.

'No, Linda.' I pulled away from her roughly. 'You're a

client.' Rule number one, never do it with the clients or the tenants. It had happened in the past and I ended up regretting it.

I spent the night back on the settee but this time I didn't sleep too well.

I wondered just how I'd explain things to Maria.

Chapter Nine

We were both up for breakfast by eight o'clock. Linda made some tea and toast whilst I sorted through my mail.

'Sorry,' she said suddenly as we sat together at the breakfast bar in the kitchen.

'Sorry?'

'About last night.'

'That's all right.' What else could I say? To have said something like, 'It's not as if I don't fancy you' would have sounded banal or, even worse, be taken as an invitation to change my mind.

Luckily, the ringing of the phone saved me.

'Molloy's Evictions at your service, unwanted tenants disposed of to order.'

'Morning, Geoff. You got the message then?'

'Certainly did.' He'd never sounded so ebullient. 'Who are we throwing out?'

I explained about Mr Lloyd and the heroin. 'If we leave pretty sharply, we might catch him before he goes out.'

'I can be there in ten minutes.'

'Make it twenty and I'll meet you outside.'

'Is this at Shelley's house?' asked Linda, who'd overheard my half of the conversation.

I nodded. 'You were going to go there today, weren't you, to sort out her things? You might as well come along now with me.'

She looked apprehensive. 'There's not going to be any trouble, is there?'

'Probably, but you'll be safely out of it in Shelley's flat. We'll go in my car,' I said, remembering her driving. 'Shouldn't take us too long – most of the traffic will be going the other way.'

Geoffrey, in his seventh-hand rusting BMW, was already at Livingstone Drive when we drew up outside. I let Linda into the ground-floor flat and told her to lock the door.

'Let's go,' I said to Geoffrey. I ran up the stairs, feeling like The Sweeney, Geoff close behind me, and hammered loudly on Mr Lloyd's door.

'I've got the keys, boss, if he doesn't answer.'

But he did. He was wearing a plain white T-shirt and striped boxer shorts. Despite the carefully trimmed beard, without his glasses he looked less academic and more aggressive than I remembered him. He had a substantial covering of body hair on his arms, legs and chest that would have precluded him from a job with The Chippendales. I barged past him into the room, closely followed by Geoffrey.

'Excuse me, what's going on here?'

'I want you out of this flat.'

'You what?'

Geoffrey had followed me into the room and we faced him together.

'You heard. *Out.* Like now.'

'What for?'

'I had to come into this flat yesterday to check a reported smell of gas and I found a quantity of heroin in your bedroom. Now, if you'd rather I went to the police, fine. We'll call them from that phone. But, from my point of view, I just want you out of here – so if you'll get your stuff together, as far as I'm concerned, that's it.'

'There's no drugs in this flat.'

'Look, I'm not arguing.'

'You can't throw me out just like that.'

'No?' I went over to his table and picked up a coffee-pot.

He watched bemused as I carried it across the room, opened the window and dropped the pot out. The crash when it hit the ground two storeys down produced a look of horror on Lloyd's face, quickly replaced by an expression of pure hate.

He controlled his temper well. 'That was a gift,' he said and started to move towards me but Geoffrey blocked the way.

'Start packing, sunshine, or we'll do it for you and, as you see, we're none too careful.'

'You're mad.'

'Blazing mad,' I agreed. 'Now are you going or will it be the CD player next?'

For a second, things hung in the balance as he glared at us with fury in his eyes. I thought of possible outcomes. As a first offender, could I expect a jail sentence for illegal eviction and harassment, not to mention destruction of property? Assuming, of course, Lloyd didn't produce a gun and shoot us both on the spot.

And then the moment passed. 'All right, I'll go, but you'll have to give me a couple of hours to sort my stuff out.'

'You can have one hour.'

'Let me call a friend to give me a lift.' He maintained his effort to be polite but underneath, I could see he was seething. 'I've been no trouble in this house, Mr Ace, and you have no legal right to throw me out. If I wanted, I could have you arrested for harassment.'

'I don't think you will.'

'Only because I have no desire to waste the energy. But I shall remember what you have done.'

'It's nothing personal,' I told him. Now that the threat of violence had receded, I was prepared to discuss the matter in a more civilised way. 'But if drugs are found on my premises, it is me the police arrest. Simple as that. Sorry.'

I stood by whilst he phoned. 'Tell me,' I said when he'd

arranged his transport, 'did you know the lady on the ground floor that died, Mrs Lunt?'

'Never spoke to her.'

'Mr Mountbatten next door reckons she's been up here.'

'Well, I certainly haven't seen her. I keep myself to myself.'

'What about Miss Barrie?'

'What about her? I don't know her. Who is she?'

'She lives on the ground floor too, opposite Mrs Lunt's flat.'

'Never heard of her.'

'I see.' I moved towards the door, Geoffrey behind me. 'An hour then.'

We went downstairs and joined Linda who was also busily packing. She'd arranged her sister's smaller belongings and papers on the table. I introduced Geoffrey.

'Will you be able to get everything in your Fiesta to take back to Nelson?' I asked.

'I think so. There's not really that much, though won't you want to examine everything for clues?'

'I already have and there's nothing that gave me any indication as to why she would kill herself.'

Whilst we helped her sort out the rest of Michelle Lunt's effects, a van pulled up outside the house and a couple of men carrying flattened cardboard boxes rang Lloyd's bell. By the end of the hour, after several trips up and down the stairs, the van appeared full.

Geoff and I went up to make sure. The rooms had been stripped of everything apart from the basic furniture, which was mine.

'I won't forget this.' Lloyd, flanked by his support army, sounded threatening but I took him unawares by going up to him and putting my hand on his shoulder.

'Write to me from your new address with proof that your utility bills have been paid and I'll refund any outstanding rent.'

He shook free from my grasp. 'Oh, don't worry, you'll be hearing from me.' The words carried enough menace to send a chill down my spine. Geoffrey moved forward aggressively but I waved him back.

'The keys, please.' I held out my hand and he put them in it. I stood aside for the men to leave then locked the door of the flat behind us before we escorted them out of the house.

'Why didn't you let me whack him?' Geoffrey complained. 'We could have battered all three of them.'

'No sense in making enemies. That's why I tried to reason with him.'

'That's bollocks. You don't reason with scum like that.'

'Maybe you're right.'

'Do you think he had anything to do with the girl who topped herself?'

'I did at one time but I'm not so sure now.'

'What about him and that Miss Barrie?'

'Don't know. I'm certain it was her who came up and knocked yesterday when I was here.'

'Perhaps he's been dealing and she's one of his customers.'

'Maybe.'

'So we should be searching her room next?'

'We'll see how it goes.' The thought of crossing Miss Barrie didn't appeal to me. She was one of those 'I know my rights' people.

We went back to Linda who'd been stacking up her sister's things ready to take away. 'Pity he didn't leave us some cardboard boxes,' I said.

'I think there were a couple left upstairs – I'll run up and see.' Geoffrey took the key from me.

'About tonight,' said Linda after he'd left the room.

'Yes?'

'Do you still want me to stay – you know, after last night and that trouble with your girlfriend?'

I couldn't see it would do any harm. The damage had already been done, insomuch as she'd already stayed with me for two nights.

Whether or not Maria would accept my explanation was another matter.

Geoffrey bore three boxes when he returned. 'Nice of Mr Lloyd to assist in our packing.'

We managed to fit all the stuff into the back of the RAV4. 'Thanks for the help,' I said to Geoffrey.

'Two flats to let now, eh boss?'

'Looks like it. I'm going to have to be more careful whom I let to. Didn't you say you had an accountant lined up?'

'And a girl working at Rushworths, the music shop. Wants one for her and her boyfriend. He's a keyboard player. They could have Lloyd's place.'

'I'll leave it to you to show them round, Geoff.'

'Are you sure?'

'Why not? After this shambles, you can't do any worse than me, and anyway, I'm going to be busy.' I looked at Linda. 'I've got to find out why Shelley Roberts alias Michelle Lunt died.'

Chapter Ten

Geoffrey went back to the office and I took Linda to lunch at Lucy in the Sky with Diamonds. The café was full but we managed to grab a table outside. Margie came out to take the order, looking questioningly at Linda and giving me a quizzical stare.

I settled for the lentil and bacon broth and Linda said she'd have the same.

'What do you think will happen at the inquest tomorrow?' she asked when Margie had gone.

'Can't see it being anything other than suicide, I'm afraid, and unless there's anything untoward, they'll release the body for the cremation next week.'

'Do you think they'll have found out if Shelley was married or not?'

'I'm sure they will.' And I was pretty certain now she would turn out to be single. Yet, even if it suited Wilbur Lunt to pretend he was married to her, what reason would she have for going along with it?

'You'll keep me in touch with your progress when I go back, won't you?' she asked.

'Of course. You're my client, aren't you?'

After the meal, I dropped her at the flat. 'I'm doing the show till seven,' I said, 'then I have a bit of business to see to. Can you get yourself something to eat from the freezer, because I don't expect I'll be back until after eleven.'

The 'business' I had was with Maria. I needed to go round

and assure her that Linda's visit was totally innocent, which, of course, it was.

Somehow, though, I didn't think my task would be so easy. The vision of Linda wandering around my flat half-dressed was one that would make most women suspicious, and in my case there was the added disadvantage of my relationship with Hilary.

Maria had never been entirely happy that I still saw someone she regarded as a relic from my past, and I don't suppose I could blame her. At least Linda was returning to Nelson straight after the inquest.

I had a few hours to kill before the show so I went back to Lucy in the Sky and ordered a pot of tea. 'Nice girl that,' said Margie. 'Bit young for you though, Johnny.'

Linda's age hadn't entered my mind. 'Nothing like that,' I told her. 'Her sister lived in one of my flats and she committed suicide last week.'

'Oh, how awful! What happened?'

I explained about Michelle and how I'd been helping Linda sort everything out. What I was doing, of course, was getting in my excuses in case Margie talked to Maria. Margie would be able to confirm to her that I wasn't lying about Linda, and that mattered to me.

Margie had always been very discreet about Hilary and Maria, both of whom she saw regularly, but I sensed she'd regard any other woman as an interloper. Or was it just guilt on my part, imagining reactions that weren't there?

I finished the tea, which I hadn't really wanted, said goodbye to Margie and walked down to the Pier Head. The wind was frisky for July. I waited for the ferry coming across and took the round trip.

Only a few school-kids shared the top deck with me, running from one side to the other, shouting and generally fooling around. They ignored me. I looked out across the choppy waters of the Mersey and tried to make some sense out of Michelle Lunt's death.

It seemed pretty certain it was suicide if only because, as far as I could work out, nobody stood to gain from her dying. Unless she was killed to keep her mouth shut, which made Wilbur the obvious suspect. Had he been under her surveillance and broken her cover?

I was no nearer an answer when the *Mountwood* docked back again at Liverpool. I disembarked, and walked into town as far as Quiggins. Quiggins is an old warehouse turned into an indoor market with stalls on three floors, selling a miscellany of designer fashions, second-hand clothes, CDs, indie records, antiques, body jewellery, bizarre gifts and all kinds of way-out gear.

Most of the customers were students and young people, fashion-conscious but poor.

In the end, I bought a pair of black Kickers. I was lucky, they had just one pair of size tens left.

On the next floor, a longhaired girl with a ring through her lip sold me a bottle of patchouli oil for my burner.

There was still over an hour to go before I was due on air so I took my time eating a sandwich in the upstairs café before strolling across to the radio station.

Ken was sorting out the mail.

'You're early. We've had a couple more people on, wanting you to open garden parties.'

'No way.' I don't do personal appearances.

'I don't blame you. Looks like yours were made for radio.' He chortled at his little joke. It was one he repeated most weeks, in various different forms.

I played a couple of Seventies disco tracks on the show, Candi Staton's *Young Hearts Run Free* and *Le Freak* by Chic. Despite Glam Rock fashions coming into vogue again, I couldn't see me digging out my fluorescent flares from the wardrobe.

I drove to Maria's flat in Blundelsands with some apprehension. It turned out to be justified, although I wasn't prepared for such a hostile reception.

She opened the front door and I stepped in but got no further than the hall.

'I go away for five lousy days,' Maria said fiercely, 'and you move some tart in.'

'Hang on, Linda isn't a tart and she hasn't moved in.'

'If she isn't a tart, why was she wandering round your flat in her knickers?'

I explained about Michelle Lunt's suicide and how her sister had come over from Nelson and had nowhere to stay. It sounded pretty plausible but it was all totally irrelevant to Maria, who wanted to know only one thing.

'Did you sleep with her?'

'No,' I murmured, 'I didn't.'

'Liar.'

'I said no, I didn't sleep with her.'

'And I say you did. You forget, Johnny, I know you.' She sighed. 'You're like all men, you haven't got the willpower to say no,' her voice changed to a snarl, 'however ugly the slut is.'

I was about to say that Linda was neither ugly nor a slut, but realised that that might not be the best line of argument.

'Look, just go, Johnny. Get out. I thought we had a relationship.'

'We have.'

'How can we, when you go off with someone else the minute I'm away?'

I opened my mouth but didn't get a chance to speak.

'And don't ring me again. It's over.' She pushed me through the door, started to close it then opened it again. 'You know, I really thought we had something good between us.'

'We have,' I protested. 'But I've never pretended I've been going out exclusively with you. You've known all along about Hilary.'

'Hilary.' She spat out her name contemptuously. '*She* was never a threat.'

'How can you say that? I've been seeing her for over twenty years.'

'Exactly. If anything had been going to come of it, you'd have married her by now. You just use each other for convenience. If your dear Hilary met somebody tomorrow, she'd be off like a shot, twenty years or not.'

I didn't know what to say. I'd never even contemplated that Hilary wouldn't always be around. But then, I didn't want to be without Maria either and, if I sometimes acknowledged to myself how selfish that was, it was something I couldn't help.

Maria was still raving on. 'I've been prepared to accept that you don't want commitment, but I'm damned if I'm sticking around while you shag everything that will open its legs for you.'

I was shocked at the language. Maria is never usually coarse. 'It's not like that . . .' I started to say, but it sounded lame and she wouldn't let me finish anyway.

'Goodbye, Johnny,' she said, and quietly but firmly shut the door.

I walked slowly back to the car and drove into town. I couldn't face Linda yet so I went to the Masquerade Club for a couple of drinks.

Tommy McKale listened to my gloomy tidings but showed little sympathy. 'Had to happen,' he said, 'the way you juggle women around. Law of averages.'

'It was a misunderstanding.'

'Always is. What's the new one like?' I explained about Linda being just a client. 'Ah!' he said. 'So you *did* get involved in that hanging business, just as I predicted. And what was it you used to say about business and pleasure?'

'I know, don't tell me.'

'Your trouble is, you're dick happy.' He sighed. 'You know, there's one good thing about old age and that's the blessed relief of impotence. Or so my grandfather used to tell me.'

'I thought that impotence was a curse. Why else are all the pensioners queuing up for Viagra?'

'They're deluding themselves. They'd be better off with bromide. Think of the trouble all this sex business causes.' I didn't need reminding. 'Don't worry about Maria though, Johnny. She must like you or she wouldn't have made such a fuss.' I hoped he was right. 'Give her a few days.' He grinned. 'When did you say Hilary was back?'

I groaned. 'Saturday. But Linda goes back to Nelson tomorrow.'

'Lucky for you. And what about the case? How far have you got with that?'

'I'm missing one American banker who isn't who he said he was.'

'The husband?'

'Supposedly the husband. But it turns out the dead wife was an undercover drugs cop and probably not married to him.'

'Heavy stuff. You sure you've not been reading too many Raymond Chandler books?'

'I know. It sounds crazy, doesn't it?'

'It's going to be difficult for you, tracing them.'

'You reckon?'

'Well, you haven't got the back-up that the police have for tracking down people. You can hardly ring the FBI for information, especially if the man was one of their own.'

I told him about the heroin find and the eviction of Lloyd. 'You want to be careful there,' he warned. 'Don't make enemies out of those people – you never know who's behind them. But I agree, you don't want that going on in your flats. Let me know if you have any comeback and I'll sort it for you.'

I knew the McKale way of sorting things from previous experience and I found it reassuring that I could call on him if necessary.

'Here.' He took a card out of his pocket and handed it to

me. 'If you get into any trouble, you can reach me at this number in the daytime.'

I thanked him and put the card carefully in my wallet.

'Do you think there's a connection with Lloyd and your dead swinger?' Tommy asked.

'I tend to think it was coincidence. Let's face it, half the students in the city probably have some sort of banned substance hidden in their gaffs at any one time.'

'But she was with the Drug Squad, remember.'

'So they say, but I can't see the two of them coming all the way from America for Lloyd. He's hardly big league.'

'How do you know that? If they weren't after Lloyd, why were they living in your house?'

I didn't know the answer to that one and, after the events of the evening, it wasn't uppermost in my mind.

I downed the rest of my drink, said goodbye to Tommy and made my way back to the flat. Linda was already in bed, propped up on the pillows, covers round her, watching *Friends*.

'You don't look very happy,' she greeted me. I said nothing but threw down my leather jacket on the end of the bed. 'You've been to see your girlfriend, haven't you?'

What is it about women and intuition?

She sat up and turned down the sound on the television. 'What did she say?'

' "Goodbye" is, I think, a fair summing-up of the conversation.'

'Oh dear, I'm really sorry, Johnny.' The words sounded convincing, though Linda didn't look completely sincere. 'Don't worry. She'll come round sooner or later.'

I'd not yet begun to consider the possibility that Maria wouldn't 'come round' – and I certainly didn't want to think about it at that moment.

'Good night, Linda,' I said wearily, and taking a pair of clean pyjamas from the wardrobe, I went back to spend another restless night on the settee.

Chapter Eleven

The inquest went as predicted. A verdict of suicide was brought in after the forensic evidence proved that no third party had been instrumental in tying the rope around Michelle Roberts' neck.

The coroner pointed out that there were no injuries or marks on the body to suggest that any force had been used or, indeed, that another person had been present at the time of death.

Then the suicide note was read out. I was hoping this would provide some clue as to why Michelle had hung herself but it was brief and non-committal. *I can't go on any more. Please forgive me. I'm so sorry*, it said.

A message was read out from Miss Roberts' partner, Wilbur Lunt, expressing his distress and sadness at the death of someone who had been very dear to him, and sending deepest apologies for his absence from the inquest due to circumstances beyond his control back in America.

'Crap,' I whispered to Linda but she was sobbing and gave no sign of hearing me.

Detective Sergeant Leary was present but I didn't get the chance to speak to him and he left immediately after the verdict.

'So that's that,' I said. 'All over.'

'Like you predicted, Johnny,' murmured Linda. 'Tidied up. Or, as you would say, swept under the carpet?'

'And it's up to me to unsweep it,' I told her, although

I wasn't sure quite where I would start. I offered to buy her lunch but she declined.

'I think I'll go straight home if you don't mind. I need to organise everything for Shelley's funeral. There's the relatives to tell. Maybe two or three of them will want to come – cousins and so on.'

'Have you decided when to have it?'

'The man at Wavertree suggested next Friday if the inquest went without a hitch.'

'Sounds OK to me. And it's going to be at the Springwood Crematorium?'

'Yes.'

We caught a cab back to my flat and I transferred all Shelley's belongings from my car to Linda's Fiesta while she went upstairs to pack her things.

'It's been really good of you to have me, Johnny.' She smiled affectionately. 'You will do your best to find out what happened to Shelley, won't you? And when you need more money, get in touch.'

'About the money, Linda – I've been thinking it over. I feel I should only charge you if I get a result.'

'But your time . . .'

'You've already paid me quite a lot by letting me keep your furniture. Now, I'm going to give this business with your sister my best shot, but to be honest, it isn't going to be easy. I don't know if I'll be able to achieve that much. I'll ring you regularly to report on my progress though, and if I do come up with something definite, we'll talk about it then.'

She was about to argue but I put my finger on her lips. 'That's final.'

'OK,' she said. 'If that's the way you want it. But I've every faith in you, Johnny. I know you'll discover why Shelley died.'

I wished I felt as confident, I thought, as she drove away in her little blue car. I wasn't even sure where to start. As Tommy McKale had said, the police had all the resources but Detective Sergeant Leary wouldn't lift a finger to help me. On the other hand, there was my old chum in the police force, Jim Burroughs. He might be able to give me some assistance.

I hadn't seen Jim for some time although I'd recently spotted a poster advertising his old group, The Chocolate Lavatory, at a Merseybeats gig at the Orrell Park Ballroom.

Perhaps, as he neared retirement age, he was planning a new career as an ageing pop star. Happily, I'd never felt the desire to resurrect The Cruzads and return to drumming.

'Johnny,' he said when I rang him, 'long time no hear.'

'You've not been into the studio lately, Jim.' Over the years, my radio programme had been quite useful to the police when they wanted to put forward some piece of propaganda or other, and Jim had never been slow to take advantage of this in the past.

'I've been off work, that's why.'

'Nothing serious?' I remembered now that the last time I'd seen him, Jim had been complaining of chest pains, but he'd dismissed them as nothing more than indigestion brought on by the stress of the job.

'They thought I'd had a heart attack at first, but it turned out to be angina.'

I'd always believed they were much the same thing but didn't say so. 'How long are you signed off for?'

'Actually, Johnny, they're talking about early retirement on health grounds. You know what it's like, they don't want us old ones around any more. It's the same everywhere. Christ, my new Chief Inspector's only thirty-eight. Experience counts for bugger all these days.'

'Is that what you want – retirement?'

'I reckon it is. I'll get a good pension and the job's not what it was. It's all red tape, and political correctness and crap like that. Hardly time to catch criminals.'

'You'd miss it.'

'I don't know. There's a lot of stress with the work which is probably why I'm ill in the first place.'

Jim belonged to the old school of policing. Nowadays, the new breed of copper would probably sue his employers for half a million pounds for exposing him to the stress in the first place.

'What would you do?'

'Well, you know the group's got back together,' he said eagerly, 'and we're doing quite well. We've got a gig at the OPB next week.'

I didn't think it would affect the ticket sales for Celine Dion if she'd been in town, and quickly changed the subject before I ended up being talked into going to watch him perform. 'I need your help, Jim, with a case.'

'You're carrying on with the private investigations lark then?'

'I guess so, although I've not got premises yet. This thing came out of the blue. One of my tenants in Livingstone Drive topped herself – Michelle Lunt.'

'I read about that in the *Echo*. One of your flats, was it? You're trying to say it wasn't suicide?'

'No, the verdict was sound but there is something odd about the set-up. Can we meet and I'll tell you about it?'

'Come round to ours tonight after you've done your programme. I'd be glad of the company. The wife watches soaps from five to nine and it drives me bloody barmy sitting in front of the box.'

I'd hardly put the phone down when it rang again.

'I've had your friend Miss Barrie on the blower,' said Geoffrey.

'Oh yes?'

'She wants you to go round and see her, something about her electric meter.'

'Why me? That's your department.'

'Perhaps she fancies you.' I never did appreciate Geoffrey's pathetic attempts at humour. 'She was most insistent *you* went.'

'Oh yes, and Everton might win the Premiership in the next twenty years.'

'Anyway, she said could you call and see her as soon as you can.'

I was curious and curiosity is always a dangerous thing with me. Gets me into no end of trouble. I heated some soup in the microwave for my lunch then set off for Livingstone Drive.

Serina Barrie was waiting for me in her flat.

'Thanks for coming so quickly.'

She was wearing a towelling dressing-gown, which barely covered her knees. Her blonde hair, which had been short when I first met her, was now brushing her shoulders and she wore enough traces of lipstick and eye shadow to accentuate her high cheekbones.

'What's the problem?' I asked in a businesslike way.

'I wanted to ask you a favour.'

'Something about the electric, I believe.'

She lowered her eyes. 'Actually, no. I just said that to your partner.'

'Oh yes?' Geoffrey would have appreciated his elevated status but I was more wary than ever of her motive and it must have shown in my voice.

'Don't worry, it's nothing awful.' She smiled, as if amused at my suspicion. 'I believe you take photographs.'

'Who told you that?'

'Roy Quantine, his name is. He said he used to live in one of your flats.'

I remembered Roy Quantine. He was a seedy little man in his early sixties. In his time he'd been a hospital porter, taxi driver, petty thief, piss artist and general low-life. I'd inherited him when I bought a house in South Albert Road and he'd occupied a grimy studio flat on the top floor.

I couldn't believe it when I'd first walked into the place. My feet stuck to the carpet, the ancient gas cooker was thick with grease, there were pots of half-dead plants all around the flat and unpleasant yellow stains on the bedsheets. The place stank of stale beer, pee and vomit.

As soon as I started to refurbish the property, I asked him to go. He wasn't too keen at first but when I threatened him with the Environmental Health Officer and the Housing Benefit Fraud Squad he disappeared within twenty-four hours and I hadn't seen him since.

As Quantine's territory was unlikely to stretch much beyond the dole office and the pub, I couldn't imagine how he'd ever encountered a young student like Serina Barrie in the first place, especially one as stuck-up and posey as she obviously was.

'You do take them, don't you?' she asked anxiously.

'I used to, but that was years ago. I don't have the equipment any more that a proper photographer would have. Or the studio, come to that.'

Years ago, I bought a second-hand 35mm Nikon and used to do wedding albums, passport photos, that sort of thing. It was just one of the jobs I did to bring in a few quid, like painting and decorating, working behind a bar or . . . playing the drums.

I must have had some eye for composition because most of the time, the results turned out well and I gained a bit of a reputation as a decent photographer which, in turn, led to more assignments.

But then videos came out, with all the special effects that I wasn't able to do, and that was the end of my career as a budding David Bailey. I became a full-time drummer with The Cruzads and the only photos I took after that were holiday snaps.

'Oh, I wouldn't need all that. All it is, I'm putting together a portfolio for this modelling agency, but on my grant I can't afford to go to a proper studio. I just need someone who has an eye for a picture, which I'm told you have.' She widened her eyes disingenuously. 'So what about it? Will you do it?'

I couldn't think of a single logical reason why I shouldn't, although every instinct warned me against it.

'Where do you want them taken? Remember, I've no studio.'

'Outside in the garden here would be fine. There's a lawn and trees. It'll be a nice background for a summer clothes collection.'

'That's what it is, is it? Summer clothes?'

'Yes. Fashion stuff, coats and dresses, not swimwear or lingerie or anything like that.'

'When were you thinking of?'

'Would there be any chance of tomorrow, only I need them quite quickly.'

'Saturday? I suppose so.' There was no match on I wanted to see. Everton were playing at Chester in a friendly. 'Providing it's not pouring with rain.'

'That's great. I'll have my changes of costume ready.'

I arranged to come round at two.

'While I'm here,' I said, 'I wanted to ask you: did you have much to do with Mrs Lunt?'

'The girl from next door, you mean, the one who died? Oh dear, the inquest was this morning, wasn't it? What was the verdict?'

'Suicide. Nothing else it could be, was there?'

'I suppose not. I hardly saw her, just the odd occasion when she was getting the milk in and we exchanged the time of day. I never had a conversation with her.'

'Tell me, was she friendly with Mr Lloyd upstairs?'

'He's gone, hasn't he? I saw him moving his things out yesterday.'

'I was told you and he were quite pally.'

She frowned. 'Who told you that? I don't think I ever spoke to him.'

I didn't mention the footsteps I'd heard on the stairs when I was in Lloyd's flat the previous day.

'Where's he gone, do you know?'

'Why should I?'

'With you both being at university.'

'I didn't know he was,' but she looked disconcerted by my questions. 'It's a big campus.'

It was also a different university but I didn't tell her that.

'So you don't know if he was on speaking terms with Mrs Lunt?'

'I'm afraid not. I'm not a very sociable neighbour, am I?' She laughed and moved to safer subjects. 'Do you think I should send flowers to her funeral, as she lived next door?'

'Not if you didn't know her.'

'No. Right then, I'll see you tomorrow. About two?'

I drove over to the office to fill Geoffrey in about the meeting. 'It had nothing to do with the meters,' I said, and told him about Miss Barrie's request. 'She's trying to make out I'm a modern-day Cecil Beaton. I'm not happy with it, Geoff.'

'It's not like you to be frightened of women.' He nudged me. 'Hey, they're not mucky photos you're doing, are they?'

'In the garden? Don't be bloody daft. It's a fashion portfolio.'

'Oh yes?' Geoffrey looked sceptical. 'Sounds like she's got her eye on you, and after all you said about keeping your hands off the tenants.'

'You're joking. Serina Barrie? I'd rather go ten rounds with Lennox Lewis. Still, I don't suppose it will do any harm.'

Why don't I ever follow my instincts?

Chapter Twelve

After the show, I drove round to Jim Burroughs' house. Jim lives in a 1930s semi in Mossley Hill, a 'naice' middle-class area not far from Menlove Avenue, John Lennon's childhood territory.

His face was pale and he'd lost a few pounds, but otherwise he looked no different from when I'd last seen him some months ago. He still had a full head of grey hair, cropped closely to his skull, and his broad shoulders weren't yet drooping despite his enforced idleness.

'I brought a couple of cans with me.' I produced a four-pack of Newcastle Brown. 'I take it you're allowed to drink?'

He grabbed one swiftly, opened it and took a long, delighted slurp. 'Mm! Not officially, but as long as Rosemary doesn't know . . . I get one glass of red wine with my dinner and that's it. What sort of life is that?'

'Better than the alternative if it kills you.' I opened a can of Scrumpy Jack.

'I've had to give up smoking,' he coughed, 'I'm on a low-fat, no-cholesterol diet, I take ten tablets a day and twice a week I have to go on this bloody machine at the gym. Nearly kills me,' he moaned.

'I thought you coppers were supposed to be super-fit.'

'Load of bollocks. When we're not sloped over a desk or driving all day in traffic jams, choking on exhaust fumes, we're getting beaten up by members of the public.'

'I bet they didn't tell you that when you joined. Mind you,

in those days, policemen wore funny hats and rode round on push-bikes, didn't they?'

We continued this badinage for a few minutes then Jim Burroughs put his can on the floor and adopted his serious Detective Inspector expression. 'Tell me about your case, Johnny. Who's your client?'

'The dead girl's sister.'

'She thinks it was murder, does she?'

'No, she's accepted it was suicide but she wants to know why.'

'Wasn't there a note?'

'Yes, but it told us nothing, just the standard "must end it all, goodbye cruel world" sort of thing.' Jim listened patiently while I told him the whole story.

'I can easily check on the girl's Drug Squad credentials,' he said. 'You think the so-called husband may have been with them as well, and the Citibank job was a blind?'

'Either that or he was the one she was after.'

'Forgive me for saying this, Johnny, but if that was the case, what were they doing living in one of your flats? I mean, don't get me wrong,' he added hastily, seeing the look on my face, 'but yours are hardly the swish upmarket apartments your average merchant banker is looking for.'

Exactly the sentiments Tommy McKale had expressed.

'He answered my ad in the *Echo*, brought his wife along to see it, they both liked it, simple as that. They spent a fortune doing it up – expensive furniture, widescreen TV, you name it.'

'Even so, the area . . .'

'They were strangers. They wouldn't know there was anything wrong with the area.'

'Come off it. Anyone can see it's bedsitland. Professional people rent purpose-built flats or posh houses. If they were genuine, they'd have been in Docklands, like yourself, or out in Gatacre or Formby. No, I think they had a reason for moving into that particular house. Who lived in their flat before them?'

'A third-year maths student, Chris Voke. He left at Easter.'

'Funny time to go, just weeks before his final exams. When did his contract run out?'

'Not until July, but his father was taken ill so he went back home. They only live in Warrington so he was able to travel in every day.'

'Convenient. For the Lunts, I mean, if they wanted to get into the house.'

'You think they paid him to move?'

Jim took another gulp of beer. 'Could be. The question is, who in your house would they be watching? Do you have any drug barons in at the moment?'

I ignored the jibe and told him about Lloyd and the heroin. 'A possibility,' he said doubtfully, 'but I don't think they'd go to all this trouble for a small-time dealer.'

'That's what I thought.' Yet now I wasn't so sure. I thought of who else was in the house. Badger? Pat Lake? Serina Barrie? None of them appeared likely contenders for Mr Big, not even Badger, despite his esoteric lifestyle.

'Maybe he wasn't small-time,' I said, but Burroughs grunted sceptically. 'Is there any chance Mrs Lunt's death could have been murder?' I went on. 'Inquests have been known to get it wrong in the past.'

'Unlikely, but always possible. I think, though, we'll have to go along for the time being with the assumption that it was suicide. Who handled the investigation?'

'A Detective Sergeant Leary.'

'I know him, and he's a right smartarse from all accounts. Didn't you get anywhere with him?'

'No. I got the impression he wanted the whole business put to bed as quickly as possible.'

'Well, manpower's short and a speedy result looks good

on the crime figures. Statistics is all they care about now-adays. They're what we're judged on, though, so you can hardly blame him. Why make work?'

'To get at the truth perhaps?' I said sarcastically but it was wasted on Burroughs.

'If a person wants the truth, Johnny, they go to somebody like you, which is exactly what's happened here. Look, I'll find you all the info on Michelle Lunt or Roberts, whatever her name was.' He coughed slightly. 'I take it I'm on wages?'

I laughed. 'I know how the police feel about back-handers,' I said.

'Of course you do,' he replied. 'We expect them. Where else would you get this information from? Does a "pony" sound reasonable?'

He was right. Where else would I get it? And twenty-five quid was cheap enough. 'I suppose so.'

'In advance.'

I handed across five five-pound notes.

'I might be coming to you for a job one day, Johnny, you never know. When you get your office sorted and I pick up my pension.'

I said nothing but held the suggestion for future consideration. I could do worse than having Jim as a partner if I ever set up the business properly. He'd have all the right contacts.

'You'll be in touch then?' I asked.

'Give it a couple of days. I'll call you next week.' He leant down and handed me the other three cans of Newcastle Brown. 'Here, take these.' He picked up the empty one. 'And this. If Rosemary finds them there'll be trouble.'

There was just one message on the ansaphone when I got back to the flat. Hilary had rung from Greece to remind me that her boat from Thassos was leaving for the mainland tomorrow morning and she would be flying out of Kavala Airport back to England mid-afternoon.

She said she was missing me and would I like to go round to hers in the evening?

She didn't ask me to pick her up at Manchester Airport, which was lucky, because tomorrow afternoon I had my assignment with Miss Barrie.

Chapter Thirteen

Next morning I dug out my old Nikon camera. It was years since I'd used it. On the odd occasions I'd wanted to take photographs, I'd tended to buy one of those throw-away jobs.

I took the Nikon to a friend of mine in Universal Studios in Dale Street to have it checked over.

'Christ, Johnny. It's a museum piece. We're on to digital cameras now and advanced photo systems.'

'Just give me half a dozen rolls of film, Tim,' I said, when he'd reluctantly ascertained that the Nikon was in fine working condition 'for its age'.

Luckily for an outdoor shoot, it was a bright afternoon and at two-thirty, I was standing in the garden at Livingstone Drive watching Serina Barrie walk towards me with all the poise of Claudia Schiffer.

'Will this do?' she asked, stopping beside a clematis bush and turning round. She wore a white silk blouse and a cream suit that, from a distance, could have been mistaken for a designer label.

'Fine,' I said. She placed her hands on her hips, tossed her blonde hair behind her shoulders and gave a sultry pout worthy of Brigitte Bardot at her best. 'Hold it there.'

I studied her image in the viewfinder of the Nikon and pressed the shutter. Then I moved around her, shooting from different angles and shouting out instructions like David Hemmings did in the film *Blow Up*.

Over the next two hours, Serina changed into lots of different tops with co-ordinating skirts and trousers, followed by poses in jeans, dresses, shorts and coats.

I took long shots, close-ups, serious portraits, fun poses and a couple of surreal things with her hanging upside down from tree branches.

'That was really good,' she said, when I'd finished the last film. 'I can tell you've done this before. Why didn't you stick at it?'

'Thought I'd be the second Ringo Starr, that's why,' and I explained about The Cruzads.

'You really ought to take up photography again,' she said flatteringly.

I held out the Nikon. 'Thanks, but I'd need a more up-to-date camera than this.'

'Funnily enough, Roy was talking about cameras the other day. Someone he knows has some for sale.'

'Quantine? I didn't know he was into photography.'

'He isn't. But a friend of his who owns a camera shop is selling up. You never know, you might pick up a bargain. Why don't you ring him?'

'Roy? I don't have his number.'

'No, the man who's got the cameras. Fisher, his name is, Clive Fisher. He lives in Kirkdale. I've got his number in the flat, I'll get it for you.'

I followed her inside and she produced a slip of paper from her handbag. 'Here we are, *Clive Fisher Photographics*,' and she handed me the paper. The phone number was written underneath.

'Thanks. I might give him a ring.' Surprisingly, I'd enjoyed the afternoon. It had brought back memories of the old days, and I felt I could get quite interested in taking photographs again.

'Be quick then, before everything's gone. It's over a week since Roy mentioned it.'

'I might just do that. Tell me, how do you come to know

Roy Quantine? He's not the sort of person who'd belong to your social circle.'

She smiled. 'What's my social circle? No, he drinks in this pub I go to. My boyfriend's studying to be a doctor and a lot of medical students drink there. Roy used to be a hospital porter and he still hangs around with that crowd.'

'Right.' I personally wouldn't have liked someone with Quantine's hygiene record wheeling me into the operating theatre.

'How much will I owe you?'

'I'll let you know later.' I'd not given it a thought. I wasn't out to make a big profit so I imagined I'd allow for the cost of the film and the prints and be happy with that.

'When will the photos be ready?'

'It's the weekend so shall we say Wednesday? Will you be in on Wednesday night?'

'I can be.'

'OK, I'll bring them round at eight after I've done my radio show.'

'Yes, I've been told you're on the radio. I listen to Atlantic 252 myself.' She said it as if the dial was permanently fixed.

Each to his own, I thought. I listen to *The Archers* but it doesn't stop me from watching *Top of the Pops*.

'Thanks again for coming,' she said, ushering me to the door. 'I'm sure my portfolio will be brilliant.'

I hoped so too and I was quite confident the prints would turn out well. The light had been good and Serina Barrie was not only very attractive but also highly photogenic and she knew how to pose in front of the lens.

I drove straight to Universal and left the films to be developed and printed, well satisfied with my afternoon's work. When I got back to the flat, I rang Hilary but there was no reply. Probably her flight had been delayed.

I took out the slip of paper Serina Barrie had given me, pondered for a moment, then dialled the number. If I was going to get involved in investigation work, a new camera could well be a useful asset, and I could claim the cost against tax. Maybe, if they were selling all their stock, Fisher Photographics might also have accessories like telephoto lenses and flashguns for sale.

I was about to put the phone down after it had rung eight times when, ''Ello?' came a gruff voice.

'Is that Clive Fisher Photographics?'

'Who do you want?'

'Mr Fisher if he's available.'

'He's not here.'

'Is that his shop or his home?'

'What did you want?'

'I believe he's got some cameras and things for sale.'

'Who are you?'

'Roy Quantine gave me your number.'

'What were you looking for?'

'A 35mm camera with telephoto lens.' I thought of what the man at Universal had told me. 'Maybe a digital camera. Have you got any I could look at?'

'He's out at the moment.'

I was becoming impatient with the person at the other end. No wonder, I thought, small businesses go bust when they have to rely on cretins answering the phone whenever they leave the shop for a moment.

'When will he be in?'

'He won't. It'll be Monday now.'

'Whereabouts are you and I'll call in on Monday.'

'I don't know. You'll have to ring on Monday.' And he put the phone down. I could see Mr Fisher being very annoyed when he returned and found out he'd missed a customer. It made me all the more determined to chase him up. I realised I'd become quite excited about taking up my old hobby again.

I left it a few minutes then rang Hilary again.

'You must be psychic,' she said breathlessly. 'I got in not five minutes ago.'

'How was the holiday?'

She'd had a great time. Her friends were a lively crowd: they'd done all the bars, visited a few ruins and she now boasted an all-over suntan, which she couldn't wait to show me when I came round.

I told her I'd bring a takeaway over about nine, give her time to unpack.

'Make it an Indian,' she said. 'I've had enough shish kebabs to last me a lifetime.'

I took the Wallasey tunnel and the M53 to Hilary's cottage, picking up a curry in Heswall on the way.

After the events of the week, I was glad to see Hilary again. We'd rarely been apart for this long over all the years I'd known her.

'I've missed you,' she said, after we'd eaten the poppadums, naan bread, chicken korma, vegetable jalfreiza and pilau rice.

'I've missed you, too.' We kissed then she pulled away and reached over for a carrier bag, which she handed to me.

'Your present.'

It was a navy-blue sweatshirt with the outline of the island of Thassos woven in light blue.

'It's lovely, sweetheart. Thanks.' I kissed her fondly.

'It's good to be home,' she sighed. 'A fortnight with the girls is long enough.'

'Where's Pepper?' I asked. I was used to seeing her tortoiseshell cat curled up on the hearthrug.

'Still at the cattery. I'll pick her up in the morning.' She took my hand. 'Come on, let's go to bed. I'm not used to this celibate life.'

It was her way of letting me know she'd been faithful although I hadn't imagined otherwise.

From time to time Hilary goes out with this surgeon, a colleague at the Royal Infirmary where she is a sister. The relationship may or may not be platonic – I don't ask – and

Hilary knows I see Maria, but we have just carried on as always, as loving friends.

I felt a certain disquiet and a curious desolation at the thought that Maria might not go out with me again. However, lying in Hilary's arms, I soon forgot about her, the Michelle Lunt affair, Lloyd, the drugs, Miss Barrie's photos and everything else.

But I wouldn't be allowed to forget any of them for long.

Chapter Fourteen

I spent most of Sunday with Hilary. We went out to lunch at the Basset Hound in Thingwall and collected Pepper on the way back.

The minute the cat was released from her basket, she ran into every room in the cottage. I said, 'She's checking to make sure everything's still the same as when she left it.'

'No,' said Hilary, as Pepper extended her perambulations into the garden, 'she's marking out her territory again. Cats have a great sense of boundary. She knows that all this space is hers, and woe betide any strange cat trying to muscle in. She'll go for them.'

'Game beggar for sixteen, isn't she?'

We sat in the garden over a long drink and watched the cat for a while.

'Anything been happening?' she asked.

I told her about Michelle Lunt's suicide.

'I hope you're not getting involved, Johnny.'

'Well . . .'

'Because it isn't really any of your business. I know how you like to interfere but it can get dangerous, and I don't want anything happening to you.'

'I wouldn't call it interfering exactly,' I began, but thought better of it and let the sentence lie. Hilary has never been keen on my proposed new career.

'And how's the lovely Maria?' she continued.

'I don't know, I haven't seen her.' I felt it unnecessary to relate the brief conversation in Maria's hallway.

'Oh. All off is it? I must say, she lasted longer than I'd have given her credit for.' She put her arms around me. 'So you're all mine again, are you?' Then her hands began to wander.

I wasn't in the mood. Her antagonism to the Lunt affair had struck a false note. I enjoyed my investigation work and perhaps that was the moment when I realised exactly how important it was to me. However much I enjoyed doing the radio programme and however involved I was in the property game, I was deadly serious about setting up as a private eye and I wished Hilary was more enthusiastic about it.

Maria had always been involved with my detective work and I knew I was going to miss her for that apart from anything else. It would have been nice to have had Hilary share it with me, as in all other respects we made an ideal team. She was outgoing, got on well with my friends, knew all the things I liked and our sex-life was wonderful.

'What's the matter?' Hilary asked. She is acutely perceptive to any changes in my mood.

'Nothing. A headache, that's all.'

'I can get rid of that for you.' She smiled wickedly and slowly removed her top. Luckily, the garden was sheltered from the neighbours' view as Hilary unclipped her peach-coloured bra, threw it into the shrubbery, and held up her pretty, suntanned boobs seductively. Her 'treatment' worked. I've always liked making love in the open air and especially in the afternoon.

I stayed until teatime and we parted on good terms. I arranged to take her to see *Godzilla* on her night off on Thursday. She liked horror films although I feared this was going to be more like a cartoon and a bad one at that.

Back at the flat on my own later, however, I started thinking about the case and realised I would have liked having Maria round to discuss it with. But I didn't feel I could ring her yet, which irritated me.

I put some blues on the CD player and hit the Scrumpy

Jack. You can't beat the blues when you're feeling depressed. If they played *Part-Time Love* by Little Johnnie Taylor on the Samaritans' ansaphone, they'd double the amount of suicides in no time.

By the fifth bottle, I'd made up my mind to find premises in town and set up an office. *Ace Investigations*, I thought, would make a good title. High up in *Yellow Pages* too. Never start a business with a Z; the punters give up before they reach your entry.

After the eighth bottle, I fell asleep on the settee and didn't wake until nine the next morning. My head really did ache now, a throbbing pain that was accentuated by the thump of the music still blasting out of the CD player; *Smokestack Lightning* was the track. I stumbled across to turn it off, banging my knee on the coffee table as I did so, sending a searing pain down my leg.

At this point, the phone rang and I knew how Quasimodo must have felt locked up in the bell-tower with a million decibels.

'Johnny Ace.'

'Christ, you sound rough.' Geoffrey seemed amused.

'What bleeding time do you call this?'

'Ten past nine on a bright Monday morning.' People shouldn't be allowed to sound so cheerful at that time. 'Whatever were you doing last night?'

'I was in here with Howling Wolf and a crate of strong cider.'

'Ah. A hangover, is it? Well, I've got more bad news for you.'

'Miss Barrie's hung herself?'

'That's bad news? No, we've got a flood at South Albert Road. Pipe under the bath in Flat Three must be leaking and the water's gone right through the ceiling of number two.'

'That's old Mrs Pemberton's flat, isn't it? She complains enough as it is. How bad is it?'

'Enough to be an insurance job.' Geoffrey knows I never

like to claim if the damage is less than £300. Every claim, no matter how small, pushes up the premiums.

'Ah – that bad. Have you rung Jack?' Jack is the foreman of my workforce.

'He's on his way over with Reg. I just wanted to get the go-ahead for the insurance. Mrs Pemberton's talking about new carpets and redecorating.'

'She would. It's a wonder she didn't have a priceless Picasso hung on the walls. Tell her to forget the carpets and we'll buy her a canoe.' I put the phone down and went to the kitchen cupboard for the Andrews. I took two teaspoons in a glass of water and prepared to face the day.

The first number to call on my pad was Clive Fisher Photographics. I hoped I'd have better luck this time.

The same youth's voice answered.

'Yeah?'

'Is Mr Fisher there?'

'He's out.'

'I'm ringing about the cameras he has for sale. I spoke to you on Saturday.'

'Oh yeah. He says you can come round and look at them.'

'Whereabouts are you?' He gave me an address in Kirkdale. 'Are you open all day?'

'Someone'll be here,' he said.

'Right. I'll be down later this morning.'

After I'd had a hot shower followed by an ice-cold rinse, I felt better. I thought I'd maybe go round a few estate agents' offices later to get an idea of what office premises were available in town. Meanwhile, I set off to find Clive Fisher's photographic shop.

The first surprise was, it wasn't a shop. The address turned out to be a terraced house in a rundown street a couple of blocks from Hawthorne Road.

I parked the RAV4 outside and, stepping round the dog-dirt on the pavement, I knocked on the front door.

The lad who opened it was about nineteen. His hair was cropped, his expression sullen and he wore a dirty polo shirt and camouflage trousers. 'Yeah?'

'I was looking for a camera shop – Clive Fisher Photographics. I was given this address but—'

'You the fella what rang about the cameras?'

Now I recognised the voice on the phone. 'That's right.'

Wordlessly, he disappeared inside, leaving me standing on the step, and returned a few seconds later with two cameras. 'Me dad's out but he left these.'

I took one from him and examined it. It was a Minolta Dynex 3000i. There was no box or case with it, nor an instruction book, but the camera appeared to be new. I couldn't see any scratches or signs of wear but I knew most camera shops dealt in second-hand gear.

I gave it him back and looked at the other one. This was a Canon and it appeared to have a fault in that I couldn't get the shutter to function.

'How much for the Minolta?' I asked, handing the Canon back.

'He wants £150 for the two.'

'I only want one.'

'Sorry, mate. He says to sell the pair or forget it.'

'What about other things? Are there no lenses or tripods or flashes left?'

'All gone, mate. You're a bit late. All that's left is these two as you see them and he wants a ton and a half.'

'But I don't need two cameras.' He shrugged his shoulders and looked bored. 'Look, I'll give you £75 for that one.' I pointed to the Minolta. 'It's a good price seeing as there's no case or instructions with it.'

He began to get shirty. 'I told you, it's two or nothing so take 'em both or fuck off.'

I made a mental calculation. Each camera would cost about £200 in the shops but that would be brand new, in perfect working order and guaranteed. Although the Minolta looked new, I couldn't be certain it was, whilst the Canon, being broken, was almost certainly second-hand and might cost a lot to repair.

'OK, I'll give you £100 for the two.' I took out a wad of five-pound notes. 'Cash.' I felt £100 for the Dynex was about right. The Canon I wasn't really interested in. 'That one's broken, you know. You'll never sell it and digital cameras are coming in now. These will soon be out of date.'

'Piss off. One fifty for the two or forget it.'

'I'll forget it.' I walked angrily to the kerb and climbed into the RAV4, annoyed that my time had been wasted, but before I could start the engine, he appeared at the driver's window. I wound it down.

'Cash, you said?'

I counted out twenty of the notes. 'One hundred pounds.'

'Make it one twenty?'

It was my turn to say, 'Piss off.'

'All right. Here, have the fuckers.' He thrust both cameras into my lap, grabbed the money out of my hand and ran back into his house.

I put the cameras on the seat beside me and drove off before he changed his mind. Half a mile down the road, I realised I hadn't got a receipt, but at the price I'd paid for the gear, I could afford to miss out on the tax relief. Anyway, I didn't feel like going back and asking for one. Mr Fisher junior was hardly approachable and probably hadn't learnt to write anyway.

I wasn't to realise it at the time, because I was too busy with the Michelle Lunt case, but not getting that piece of paper was a major mistake. I certainly could not have bargained for the horrendous consequences.

Chapter Fifteen

It was Tuesday morning when Jim Burroughs rang me. I'd spent most of Monday looking at premises in different parts of town but there was nothing that took my fancy.

'I'm at the office this morning,' I told him, 'but come down to The Diner at one, Jim, and I'll buy you lunch.'

The Diner is on the ground floor of the Royal Liver Building and it caters for the people who work on the nine floors above. I think it must be subsidised because the prices are cheap and the food's good.

Jim Burroughs turned up in a grey three-piece suit and could, for all the world, have been another insurance salesman except nobody working on the upper floors these days seemed to be over twenty-nine.

'Well,' I said, when we'd carried our meals over to the far end of the hall, close to the fountain, 'what have you found out?'

'Bloody hell, give me a chance. Eat first, talk later, eh? Pass the salt, will you?'

'It's bad for your blood pressure.' I handed it to him and he sprinkled it liberally on his chips.

'If I don't have it, it's bad for my temper and that sends my blood pressure up anyway.'

His condition didn't seem to have affected his appetite. He munched his way through his mixed grill with enthusiasm, occasionally allowing globules of fat to run down his chin, eventually to be wiped off with the back of his hand.

'You certainly know how to eat with finesse,' I said. 'Must be all those Masonic dinners.'

'Fookorph,' he spluttered, releasing pieces of black pudding into the air, but I caught the meaning.

'Michelle Lunt,' he said finally, wiping his mouth with a napkin. 'A mystery lady and no mistake.'

'How much of what the solicitor said was true?'

'Most of it. She was part of a nationwide team set up to investigate a major drug ring.'

'In Liverpool?'

'Apparently.'

'What do you mean, apparently?'

'Nobody's saying much, Johnny. I don't even know where she was stationed originally.'

'Aren't the police following it up?'

'I'm afraid not. The case is dead and buried as far as our lot are concerned.'

'Did you speak to Detective Sergeant Leary?'

'I spoke to John Sutton who's Leary's boss.'

'And?'

'He was very cagey. Just said the case was closed and that the deceased had been a serving officer with another force who had been duly informed. He wouldn't tell me which force that was.'

'Why not?'

'I don't know. Like you say, there's something odd about the whole set-up, but when I ask questions I come up against closed doors.'

'What did he say about Wilbur Lunt?'

'Never mentioned him.'

'Didn't you ask?'

'Of course I asked. Sutton said Leary had spoken to Lunt and, as far as he knew, Lunt had returned to the States.'

'And they left it at that?'

Jim Burroughs put on his exasperated expression. 'Look, Johnny, you must realise, the only matter our people were dealing with was a suicide. The woman had left a note saying she intended to kill herself, and Forensic found nothing to suggest otherwise, so what else is there to investigate? Nobody's made a complaint.'

'But I told Leary about Wilbur Lunt not working for Citibank and giving a false telephone number and references.'

'That's between you and him though, nothing to do with his wife's death.'

'But, of course, she wasn't his wife, was she? Furthermore, Leary knows Lunt lied about meeting Michelle's mother.'

'So what? Strange, I'll grant you, but nothing criminal in it.'

I tried another tack. 'If Michelle was with the police, and we know Wilbur wasn't with Citibank, who was he with? Was he with the police too?'

'Unlikely, I'd say. Anyway, he was American, wasn't he?'

'So he said. I wonder why he lied about being with Citibank?'

'Who knows? He may have had a million reasons, even quite innocent ones. Maybe he just didn't want you to know what he did for a living. Perhaps he was a condom salesman and he found it embarrassing to tell you.'

'He went to extraordinary lengths to hide it, whatever it was. One thing's for certain, he was earning big money from somewhere, judging by the furniture he put in the flat and the car he drove.'

'I thought the car was hired.'

'It's not cheap even hiring a Merc, Jim.'

'When he paid you, were his cheques from Citibank?'

'Oh yes, and the standing order for the rent, but all that proves is that he has an account there, not that he worked for them.'

'Which he didn't.' Jim Burroughs took out a white tablet

and popped it in his mouth. 'Indigestion,' he explained. 'Brought on by the blood pressure tablets. These help the indigestion but they usually give me a terrible headache.'

'Don't tell me, so you have to take another tablet for your head. Have you ever thought the drug companies planned it that way?'

'Probably.' He swallowed the tablet with the dregs of his tea. 'So I'm afraid that's all I can tell you, Johnny.'

'Can you find out if Wilbur Lunt did fly back to America?'

'You think he may still be in the country?'

'Could be. I'd like to know why he came over here in the first place.'

'To be with his wife – sorry, his girlfriend.'

'So she's working on an important case and he's just along for the ride.'

'Why not?'

'Unless he was working with her, maybe as her cover.'

'In which case he'd be on the payroll as well.'

'Would you be able to trace him if he was in the police?'

'I could try, I suppose.'

I stood up. 'Have a go for me, Jim. I need to know who Wilbur Lunt really is. Who does he work for and has he done a runner? If so, I reckon we'll have a job finding him, and he's the most likely person to know why Michelle killed herself.'

'If you don't mind me saying so, Johnny, this is a bit of a daft project you've taken on.'

'Why's that?'

'Well, nobody stands to gain anything even if you do get a result. The girl's dead, nothing's going to bring her back. There's no crime to solve, everyone agrees it was suicide – the legacy's gone to the rightful beneficiary, so why bother?'

'Let's say I'm curious. There's obviously some big mystery here and I want to know what it is.'

'And why should the sister spend half her inheritance chasing up motives and reasons which may never come to light even if we do find Lunt? Let's assume Lunt and the dead girl were a couple; however close he was to her, he might not know why she topped herself. Nobody can be privy to another person's thoughts, Johnny. What I want to know is, what does your client hope to gain?'

'Peace of mind, Jim, I daresay. And there's quite a few people in the world who'd pay good money for that.'

After I left Jim Burroughs, I walked back to the flat and gave some thought to Michelle Lunt. I knew nothing whatsoever about her. Furthermore, I was unlikely to find out anything from other sources.

Linda could only tell me about the person her sister had been ten years or more ago. None of the people at Livingstone Drive had had a decent conversation with her, and her life before she came to Liverpool was a complete mystery. Her occasional postcards and phone calls to Linda containing the barest details of her movements may not have been telling the truth.

The only person I knew who could tell me a thing about her was Wilbur Lunt. Everything rested on finding him.

I gave Linda a ring to keep her up to date on my progress or lack of it but only got her ansaphone. However, she rang me back just before I left for the radio station.

'You think the police are hiding something?' she asked. 'Why would they do that?'

'If it was part of an ongoing investigation, they might be keeping things under wraps.'

'Something to do with Shelley working on a drugs case, you mean?'

'Yes.' I suspected there was more to it than that but I saw no point in alarming Linda.

'Are there many people coming over for the funeral?' I asked.

'Only me. Our cousins are sending flowers and she never
kept in touch with any of her schoolfriends.'

'What about your father?'

'I wrote and told him when she died but I've not had
a reply.'

'Isn't he on the phone?'

'Unobtainable. I think they must have moved again. I
didn't get a Christmas card last year – I told you, didn't I?
I suppose he wants to forget the past and start a new life.'

She seemed very philosophical about it. I would have
been very hurt to have been discarded in such a way by
my parent.

'There's not going to be a big turnout then?'

'Only you and me so far, unless Shelley's employers turn
up. I assume that Wilbur Lunt won't be coming.'

'Unlikely. As for her department, I don't know. As a
matter of courtesy, you think they'd send a representative.'

'Will you meet me there then, at the Crematorium?'

'Yes, that's fine. Say quarter to eleven.'

'Maybe we could go out later for a meal?' She sounded
desolate but taking her up on it presented difficulties. Hilary
would be staying over on the Thursday night, which meant
she might still be around on Friday daytime.

'I've got a meeting with my architect at two,' I lied, 'but
I'll see what I can do.' Linda was also my client, another
reason for keeping her at a distance.

'What was that record you played last night, something
about a cemetery?' Ken asked me when I arrived at the
station.

'*Part-Time Love* by Little Johnnie Taylor, why?'

'Someone wanted to buy it.' He sounded surprised.

'You see? I told you my listeners were people of dis-
cernment.'

'Nonsense. Your whole show last night was most depres-
sing. All that wailing stuff – morbid, I call it.'

'I felt morbid and, what's more, I feel just as morbid tonight. So be warned.'

I wouldn't last two hours on a commercial station with a computerised playlist and a script written by someone else.

'Hey, Ken,' I said, as a thought struck me. 'You're keen on photography, aren't you?' I recalled interminable sets of holiday snaps he'd shown me over the years, taken in places like Cornwall and Bognor Regis. Not for Ken the delights of Paris or the Caribbean. The Isle of Man was abroad to him.

'Why?' He sounded suspicious.

'I've got a camera I might want to sell, that's all. A Canon.' I told him the model and explained how I'd bought two in a job lot. 'Better than that old compact thing you've got.'

'Why are you selling that one rather than the other? Is there something wrong with it?' How paranoid can you get?

'No, it's new.' I'd no intention of selling it until I'd had the fault fixed. 'The bloke I bought it off has retired and sold his stock off, that's all.'

'Bring it in, I'll have a look at it. I'm not promising, mind.'

Next morning I went down to Universal Studios to collect the Serina Barrie photos. I took with me the two cameras I'd bought from Clive Fisher's son and, as an afterthought, my old Nikon.

'Can you mend this, Tim?' I asked, handing across the Canon. 'I can't get the shutter to work.' He took it from me and disappeared into the back. A couple of minutes later, he emerged smiling.

'All fixed.'

'That was quick.'

'It wasn't difficult. It only needed new batteries.'

So the camera had been used before. All the same, it looked pretty new. I showed him the Minolta Dynex. 'Have you got a telephoto lens that would fit this and, if so, would you take my museum piece in part-exchange.'

Tim smiled. 'I was only joking about it being a museum piece, you know.' He opened up the Nikon and checked it over. 'Ah, they don't make them like this any more.'

'What do you think then?'

'I've got a 28–200mm zoom lens here that would do you perfectly for the Dynex. Give me the lens that's on it now plus the Nikon and we'll call it a straight swap.'

It seemed fair to me. 'You're on.'

He checked over the Minolta for me, fitted the zoom lens and put a film each in both the Minolta and the Canon.

'There, you're all set up now. Going back into the business, are you?' Tim remembered me from way back in the *Ace Photography* period.

'No, strictly amateur these days. Are my prints ready?'

'I've got them right here.' He passed over six packages held together by a wide elastic band. 'Nice girl.'

'She wants to be a model.'

'Bit young for you.'

'She's a tenant, Tim.' I opened up the top envelope and flicked through the prints. Serina Barrie in leather trousers and a short halter top looking very fetching. 'I'm glad I got the 8" by 6" size. Not bad, are they?'

'They're very good. You could do this professionally, you know.'

'I suppose in a way this is a professional job. She wants them for her portfolio when she applies for work with modelling agencies.'

'They won't let her down.'

I gathered my cameras and paid for the prints and batteries.

I took the Canon with me to the station and showed it to Ken. 'Perfect working order,' I said, 'plus new batteries and a film in it. What more could you ask for?'

'How much?'

'They're two hundred new.'

'I thought you said it was new.'

'Display model, Ken, that's why there's no instruction book or box.'

'Or guarantee. What if it goes wrong?'

'If anything goes wrong within six months, I'll give you your money back. I can't say fairer than that, can I?'

'So what do you want for it?'

'A ton.'

He pursed his lips. 'Sounds expensive. I'll give you seventy-five.'

'Sorry, Ken. I couldn't let it go for less than a hundred. It's not even half price.'

'Oh, very well, go on, I'll have it. You'll have to wait till Friday for the money if that's all right?'

I told him it was. I was well pleased with the deal and so should Ken have been. At £100, the Canon was a bargain. As for me, all it had cost me was my old Nikon and the price of the batteries. In return I'd acquired a new Minolta Dynex with zoom lens worth about £300. Celebrations all round.

After I'd done the programme, I drove straight to Livingstone Drive. I was looking forward to seeing Miss Barrie's face when I showed her the photos. I was sure she'd be well pleased with them.

It was shortly after eight o'clock when I pulled up outside the house. I could hardly believe it was only a fortnight since Michelle Lunt was found hanging in the front room of No. Three.

Geoffrey had now re-let the flat, to the accountant he'd mentioned, and the keyboard player and his girlfriend were installed in Mr Lloyd's old place.

I let myself in the front door and rang Serina Barrie's bell. Nobody answered. I rang again and knocked loudly, in case the bell wasn't working. No reply.

I gave it another couple of goes before the door on the other side opened and a youth with glasses and a shock of curly hair peered out from the Lunts' erstwhile home.

'Can I help you?'

'You must be Giles,' I said. 'Johnny Ace. I'm your landlord.'

'Oh, hello.' He held out his hand. 'Pleased to meet you.'

'Settling in, are you? Has Geoffrey fixed you up with everything you need?'

'Yes, everything's fine, thanks. I only moved in yesterday. The furniture's first class.'

I wondered who'd paid for it if it wasn't Citibank. 'Better than your average flat. They're not all like this. You got lucky.' So had I, although I didn't feel I'd done too much yet to justify owning it.

'I'll say.' He glanced across to Serina Barrie's door. 'Has somebody moved in there?'

'How do you mean? A girl called Serina Barrie lives there. She's been here nearly two years. Haven't you met her?'

'But that flat's empty.'

'What?'

'The guy on the top floor, with the Rastafarian hairstyle, he told me. She left on Sunday night.'

'You're joking!'

I ran to the car to fetch my set of spare keys and opened Miss Barrie's door.

Giles was right. The room was stripped of every trace of Serina Barrie. I checked the bedroom, bathroom and kitchen. Not so much as a pair of tights, a toilet roll or a loaf of bread to show anyone had recently lived there.

Serina Barrie had completely disappeared.

Chapter Sixteen

'Sunday night she went, man. Two big guys with a hire van came and shifted all her stuff. I passed them in the hall.'

I was in Badger's flat and he was filling me in on the details of Serina Barrie's unexpected departure. 'Did she say where she was going?'

'Never spoke to me. But then, she never spoke to anyone, stuck-up bitch. Had she paid her rent?'

'Yes, but I saw her on Saturday and she never mentioned leaving.'

There was something very strange about the whole thing. What had made her suddenly decide to leave? Or was it planned? But, if she did know she was going, why had she asked me to bring the photos round on Wednesday? It was more likely that something had happened between Saturday afternoon and Sunday evening.

'Did she look . . .' I searched for a word '. . . distressed?' Suggesting she was being kidnapped or fleeing from some imminent danger sounded too far-fetched yet I did feel her departure might have sinister overtones.

'No. She was hustling the guys, giving her orders but she seemed in control of things. Why? Do you think something has happened to her?'

'I don't know.'

Badger followed me downstairs for an inspection of Miss Barrie's former home.

'Man, this house is getting dangerous. First the swinging sister, then Mr Needle and now the lady with the vanishing trick, all in a few days. Maybe I should be putting steel shutters over my windows.'

Giles, who was still hovering in the hall, listened in alarm. 'He's only joking,' I quickly reassured him. 'It's a very quiet house really.'

Badger said nothing but rolled his eyes like Al Jolson.

'You've no friends looking for accommodation, have you?' I asked Giles, as I shut the door of the empty flat behind us.

'Not at the moment, I'm afraid.'

'I might know someone,' offered Badger. 'He sells *The Big Issue* in town but he's also a poet and he runs a duty-free beer and spirits operation with a couple of other guys. Did you know you can make more money bringing booze over from the Continent than you can cocaine?'

'I don't think it's quite what I'm looking for,' I told Badger. 'I'll leave it to Geoffrey to find a suitable applicant.' If he couldn't come up with another accountant, I thought I might try the convent. A working nun sounded like a reasonable bet.

Geoffrey was surprised when I went into the office the next morning with the news of Miss Barrie's departure.

'Mind you, boss, you always did say there was something not quite kosher about her.'

I told him about the photo session and showed him the pictures. 'Not bad, are they?'

He sifted through them slowly. 'Bloody good. You ought to take it up.'

Perhaps, I thought, I should turn to photography rather than detecting. Not only was I getting nowhere fast with Wilbur Lunt, but I now had a mystery of my own to solve. What had happened to Serina Barrie?

'Whatever else she is, she's a good-looking bird,' said Geoffrey.

'Wherever else, you mean.'

'Ring the university,' suggested Geoffrey, and he fetched

me her papers from the filing cabinet. 'The Bursar should be able to tell you where she's moved to if you explain you're her landlord. They're not keen on students reneging on tenancy agreements. Gets the uni a bad name.'

'I'll give it a try but I don't think we'll learn anything. The odds are she's not told them she's moved.'

The truth was slightly different. I eventually tracked down the right person in the Registrar's department, who informed me that Serina Barrie had left her course at the end of her second year, a few weeks ago. The woman had no idea where she had gone.

'So what's she been doing since June?'

'I don't know, Geoff. Modelling maybe?' Yet, on Saturday, when I'd mentioned university to her, she had led me to believe she was still a student.

'Her rent's gone through with no trouble.'

'It's due again on Saturday. I bet we don't see it.'

'I'll get an advert in the *Echo*. That's three empty flats we'll have had in a fortnight.'

'And all of them in unusual circumstances.'

'Do you think there's a connection?'

'Not really. Miss Barrie was here well before Lloyd and the Lunts. Did she have any regular visitors or maybe a boyfriend living in?' Tenants did not always think it necessary to inform their landlord when they moved new partners in.

He thought. 'Not that I know of. I've only been in the flat a couple of times since she moved in, to get her to sign the new tenancy agreements when they came due, and she was on her own each time.'

I drove back to the flat and threw the photos on the coffee table. I wondered if she would ring me to ask for them but somehow I doubted it. But why ask me to take them if she'd no intention of collecting? Was she really in some sort of trouble?

I was glad to be going to the cinema that night. I needed

the light relief. I picked up Hilary from work and we drove
to the Plaza at Crosby.

Some time ago, the old Apollo Cinema opposite the
Library shut down and a group of neighbours, concerned the
locals would have nowhere to go at nights, banded together
and took over the lease. They put a couple of extra screens
in, reopened it as the Plaza and now they run it as a charity.
All the workers are unpaid volunteers.

I believe an enterprise like that should be supported so I
go there in preference to the multiplexes that are run by the
big conglomerates. Also, the seats are more comfortable at
the Plaza.

Godzilla wouldn't have been my choice of film but after
the upsets of the last few days, I was prepared to accept that
a bit of escapism might not be a bad idea.

We stocked up with popcorn and drinks, said hello to Jan
in the ticket booth, and went into the auditorium.

As it turned out, I thought the film was crap. 'For kids,
that's all,' I said but Hilary had loved it.

'You've got to admit the effects were good.' Give her
a few obviously fake monsters running round and a bit of
gore and she's happy.

'It was more like a computer game than a film.'

I sounded impatient and realised it was because I had so
much to think about I could scarcely give my attention to
Hilary. Some of it was due to the Maria situation, especially
as Waterloo and Crosby was Maria's territory. Also, I had
Michelle's funeral to face the next morning, and all the time
the mysteries surrounding Wilbur Lunt, and now Serina
Barrie, were at the back of my mind.

However, Hilary had one unfailing way of gaining my
full attention. The film had finished early enough for us to
snatch a late pizza round the corner at Nicola's before we
went back to the flat for the night.

'Do you know, it's over three weeks since I was in this
bed with you?' Hilary put her hand beneath the sheets and

pressed her warm naked body against me. 'Love you,' she murmured.

'Love you, too.'

Hilary flung off the duvet, sat upright and stretched out her legs. 'Sit up and put your legs round me,' she said, 'and put mine round you.' I obeyed. 'It's called "boats",' she said. 'There's a feature on positions in this month's *Company* magazine, complete with pictures.' We inched forward until I was inside her.

'Remember *Chantilly Lace*,' she whispered, as we undulated gently to and fro. Hilary and I play this game where one of us does a mime and the other has to relate it to a well-known song. 'Well, this is *Ride Your Pony*.'

'Could have fooled me,' I groaned. 'I thought it was *Up, Up and Away*.' We kissed as we made love and finally toppled over and fell asleep in each other's arms.

But we didn't get the full eight hours.

We were woken by a furious banging that sounded like a dozen battering rams at my front door. I reached for the clock radio on the bedside cabinet. It read 6.30 a.m. Too early for the postman, and the caber-tossing festival hadn't reached Liverpool yet.

Hilary jumped up in terror. 'Someone's trying to break in,' she cried. 'Oh God, phone the police.'

'It's just someone at the door,' I reassured her. 'I'll go and see who it is before they smash the panels in.'

'Be careful, Johnny,' she cried.

'You stay there.' I jumped out of bed, pulled on a dressing-gown and ran through the hall. The hammering continued.

I looked through the spyglass. A distorted, bearded head faced me, shouting the words, 'Open up!'

Making sure the security chain was on, I opened the door a few inches. 'What the hell—' I began. The bolt holding the chain split from the door casing as a group of men slammed the door wide open.

Hilary screamed.

There were six of them, all in dark sweaters and jeans. I thought they'd come to kill me. Who had I seriously upset recently? The men surrounded me. I couldn't get to the phone to ring the law. Could I make it down the stairs to the car?

One of the men pushed himself to the front. His face looked familiar – pock-marked skin, yellow teeth and a bulbous nose.

He flashed a card in front of my face.

'Detective Sergeant Leary, Merseyside Police. I have a warrant here to search these premises for stolen goods.'

'You're joking, there's no stolen goods here. What's going on?'

Hilary, wearing my Freshfield Animal Rescue T-shirt, came running out of the bedroom. For a second, an image of Linda Roberts in her Everton T-shirt flashed into my mind. 'What's happening?' she cried.

Leary ignored us both. Turning to his men, he ordered them to search all the rooms. Two of them marched into the bedroom and started pulling out the drawers, tossing my socks and underwear on the floor after feeling inside them. I watched from the doorway as they took my wallet from the dressing table and searched carefully inside the compartments.

'If it's drugs you're after, you're wasting your time.'

Leary loomed beside me. He gave no indication that he had ever met me before and the patient, civil manner he had displayed at Livingstone Drive was replaced by an offensive familiarity. 'Actually, matey, we're looking for stolen cameras.'

'Well, my camera's on that bookshelf in the corner.' I pointed into the lounge. I was worried now. You can't hide a camera in a wallet. If they weren't looking for drugs, were they planting them? If so, why?

'Here's one of them, guv.' The big, bearded constable,

who could have found work as an extra in *Planet of the Apes*, walked out of the lounge with my Minolta Dynex in one large hairy hand. 'The numbers match.'

'Right. Keep on looking. See if you can find the other one.'

'Hang on . . .' I started to protest but he interrupted me.

'Save it and get dressed. We're taking you in.' He gave a triumphant leer. 'We've got you good style, you bastard. You're under arrest.'

Hilary looked on in alarm.

'What for? I've done nothing.'

'Handling stolen goods. That'll do for starters.'

'If you mean the camera, I bought it from—'

'Don't tell me. A man in a pub.'

I tried to contain my anger. 'I bought it from a man at a house in Kirkdale. I can give you the address.'

'What was his name?'

'Er . . . I don't know. His father's—'

'I'm not interested in his father, what was this man's name?'

'I don't know, but—' Leary never allowed me to finish one sentence.

'You don't know his name? What a surprise!' Leary's tone gave new meaning to the word sarcastic.

'I can tell you where he lives because I went to his house to buy the cameras.' I gave him the address but he made no attempt to write it down.

'Oh, so you admit there were two cameras?'

'I never said there weren't.'

'So where's the other one?'

'I sold it.'

He didn't ask me to whom. 'At a vast profit, no doubt.'

'I did all right on the deal. Not a crime, is it?'

'How much did you pay for them?'

'A hundred pounds.'

'For the two?' I nodded. 'What you're saying is, you bought the cameras at such a cheap price that any reasonably intelligent person would have known they were stolen.'

'Not so. There was no guarantee with them, no instructions. In fact, one of them wasn't working.'

Then came the killer question. 'Did you get a receipt?'

What could I say? 'No, but—'

'But you'll be able to trace the cheque.' He knew the answer to that, which was why he'd asked the question.

'I paid cash. It helps when you're bartering.'

'Why didn't you get a receipt?'

I tried to explain how I was in the car at the time, ready to drive off when the lad ran out with the cameras but Leary interrupted again.

'You didn't get a receipt because they were stolen and the person you bought them from wouldn't put his name to them; you knew they were stolen and didn't expect him to.'

'No!'

'Do you often go around with a pocketful of cash on these buying sprees?'

'I've got flats. I'm always buying furniture and things second-hand.'

'All suspiciously cheap?'

'You get a bargain from time to time.'

'I bet you do. Now where's the other camera?'

'I told you, I sold it.' I gave him Ken's name. 'I don't know his address but you'll find him at the radio station.'

'Right. Get some clothes on. You're coming with us.'

'What for? I've told you where I got them.'

'You've told us nothing. Johnny Ace, I'm arresting you for—' Hilary screamed and tried to come between us but one of the policemen dragged her away.

'Leave her alone,' I shouted.

Leary finished the caution. 'Now get dressed,' he said roughly.

I went into the bedroom. One of the men had the bed-clothes on the floor and was looking under the mattress.

'It's in a striped bag marked "Swag",' I said. 'A hundred grand in forged notes and the silverware from the great Knowsley Hall robbery. And while you're at it, Lord Lucan's hiding in the Priest's Hole in the bathroom.'

He said nothing. He didn't even turn round. I said no more but pulled on a shirt and jeans. I wasn't expecting to be away long.

I wasn't expecting handcuffs either. Leary grinned as he fixed the steel bracelet on my wrists.

'What the hell is this about?'

'You'll find that out at the station.'

'I want to ring my solicitor.'

'Time enough for that later.'

'Hilary,' I shouted, 'Ring Alistair Crawford at Goldbergs and tell him what's happened. Which station are you taking me to?' I asked Leary.

'St Ann Street.' He was reluctant to part with the information.

'You got that, Hil? Tell him to get down there as soon as he can.' Which would be at least two hours, I thought, as Goldbergs didn't open till nine.

Happily, none of the neighbours saw our procession as we made our way down to the police cars. I sat in the back next to Leary.

'Why aren't you investigating Wilbur Lunt?' I asked him. He didn't reply. 'Because there's something fishy about his wife's suicide and you know it.' He remained silent. I gave up and looked out of the window as we drove up Islington.

'How long do you intend to keep me? I've got to be at Michelle Lunt's funeral at eleven. I suppose you knew about that?'

He remained silent.

At the station, the belt was removed from my jeans and

my fingerprints were taken before I was pushed into a cell and locked up.

At half-past nine, Alistair Crawford arrived, a shambling figure in his pin-stripe suit and long grey hair curling over his collar. He carried a black attaché case and an umbrella, which hadn't kept the rain off his trousers.

He looked worried.

'What's all this about, Johnny?'

I told him everything that had happened since Hilary and I were first woken up. All the while, a police constable stood impassively at the door of the cell, looking into space. 'I thought we were being burgled. Hilary was going to ring the police when we found out it was the law.'

'What were they looking for?'

'They said cameras, but as they were looking inside my wallet, I suspect they were looking for drugs.'

'I take it they didn't find any?'

'No, but I was terrified they were going to say they had.'

'Plant them, you mean? It's not unheard of, not unheard of at all.' Experience had made Alistair as suspicious of the police as I was. 'So what have they charged you with, if it wasn't possessing drugs?'

'Handling stolen goods. The cameras.'

'They found cameras then?'

'One camera.' I told Alistair the full story and he listened quietly. 'I told them who I'd bought it from and who I sold the second one to but they didn't seem interested.'

'Have you made a statement?'

'No. They said it could wait till later.'

'I don't like this, Johnny. It smacks of conspiracy.'

'But why? I haven't done anything.'

'Look, I'm going to get you out of here then I'll arrange for you to see Brendan Butterworth. If this case ever gets to court, you'll need a good barrister so we might as well involve Brendan at the start.'

'But surely it won't come to that, Alistair? I've never been in trouble in my life apart from the odd speeding ticket.'

'Yet six policemen dressed like villains force their way into your house in the early hours of the morning. Someone's got it in for you, Johnny.'

'But who?'

'You tell me. You're the private eye, or so I believe.' He smiled grimly. 'Time to start investigating your own case.'

Chapter Seventeen

I made it to the Crematorium with two minutes to spare, thanks to a taxi driver who could have given Damon Hill a run for his money.

Linda was already there, looking waxen-faced. She threw her arms round me when I ran in.

'I thought you weren't coming,' she whispered.

The service was brief and efficient. An elderly vicar ran through the prayer book at some speed then paused to say a few words about the deceased, whom he'd never heard of until a few minutes before.

'I never knew Miss Roberts,' he chanted in those high tones that the clergy affect, 'but people tell me she was a kind person who will be missed by her many friends . . .'

I glanced at the empty benches around us and said nothing. He droned on.

Of course, with so few people going to church nowadays, not many vicars have the advantage of a personal acquaintance with the deceased. They need to rely on information supplied by a third party, but what if they asked someone who didn't like the deceased? They could put the boot in good style.

'I never knew Mr Ace personally, but I am told he was an unpleasant man, involved in many notorious scandals and a person who often sought the company of young ladies of doubtful reputation.'

A whirring noise jerked my mind back to the present. The vicar had pressed the button under his desk to close the curtains. Seconds too late, a scratched recording of *Onward Christian Soldiers* filled the room, to disguise the rumbling sound of the conveyor belt carrying the coffin on its path to the incinerator.

'Sorry I was late,' I said to Linda after the final prayers had been said and we were back outside the building, examining the wreaths and flowers.

There were four large wreaths and four sets of flowers. I examined the labels. Linda and I had each sent a wreath, another was from Merseyside Police and the fourth one bore an emblem of the Crown and a hand-written inscription, *To Michelle, from her colleagues.*

Some colleagues, I thought. Couldn't be bothered to turn up in person.

I recognised Pat Lake's handwriting on a large bouquet of roses bearing the inscription *From the tenants of Livingstone Drive* and another floral tribute with a card that read, *Love, Wilbur.*

'At least he made a gesture,' I said.

The other two bouquets, I presumed, were from the cousins, Tom and Olive and Leslie and Pauline.

'Not much to show for her thirty years on earth, is it?' remarked Linda bitterly. 'Eight bunches of flowers and only two people to see her off.' I had to agree with her.

'Shall we go for something to eat?' she said next.

'Linda, I'm sorry, I can't. Something terrible has happened.' I told her briefly about my arrest.

'Johnny, that's awful! What are you going to do?'

'I'm seeing my solicitor in five minutes. The odd thing is, the Sergeant who arrested me was Leary, the one at your sister's suicide.'

'Do you think there's a connection?'

'That's what I want to find out. Look, I'll give you a ring tomorrow and let you know what's happened.'

'Should I hang around and meet you later?'

I thought of Hilary back at the flat. 'No. I don't know how

long I'll be. I might have to meet barristers or something. I'll ring you at home.'

Half an hour later, I was sitting in Alistair's old-fashioned office in Dale Street. Eunice the receptionist had brought up a pot of Darjeeling tea served in china cups, and we were puzzling over how my predicament had come about.

'The police knew about the cameras,' said Alistair. 'They knew you'd bought them and they knew they'd find them at your flat. So, the big question is, who told them?'

'I've no idea.'

'Well, let's take things backwards. How did you first find out about these cameras being for sale?'

'This girl who lives in one of my flats. She told me about them.'

'And she'll testify to that, will she?'

'Of cour—' I stopped. Serina Barrie had disappeared. Alistair raised a bushy eyebrow at my sudden halt. 'She's done a runner, Alistair, she's disappeared.'

He didn't look surprised. 'Had she been with you long?'

'Yes. Nearly two years.'

'Strange that she should leave at this particular time. How did she come to know about the cameras in the first place?'

'From an ex-tenant of mine that she knew – a down-and-out called Roy Quantine. You may remember him. It was when I first bought South Albert Road – he lived in the attic. It was like a pigsty and I threw him out.'

'So that's one person with a grudge against you?'

'Oh, come on Alistair, it was years ago.'

'He wasn't the one actually selling the cameras though?'

'No, that was someone called Clive Fisher. I'd never heard of him before then. Miss Barrie told me he had a photographic shop but he'd recently retired and was selling off his stock.'

'You went to this shop?'

'No, to his house. He lived in this terraced place off

Hawthorne Road, between Kirkdale and Bootle. I didn't see Clive Fisher himself, it was his son.'

'Or so he told you.'

'What?'

'Never mind.' He reached up and pulled down a *Yellow Pages* from a shelf above his head. 'I'd like to bet there's no Clive Fisher anywhere in here.'

I felt sick. I looked for *Photographic Retailers* but I knew Alistair was going to be right. There was no entry for Clive Fisher under any heading remotely connected with cameras or photography, and no entry for anyone called Fisher at that address in the Liverpool residential phone book, which we consulted next.

'He could be ex-directory,' I pleaded, but I knew it was a false hope.

'So you don't know the name of the man you purchased these cameras from, and you have no receipt?'

'I know the address and I have a phone number.' Whether the phone was in that house, of course, was debatable. 'I gave them both to Leary.'

'The Sergeant in charge?'

'Yes. And here's another funny thing.' I recounted the story of Michelle Lunt's suicide and my conversations with DS Leary.

'It may or may not have a bearing on this matter. Too early to say. What happened to the other camera? Did you sell it? You say they only found one.'

'I sold it to Ken, my producer at the radio station. I told Leary.'

'What sort of money are we talking about on these transactions?' When I told him, Alistair's face fell. 'You did very nicely on this deal, didn't you? You bought two brand new cameras for one hundred pounds and soon afterwards sold just one of them for the same amount. It would be hard to persuade a jury that you didn't suspect there was something not quite right about such a deal.'

'What do you mean, jury?' I cried. 'Surely this won't go to Crown Court?'

'I don't think you realise how serious this is, Johnny. For a start, a criminal record will affect your credit rating, the end of you borrowing money for property deals. You'll find it very difficult to get insurance on anything. Apply to travel to the States and you won't be granted a visa. That's in addition to any fine or prison sentence.'

I felt drained. 'I've been set up, haven't I?'

'Without a doubt, but by whom?'

'Do you think the police are involved?'

'I'd say there was a good chance, if only because of my basic mistrust of our noble boys in blue based on my years of experience in the legal profession. I can see a lot of planning behind all this, Johnny. You've made a serious enemy somewhere along the line.'

'So what do I do?'

'Well, I'm going to arrange a meeting, as I say, with Brendan Butterworth. I'll try and fix it for Monday. Meanwhile, I shall find out from your friend DS Leary what exactly these charges relate to.'

'What can I do?'

'You can go off and do some detecting on your own account. Have you no friends in the Force who'll help you? I should have thought, with your contacts . . .'

I knew that must be my first step. Jim Burroughs. I thanked Alistair and went outside into the road. Dale Street looked the same as ever, buses hurling down it trying to beat the lights, secretaries braving the rain to run across to sandwich bars, yet I felt different. I felt as if I was watching it on TV and I wasn't really there.

I rang Jim from a phone box and arranged to go round the next morning, then I took a taxi back to the flat.

Hilary was still there when I returned, waiting for me with great trepidation. 'Whatever was all that about?' She threw her arms around me. 'I thought I'd never see you again. I was so frightened when those men broke in.'

I told her about Serina Barrie and the cameras. I didn't mention the connection, if indeed there was one, with Michelle Lunt.

'They're not going to charge you, surely?'

'They already have.'

'Oh Johnny, how have you managed to get involved in trouble again?'

'Fate, I suppose, but this time it's nothing to do with anything I've done. Do you want some lunch?'

'Where shall we go?'

'I thought we'd microwave something from the freezer. I don't really feel like going out at the moment.' I wanted to grab some food then have a long hot bath to rid myself of the odour of the cell, not to mention the inkstains on my fingers.

'If you like.' She looked worried. 'The police won't come back, will they?'

'No.' I didn't know why they'd come in the first place. Who had told them those cameras would be in my flat?

Hilary had to leave for work soon after we'd eaten lunch, which suited me. I needed some space to try and get a grip on events.

'I'll be back tonight,' she promised. 'Don't get into any more trouble.'

Thinking about it, I concluded that the people I urgently needed to speak to were Fisher and Quantine. They seemed to be the ones behind all this. Quantine I would have to search for, but I knew where Fisher was. I just needed to get to him before he, too, disappeared.

In the end, I had a shower, which was quicker, then got out the RAV4 and drove to Kirkdale, trying to avoid speed traps along the way. The terraced house looked exactly as I'd left it a few days before.

I knocked loudly on the door and waited. I heard shuffling and the sound of a bolt being drawn then the door opened a few inches and an old woman in a headscarf and a multi-coloured chainstore frock peered out.

'What is it?' She had no teeth and her nose protruded like a beak, giving her the appearance of a rare species of parrot.

'I'm looking for Mr Fisher.'

'Who?' she shouted, and peered at me as if not quite sure I was there at all.

'Fisher.' I spelt it out.

'No one of that name here.'

'I came here on Monday and saw him. At this very door.'

'I'm on me own in this house, luv, have been for thirty years since my Albert died. It was his liver. I told him about the drink but he took no notice.'

'A boy of about nineteen was in your house this week. He came to the door and spoke to me.'

'He must have been a ghost then because he doesn't live here. I wish he did. It's no fun on your own when you're my age. I'm eighty-four next birthday.'

'Can I come in for a minute?' I felt there must be traces of him somewhere in the house.

'No, you can't. Who do you think you are? Where's your ID?'

'I don't have any. Look . . .' I put my foot in the door as she tried to close it.

She opened it again and shook her stick at me. 'Bugger off or I'll call the busies.' For a moment she hesitated as if deciding whether to strike me or not. I quickly removed my foot and she slammed the door in my face.

Chapter Eighteen

I could see no point in knocking again. Better to call back later, after I'd done the programme, and see if somebody different came to the door. Like Mr Fisher.

The next person to see was Quantine, except I'd no idea where to find him. Miss Barrie had said he hung out at a pub frequented by medical students which suggested somewhere near the hospital or the university. I should have asked Hilary about it.

In the end, I drove out to Walton to the old Carnegie Library and asked to see the electoral roll. The only person listed for the house I'd just left was a Violet Parker. So who was 'Fisher' and how had he come to be in the house without the old lady, who presumably *was* Violet Parker, knowing he was there? Unless, of course, she was in the plot too.

I felt I was becoming paranoid, but don't they say that even paranoids have enemies?

I couldn't help a rueful smile as I left the Library. A week ago I'd have rung up Maria to get this information for me. Somewhere along the line, I was going to have to see her and try to straighten things out between us, but there was no time for anything else before the show and I needed to have a word with Ken.

'About the hundred pounds,' I told him. 'You don't have to give it me after all.'

His face brightened. 'You mean, the camera is a present? That's a kind thought, Johnny. Of course, with what you earn . . .'

I cut him short. 'The police will be picking the cameras up any time if they haven't already.'

'What?'

I explained to him that the cameras had been stolen.

'And you didn't know?'

'Of course not. I'd never have bought them if I had. Credit me with some scruples.'

'But I've taken some photos already.' He looked crestfallen.

'Then take the film out before they come to pick it up. Sorry about this, Ken, but look on the bright side – you've had the film for nothing.'

'Oh yes, ninety-nine pence aren't they, at Max Spielmann? You always were big-hearted, Johnny.' He marched gruffly into the studio. 'I suppose you'll be playing *Picture of You*,' he shouted through the intercom.

Joe Brown. Nice to know he'd got some sense of humour left. 'No,' I shouted back, '*Flash Bang Wallop* – Tommy Steele.'

Normal relations were restored and I proceeded to do the show but, three hours later, I was back in Kirkdale knocking at the old lady's door. This time she didn't answer. I waited a few minutes then banged again. I could see no flickering light from a television when I peered through the nets in the front room.

I walked down the street until I came to an entry and found the ginnel that ran along the backs of the houses. I counted carefully till I came to the right house and started to hoist myself over the locked back gate. All was in darkness.

'What the fuck are you doing, mate?' I turned round, lost my balance and dropped down to face a burly man in anorak and jeans. He was about fifty and a couple of stones heavier than I was. 'You were breaking in, weren't you?'

The first punch was unexpected and caught me off balance. It landed on the side of my cheek and I fell to the ground, whereupon he kicked me twice, hard, in the ribs. I tried to get up but as I did so, his fist thudded against my jaw and I passed out completely.

When I came to, probably only a minute or two later, he'd gone. I rolled to a sitting position and leaned against the wall. Blood was trickling from my mouth and my ribs felt as if Hannibal had just crossed over them with his elephants. A couple of teeth seemed to be loose and a searing pain shot through my head when I moved it.

As I sat there, a brown dog wandered over and relieved itself against the adjacent gatepost before trotting across to sniff me. It licked my face and smiled at me. I'd never seen a dog smile before and was impressed. I stroked its head; its coat was rough and wiry like a pan scourer. The brass nametag on its collar read *Roly* but there was no address or phone number.

I struggled to my feet, holding on to the post. The dog licked my hand and wagged a crooked stump that almost qualified as a tail. My jeans and shirt were covered with dirt and mud from the litter-covered ground and I'd cut my hand on some broken glass.

I wondered why I'd ever wanted to be a private eye, but this incident had nothing to do with the Michelle Lunt affair. This was my very own problem and only I could deal with it.

I stumbled back down the alley, wiping my hands on my shirt. The dog followed me.

'Hey mister, are you a burglar?' Four kids, all under ten, blocked my entrance to the street. Dickens would have called them ragamuffins; their clothes were torn and dirty, but they all sported designer trainers.

'He's been robbin' those houses.' The tallest one spoke, in a high Scouse voice.

'Give us some money, mate, or we'll tell on you.' This from a kid who had the pinched face of a young Fagin and the physique of an undernourished orphan.

'Fuck off, Jason. We'll fuckin' have it off 'im.'

The other two just stood there trying to seem menacing. I imagined how they might have looked less than five years ago in the school nativity play, dressed as shepherds or angels. At what point did childhood innocence end nowadays?

'You lot live round here, do you?' I asked them before they'd decided whether to attack me or not. My ribs didn't feel up to another battering.

'We might.'

'Do you know who lives at number twelve?'

'What's it worth?'

I produced a pound coin from my pocket and tossed it in the air. The lad called Jason jumped quickest to grab it. 'Some old woman.'

'On her own?'

'Yeah.'

'She's a witch,' broke in one of the others. 'She comes out screaming at us. We knock on her door and put things through her letterbox.'

Not so different from Victorian kids really. How come they weren't indoors playing computer games all day long like the papers led us to believe?

'Does she have any family come and visit her, someone about nineteen or twenty?'

They looked at one another. 'Not seen no one,' said Jason and the rest shook their heads.

'Hey, what you doing with that dog, mister? Are you stealing it?'

'Do you know who it belongs to?'

The tall one assumed the role of spokesman. 'It was Mr Ryall's. He used to live at number four but they put him in an 'ome last week. His family came and took his stuff but they left the dog.'

'Left it?'

'They said it'd find an 'ome. Someone'd take it in.'

'It doesn't look like they have.'

'Why don't you 'ave it, mate? Come here, Roly.' The creature ambled towards him, wagging its stump.

'Where's it been sleeping since its owner left?'

The lad shrugged. 'It's been out on the street.'

'In a shed at the end of the old man's yard,' the youngest child piped up.

'And who's fed it?'

They looked at one another. 'Dunno. Gets scraps where it can, I s'pose.'

I held the dog's thin body and felt its ribs protruding through the light brown fur. It licked my hand again.

'You take it,' said Jason. 'It'll starve in the end, or get run over.' He gave the dog a pat.

'Hey, are you all right, mister? You're bleeding.'

Someone had noticed. I wiped my mouth with the back of my hand then realised that most of the blood was coming from the hand. I wrapped a handkerchief around it. There seemed to be slivers of broken glass under the skin.

'Yes, thanks. I fell, that's all.'

'Someone's duffed you up, haven't they? Was you out shagging and her old man came home?'

They followed me as I walked to the car, Roly close behind me. When I opened the door, he immediately jumped on to the driver's seat.

'Looks like he's yours, mister.'

I wasn't sure. Kidnapping a dog might not rank as high as receiving stolen goods but I'd no wish to add to my escalating criminal record. Nonetheless, I shut the animal in the car and walked back to number Four.

'I told you, he's gone in an 'ome,' persisted the tall lad. 'Nobody lives there no more.' He seemed to be speaking the truth because, when I peered through the letterbox, I saw a build-up of mail in the hall.

'OK – I believe you. I'll see the dog gets a good home.'

The dog was looking anxiously out of the windscreen as I returned to the car. I manoeuvred it, wagging tail and all, on to the passenger seat and set off for home. On the way, I stopped off at a Spar for a couple of tins of Chappie.

'I wouldn't like to see what the other fella looks like,' grinned the lady behind the counter. Her black hair, streaked with grey, was swept up in a Sixties' beehive and she was two stone over the wrong side of fifty but her cheery manner probably kept the locals out of the hypermarkets.

In return, I was too tired to offer anything other than a wan smile. I'd had enough for one day. It was barely fourteen hours since the police had forced their way into my flat, but it seemed a lifetime ago.

Since then, I'd been charged with a crime I hadn't committed, my main alibi had disappeared, I'd been beaten up and I'd somehow acquired a dog, an animal not permitted to reside within the confines of the Waterloo Dock apartments.

What more could go wrong?

Luckily, Roger the security guard was nowhere around when I drove into the car park, and the creature trotted happily after me up the stairs.

By the time Hilary arrived just after midnight, I'd cleaned myself up, removed the bits of glass from my hand and bandaged it the best I could.

'Whatever's happened now?' she cried. Then: 'And what, in heaven's name, is *that*?' as Roly bounded towards her.

'I'll tell you in bed. It's a long story.'

'First of all, I'm going to dress your hand properly.' She took her scissors from her uniform pocket to cut off my bandage. 'Have you any other injuries? You're talking funny.'

'I took a punch on the jaw. I think a couple of teeth are loose.'

'Your face is all swollen.'

'My ribs hurt too but they're not broken. Just sore where I was kicked.'

'Is this all to do with these cameras?'

'Sort of. I was looking for the man who'd sold them to me, but he'd disappeared.'

'Oh Johnny!' Hilary sighed with exasperation. 'Why don't you let the police solve it?'

There was only one answer to that and it wasn't a pleasant one. 'Because, my love, they're not on our side.'

After Hilary had completed her nursing duties, she made a drink whilst I fed the dog. 'Is he staying?' she asked as he wolfed down the full contents of the tin.

It was something I hadn't considered. I'd brought him home on an impulse when I thought there was a good chance of him not surviving the week. That and the way he smiled.

I tried to explain that to Hilary. 'Very sweet,' she said, 'but where's it going to sleep?' Hilary was a cat person. Dogs she tolerated.

In the end, the decision wasn't mine. Roly settled himself on the foot of the bed and put his head down.

'I should have had him last night,' I said, 'to see off the intruders.'

'Doesn't look like a guard dog to me.' Even in repose, his face was set in a satisfied grin. Hilary looked alarmed. 'These people who beat you up tonight, do you think they'll come back?'

'There was only one of them and no, because he didn't know who I was. He mistook me for a burglar and caught me by surprise before I had a chance to defend myself.'

I didn't feel I'd acquitted myself well in the encounter and thought I would be advised to restrict my future opponents to people over seventy or under twelve, and then only fight them when they were ill.

'You must leave it alone,' Hilary insisted, 'before you get seriously hurt.'

But that was one thing I couldn't do. I had to locate Roy Quantine and I had to find out why the police were prosecuting me. Would Detective Inspector Jim Burroughs be able to help me?

Chapter Nineteen

'Did you bring any Newky Brown with you this time?' Jim Burroughs sat beside the gas fire in his lounge, looking much brighter than on my last visit.

'Sorry, Jim. Rosemary frisked me at the front door.' He looked alarmed until I produced a can from the inside pocket of my leather jacket and handed it over.

'I'll have it this afternoon when she's out shopping.' He hid it down the side of his chair and caught his first glimpse of Roly who lay panting on the rug. 'What the hell is that thing doing there?'

'That's my new minder. Cheaper to feed than Geoffrey.'

'Funny-looking, isn't it? What make is it?'

'Breed, Jim, is the term I think you're looking for. He's a bit of a mixture really, is Roly, but I reckon he's mostly lurcher with a touch of deerhound somewhere along the way.'

'You make him sound like a cocktail.'

I took off my jacket and slung it over the chair back. 'It's hot in here, Jim.'

'Not when you're sitting down all day, it isn't.'

'You need exercise, didn't the doctors tell you?'

He ignored me. 'Who's been giving you a going-over?'

My jaw was swollen and my face was oddly crooked when I talked. I'd made an appointment with the dentist for Monday

'Nobody important. Look, Jim, I'm in big trouble. I need your help.'

For the next ten minutes he remained silent while I went over every detail of the previous day's events. By the time I'd finished, he looked very worried.

'Something's seriously wrong here, Johnny. You've been stitched up big time and no mistake, but by whom?'

'Christ knows, Jim.'

'And why?'

I held up my hands. 'Pass.'

'So what can I do to help you?'

'For a start, do you know anything about Roy Quantine, because he's the person I need to find.'

'Oh, I know Quantine all right.'

'You do?'

'Certainly. He's got form and he's also a snout.'

'Where does he hang out?'

'On a Saturday night? Let me think. You might find him at the Stirling Club just outside town. They have a cabaret night, a couple of turns and a disco. He used to hang out there.'

'God, we used to play at the Stirling back in the Seventies. That's been going some time, hasn't it? I haven't been in for years.'

'It still gets packed out, especially of a weekend. Quantine'll probably be there with his missus. He married that redhead who used to work in the massage parlour in Duke Street before they burned it down for the insurance.'

'He must be involved somewhere along the line.'

'Got some sort of grudge against you, has he?'

'I threw him out of a flat, but that was years ago.' I couldn't see him doing this off his own bat. The question was, who had put him up to it?

'Not much progress yet with the other business,' said Jim. I immediately felt guilty because, since my arrest, I had given no thought to Linda and her sister. 'But I reckon you've got enough on your plate at the moment without worrying about that.'

I was forced to agree. 'How did your gig go at the OPB?'
I asked, remembering his excitement over the occasion.

'We had to pull out. Rosemary wouldn't let me go. I
believe Johnny Guitar and The Undertakers both went down
a storm, though. You know, it's a pity Kingsize Taylor can't
be persuaded to go back onstage. He was brilliant. I heard
this record company in Manchester offered him a fortune
to record but he didn't want to know. I wish they'd offer
it to us.'

I couldn't work up too much enthusiasm over rock'n'roll.
After hearing Jim promise to have some news for me in the
early part of the week, I set off for my second appointment
of the day. At the vet's.

'I'd say he was about four years old and, apart from being
underfed, which is a damn sight better than being overfed,
he's in pretty good condition.'

The white-coated vet had Roly on the table in his surgery
and was proceeding to stick a needle into his side.

'I'll give him a jab in case he's not had any before, then he
should be right as rain.' Roly yelped as the needle went in
and a platinum-blonde nurse held him firmly in her grasp.

The surgery was in Crosby, less than five minutes' drive
from Maria's. It seemed as good a time as any to call and
try to patch things up with her. She might be sympathetic
to my injuries and, also, I had Roly with me. Maria liked
dogs and I needed every ally I could muster.

I drove over to her flat and, with Roly trotting by my
side, went across and rang the bell. There was no answer.
I tried again but to no avail.

Part of me was relieved that there would be no confron-
tation, but I knew that the longer I left it, the more likely
it was that Maria might meet someone else. I didn't want
that. I missed her, especially with this new trouble hanging
over me.

If only Linda hadn't been in my flat just at that one
moment. I remembered that I hadn't phoned her and it was

Saturday. I'd nothing to report, but I'd promised her after the funeral that I would stay in touch. In the circumstances, I was grateful when her ansaphone picked up the call. 'It's Johnny Ace, I'll call back,' was all I said, then I went home to rest.

Eight o'clock found me outside the Stirling. Jim was right: the side streets all around the club were already filled with parked cars and I was lucky to find a space only a couple of blocks away. I gave 50p to the kid who offered to 'mind' the RAV4 for me. Why argue when you can't win?

'A busy night,' I commented as I paid my money at the door. 'Who's on?'

The burly doorman didn't look up as he took my ticket and ripped it savagely in half. 'The Bootles and Jackie Hamilton. Standing room only tonight, mate.'

I wasn't surprised. Jackie Hamilton was a legend on Merseyside and most people in the business agreed he was the best comedian the city had produced since Robb Wilton.

I bought a drink and stood by the bar watching the place fill up. There was no sign of Roy Quantine.

The Bootles came onstage at nine. They'd been going longer than most Merseybeat groups but none of them were retired gravediggers or dentists who'd gone back to it in their dotage. The Bootles were pros, a band who'd never stopped working since the Sixties.

'All right you lot, get yer arses on the dance floor.' The diminutive drummer screamed instructions to the audience with abrasive exuberance as the group stormed into their first Beatles number.

A few people took to the floor but most stayed in their seats, drinking and chatting as the group worked their way through the Lennon and McCartney songbook.

The Bootles finished their first spot and I got another drink in. By the time Jackie Hamilton came on, you couldn't have squeezed Kate Moss into the club.

Jackie's delivery has always been deliberately slow and halting, it's been his trademark through the years, but as age and a few thousand gallons of best bitter have taken their toll, the stumbling has become exaggerated and the fans hold their breath willing the next words out of him.

'My mate keeps a public toilet in town,' he began, 'but he doesn't like it any more.' He stood there looking doleful as if he couldn't quite remember what came next. The audience giggled expectantly. 'Says the place is full of perverts and queers these days.'

A cheer went up. George Michael had recently been arrested for lewd behaviour in a Los Angeles lavatory. Jackie was nothing if not topical.

'The other day . . .' He struggled for the words. 'The other day . . .' He broke off to cough.

'He's pissed,' someone in the audience said loudly and with relish. 'He's bloody pissed.' He roared out, 'Good on yer, Jackie!'

'The other day, a fellow came in for . . . for . . .' the crowd were on the edge of their seats, mouths open like rows of hungry goldfish, egging him on '. . . for a shite.' Pause. We all waited for the punchline. 'He said it were like a breath of fresh air.'

Laughter, whoops of approval and sustained applause. Someone passed half a pint of beer up to the stage. The Old Master had done it again. I looked round at the happy faces and I saw him. Roy Quantine!

He was sitting at the far end of the club, his wife next to him, their eyes intent on the stage. I elbowed my way through the crowd until I stood right behind them. He hadn't seen me.

The little man looked much older than when I'd last seen him. I expect he would have said the same about me. His face was lined and sunken as if he needed built-up dentures to flesh his cheeks out.

I waited until Jackie Hamilton had finished his act, to

a standing ovation, and Quantine rose to go to the bar. I followed closely behind him and when he'd placed his order, I tapped him on the shoulder.

'Hello, Roy. Long time no see.'

He spun round, looked blank for a moment then, when he recognised me, his eyes darted round the club as if seeking a means of escape. But I was standing too close to him.

'What do *you* want?' he said narkily.

'I want a little chat, Quantine, about cameras.'

'Eh? What you on about? Nothing to do with me. I don't have any cameras.'

'I was thinking about your friend, Mr Fisher.'

'I don't know anyone called Fisher.'

'I think you do. Serina Barrie told me all about you and Mr Fisher.'

'Who's Serina Barrie when she's at home? You're mad, Johnny Ace. Now fuck off or I'll—'

'You'll what? Start a fight in the Stirling? The bouncers will have you laid out in the gutter in thirty seconds.'

'The same applies to you,' he said cockily. 'You can't touch me.'

'No, but I'm going to follow you quietly home then I shall come in and have a few words with you, in private.'

'And what if I won't let you in?'

'You're five foot seven, you're turned sixty and you wheeze like an old pig with asthma. I'm six feet one, fit, and not averse to hurting you. I don't think you'll stop me.'

My words sounded convincing but, as I said them, I was aware of the pain in my ribs every time I breathed and my jaw didn't feel it would stand another right hook like the one the night before.

'I don't know,' he sniggered. 'It looks like someone's had a good try already.'

I suddenly caught sight of a man staring directly at us from the opposite end of the bar. He was about thirty, with sleek black hair and thin lips, and he was wearing a high-collared, three-piece navy suit. He could have doubled for Al Pacino in any gangster movie.

On an impulse, I put my arm around Quantine's shoulders, smiled at him and said, 'Thanks, Roy. Thanks a lot.' I instinctively felt that the 'man from *Godfather*' was connected in some way with Quantine and that, by giving the impression that Quantine was co-operating with me, I might stir up something.

What I did do was effectively sign Roy Quantine's death warrant.

'If you'll excuse me,' said Quantine, 'I'm going to the Gents.'

He pushed me aside and I let him go. I reckoned he wouldn't leave the club without his wife and I could keep an eye on her.

I ordered another half of cider and waited for him to come back. I didn't notice the stranger depart but he was no longer standing beside the bar when I glanced across.

A couple more minutes went by, Quantine hadn't returned and I began to feel a little edgy. The barman brought my drink, took a little time over the change, and still there was no sign of my ex-tenant.

I gave it another five minutes. As Jackie Hamilton had said, Who knows what people do in toilets these days? I finished the cider, left my glass on the bar and made my way to the Gents. Three men stood at the urinals, all of them younger than Quantine. A man was washing his hands at the sink and another was using the hand-dryer. Both men were black.

I walked across to the row of cubicles, pushing at each door with my foot. Two were empty and swung open, two were occupied. The last door opened halfway but there was something blocking it. I peered inside.

Roy Quantine lay in a pool of blood behind the door, his eyes wide open with horror and his throat slashed from side to side. The blood that had spurted from the opened artery was already trickling slowly towards the washbasins.

He wouldn't be telling me anything.

Chapter Twenty

The Bootles never got to perform their second spot. An off-duty detective who was in the audience took charge until the squad car arrived and, by the time the forensic people, the photographers and the press had moved in, I was lined up with the rest of the punters waiting to be asked what I'd seen.

The investigating officer was, thankfully, not DS Leary but a Detective Inspector named Andy Fletcher. I told him the truth, or a reasonable version of it.

I'd been exchanging harmless pleasantries with a man whom I knew slightly. He'd excused himself to go to the Gents. I had waited for my drink to be served then I, too, answered a call of nature and, to my horror, found this man slumped behind the lavatory door. I had immediately cried out to attract the attention of the other users.

The reasons for my scream were simple. The person who finds the body draws the shortest odds on the suspect list so I wanted witnesses around when I discovered Quantine. Of course, I didn't tell Fletcher that.

It transpired that one of the black guys in the cloakroom was an off-duty detective; he had ordered the bouncers to seal the doors and had immediately phoned for his colleagues.

Theoretically, therefore, the murderer should still be in the club. Except I didn't see the navy-suited man anywhere about and I wondered how many others had slipped away.

That somebody had absconded was not in doubt, as there seemed to be no trace of the murder weapon. Everyone in the club was searched and a team of uniformed police was shipped in to give the premises a thorough going-over, but I knew the knife would be long gone.

It was three o'clock before I was allowed to leave. By then, the mood had turned pretty ugly. Women were wailing about babysitters, the odd brawl broke out and the band members were arguing about loading up their equipment.

I was worried about Roly. He'd been in the flat for a good seven hours on his own and I didn't know how house-trained he was. However, when I got back, he was stretched out on the settee, fast asleep.

'Exercise time,' I told him. I found a piece of rope to thread through his collar and we took the lift down. He didn't seem enthusiastic but, at that hour of the morning, neither was I.

Even this late, a few people were still staggering down the dock road as we walked up to the Pier Head, Roly sniffing his way along the gutter.

Events, I felt, had taken a sudden turn for the worse. Serina Barrie and young Fisher had disappeared and now Quantine had been killed, to prevent him talking to me. There was nobody left who knew about the cameras.

The people who had set me up for this trumped-up charge were not fooling. But why? What was their motive?

All was still by the Landing Stage as we walked round the Liver Buildings and back to the empty flat. I wished Maria had been waiting there. Apart from her company, she had always been a sounding board when I'd been involved in my investigation work, and that was something I badly needed right now.

I didn't sleep well. My ribs and jaw were stiffening as they began to heal and the nagging ache kept me awake.

At nine o'clock, I was back in the RAV4 heading towards Blundelsands but, once again, Maria was out. 'She must have gone away for the weekend,' I murmured to Roly. He gave a sympathetic smile. I wondered if this represented empathy with animals on my part, or was it the onset of senility? Next I'd be doing a Shirley Valentine and talking to the cooker.

I returned to the flat and rang Linda Roberts. 'At last!' She sounded relieved. 'I've been so worried about you. I've rung a few times but you were never in. Has anything happened about the cameras?'

'No, unless you call me being beaten up and then finding a man with his throat cut in a nightclub lavatory progress.'

'You are joking?' she asked. 'You're not, are you? Look, why don't you come over and tell me all about it?'

I couldn't think of anything better to do. Getting out of town for a few hours might give me a new perspective on it all, and there was nothing I could do on a Sunday anyway.

'Do you mind if I bring a friend?'

The question must have caught her off-balance because she sounded guarded. 'Who exactly?' Had she thought I'd meant Maria?

'He's brown, has only half a tail and answers to the name of Roly.'

'I didn't know you had a dog.' She sounded delighted. 'I hope he won't attack Emily.'

'I'm sure Emily will scare him to death.'

The journey time to the Pennines has been cut substantially since the M65 was extended up to the M6, cutting out the twelve-mile slow crawl around Blackburn.

As I drove, I tried to make some sense of the last few days, but I couldn't get my head round it at all. I realised, too, that I had absolutely nothing to tell Linda about her sister's death. Just like with the cameras, everyone connected with the Michelle Lunt case had disappeared.

I'd never bothered to find out where Nathan Lloyd had moved to, and maybe that was a mistake. He was the last possible link with Michelle. I consoled myself with the thought that he probably wouldn't have told me.

Linda lived in a small terraced house half a mile outside the town centre. The streets hadn't changed in Nelson in the hundred years since they housed the workers in the cotton mills.

Outside the town, the rolling moors showed what life had been like in the area before the Industrial Revolution, when everyone lived on smallholdings and did their weaving at home in their stone cottages.

The papers keep telling us that the new technology will send us all back into the country to run computer-based 'cottage industries' from home, but it hasn't happened yet.

If you believe the boffins, none of us will need to go out of our front doors in another twenty years. All communication, shopping and general chatting will be done by e-mail and, instead of watching football matches in stadiums, we'll play cyber games against people on other continents.

What we'll do instead of sex I've yet to find out, but I'm sure they'll think of something.

I parked the car right outside Linda's house, behind her Fiesta, and rapped on the brass knocker. As soon as she opened the door, Roly bounded into the front room after a longhaired ginger cat, which immediately jumped up on to the windowsill and spat at him until he backed away.

'Sorry,' I said. 'I should have put him on a lead.'

Linda patted Roly affectionately on the head. 'He's fine, aren't you, boy?' He nuzzled her with drooling lips. 'Where'd you get him?'

'He befriended me when I was lying beaten up in a gutter. Look, do you fancy lunch and I'll tell you all about it in the pub.'

'No need for the pub. I've cooked us something.' She led me into the back room, which she'd turned into a breakfast kitchen. A stripped-down oak table was set for two and she pointed to a cushioned bentwood chair for me to sit on. The cushions and the curtains were of the same fabric, very Laura Ashley.

'Did you make the curtains?'

'Of course. And all the rest in the house.' The decorating was all her own work as well. The dark green wallpaper with flashes of red suited the room. It was offset by brilliant white paintwork, which helped keep it light.

On the wall were two tapestries in matching frames, both depicting vases of flowers.

'Did you do those too?'

'Yes. Do you like them?'

'They're very good.' I wasn't an expert on tapestry 'Colourful and they match the wallpaper.'

She served up a chicken casserole. 'I'll put some in a bowl for – Roly, did you say he's called? And I got a four-pack of cider in for you,' she said.

The chicken was tender, cooked in a French sauce with root vegetables. When we'd finished, we took our drinks into the lounge.

'Right,' she said, 'I want to hear how you came to ge beaten up.' She suddenly looked worried. 'It wasn't anything to do with Shelley, was it?'

'No, it wasn't. At least, I don't think so.' Other than the fact that Nathan Lloyd, Serina Barrie and Linda's siste had all lived in my house, I couldn't see a connection And yet . . .

I'd told her at the funeral about being arrested but nov I filled her in with all the details – describing the photo session with Serina Barrie, buying the cameras, looking fo Fisher and ending with the attack in the entry.

'Oh Johnny, that's awful. But the police – I never knew they were allowed to lie.' I laughed at her innocence.

'I don't know that they're allowed to,' I said, 'but the say in Liverpool that if a cop tells the truth on the witnes stand, he's sent to Coventry by his mates for letting the side down.'

'What are you going to do?'

'Find out who stole the cameras in the first place, if

can, or try to trace Miss Barrie. I just hope she doesn't end up like Roy Quantine.'

I told her about the murder and she looked horrified. 'And I'm making you waste your time on my sister.'

'Correction. You hired me to investigate your sister's death and I don't intend to neglect that. In fact, I'm seeing my friend Jim Burroughs tomorrow morning.'

'Is that your policeman chum?' I nodded. 'They're not all crooked then?'

'To a degree,' I said. 'But Jim would be crooked on my side. At least, I think he would.' Now I was getting paranoid again.

'The people who murdered this man – they won't be after you, will they?'

It wasn't something I'd considered, but having the possibility put to me didn't make me feel any better.

After the late lunch and four cans of cider, weariness overcame me. I was tired to my very painful bones. Linda kindly invited me to stay the night and recuperate in her cosy bed.

'You'd never fit on my small couch,' she pointed out, 'and you gave me your bed so it's only fair I reciprocate.'

I went to bed early, woke equally early next morning, dressed quietly and left before the morning rush-hour. On the way out, I promised a half-asleep Linda that I'd ring her with the latest news.

I had a busy day ahead. Now I had two major cases to solve.

Chapter Twenty-one

First thing Monday morning, I dropped Roly off at the office He growled nastily when Geoffrey reached out to stroke him. 'He'll get used to you,' I said. 'Just don't put your fingers too close to his mouth.'

'Don't be too long,' warned Geoffrey. 'It looks vicious.'

'Rubbish,' I said. 'He's smiling at you. I'll be back as soon as I've had my mouth fixed.'

My dentist was a stout man in his late fifties with thick hair growing on the back of his hands. He had a faintly Polish accent and, when he opened his mouth, I noticed he sported a gold tooth, something you don't often see nowadays.

'Somebody didn't like you, heh?' he laughed, as he examined my injured jaw and gently prodded the two loose teeth.

'Something like that. Can you fix them, or will they have to come out?'

'Goodness me, come out? I should think not. No teeth leave my patients unless it is absolutely necessary. Life threatening, you understand? Open wide, please.'

It took Mr Stellman a quarter of an hour using various frightening-looking instruments and some sort of fixative but eventually he stood back with a grunt of satisfaction and pronounced the recalcitrant teeth fixed. I was not to chew on them that day, nor drink anything hot. I thanked him, paid the receptionist and moved on to my next appointment, at the solicitor's.

If anything, my newly acquired barrister was larger than the dentist. Brendan Butterworth grew outwards from his neck in a curve, which reached its zenith somewhere around his navel and disappeared dramatically between his outsize thighs.

He wore a black pin-striped suit with a gold watch-chain hanging over the waistcoat. A band of thick silver hair circled his bald head but his outstanding feature was a pair of bushy white sideboards.

Why do solicitors and barristers always look as if they've stepped straight out of a Victorian melodrama? Alistair's office had hardly changed since the turn of the century and he and Butterworth could have done *Stars in Your Eyes* as Scrooge and Mr Pickwick.

He shook my hand vigorously. 'Mr Ace. So pleasant to meet you in person. I often listen to your radio programme when I'm returning from the courthouse.'

His voice boomed at the lower end of baritone but it was lightened by a pronounced Irish lilt.

'Shall we go over to Toffs,' suggested Alistair, 'to save us being interrupted by the telephone?'

We all trooped off to the wine bar further along Dale Street and settled ourselves in a quiet corner downstairs with tea, coffee and croissants for them and an orange juice for me.

'Right,' began Alistair. 'Just to bring you up to date with progress.'

'There's been progress?' I asked.

'Of sorts, but not too promising for you, I'm afraid.'

'In what way?'

'Well, apparently those two cameras were stolen some months ago from one of the stores in the city centre.'

'That long ago? Where've they been until now? And who took them?'

'I can answer the last question. Your friend Roy Quantine. He was up for some petty theft or other and asked for a

number of other offences to be taken into consideration
Your stolen cameras were one of them.'

'So why didn't the police get them back then?'

'He'd already passed them on. I've not been able to find
out who subsequently acquired them, but nobody else has
been charged with any offence relating to them.'

'I don't understand. So why are they charging me?'

'Ah, exactly. Now here's where we have the problem.'
Brendan Butterworth spoke for the first time. 'Why are the
police so anxious to pin the crime on you when they seem
perfectly happy to let the others go?'

'Precisely,' agreed Alistair. 'What you need to do
Johnny, is get hold of Quantine and make him tell you
who he sold the cameras to.'

'You mean you haven't heard?' I knew Alistair was old
fashioned and his practice dealt more with conveyancing
than with criminal matters, but even he must have seen the
Daily Post headlines – MAN SLASHED TO DEATH IN CLUB

'Heard what?' Both men asked the question in unison.

I told them about the events at the Stirling Club. 'It's
been on all the local radio stations and it's front page in
today's *Post*.'

But Alistair had been away for the weekend and Butterworth
lived in Alderley Edge in Cheshire, beyond the circulation
of the Liverpool paper. 'I didn't notice anything in the
Telegraph,' he commented, 'but murders are ten a penny
these days. Maybe if he'd been a cabinet minister . . .'

I was anxious to get back to the matter in hand. 'The
point is, has his death got anything to do with me?'

'Well, you found him,' said Butterworth. 'Rather
coincidence that, or was it?'

I explained how I'd been intending to question him.

'But his chums got to him first, to shut him up?'

'That's how it looks to me. But what could he tell
me?'

'Ah, the million-dollar question. Of course,' he carried

on, 'as the person who found the body, you'll be one of their main suspects, will you not? Was it the same policeman?'

'No. And I made sure people around me saw me find him. I shouted out.'

Butterworth shook his head. 'A clever killer would do that. Slash a man's throat with one hand and cry, "Help, someone's been hurt!" as he threw the knife out of the window.' The barrister's voice rose to a crescendo as he acted out his scenario and I could see him being an impressive figure in court.

'No knife,' I said, 'inside or out, which puts me in the clear. I think.' I was beginning not to be sure about anything any more.

'Who else is left who knew about the cameras?' asked Alistair.

'Only Miss Barrie, who first told me about them but she's gone AWOL.'

'She'll be next on the slab,' predicted Butterworth, 'assuming they find her body at all, of course.'

We all sat back and contemplated this.

'Could there be any connection between this and Michelle Lunt's suicide?' I asked. Butterworth raised his eyebrows and I spent the next ten minutes filling him in.

'So this DS Leary was in charge of that case and he was the one who arrested you?'

'Yes, but I can't see any connection.'

Neither could Brendan Butterworth. Alistair told him of my aspirations to become a private investigator and the barrister commented that it appeared that I had enough work to last me until Christmas.

'Getting back to business,' he said, 'you'll be receiving a date to attend the Magistrates' Court. I'm going to try to get the case stopped before it reaches them. If I can't and the case goes ahead, I want you in front of a jury rather than a bunch of local bigwigs. Magistrates have this ridiculous notion that everyone but the police are liars whilst the police themselves are saints. Did you ever hear anything more ridiculous? You think they'd have learnt by now.'

I didn't like the thought of the case getting to court at all. It was the sort of publicity I could do without, especially at a time when I wanted to start up in the investigation business officially.

'Try and get hold of this Barrie girl,' were Brendan Butterworth's parting words. 'See what she can tell you.'

'I thought you said she'd be dead.'

'In which case,' he smiled, 'you'll be needing the services of a medium. Nice to have met you, Mr Ace. Play some more Barry Manilow on your programme, would you? My wife's very keen on him. Don't worry. We'll beat the bastards.'

I wished I could share his optimism. I felt like a drowning man coming up for the third time with the waters closing over his head.

I wanted to ring Maria to invite her to lunch but I was frightened she'd put the phone down on me. Hilary was working a full day at the hospital. In the end, I stopped off at The Diner where I ate a curry and read the early edition of the *Echo*.

The Roy Quantine murder had been relegated to page three. Police were now saying it was a gangland killing, probably to reassure the public that no innocent people were likely to be attacked at random by some crazed psycho.

If it was a gangland killing, I wondered who was in the gang.

I finished the meal and drove back to the office to pick up Roly, stopping on the way at a little pet shop in Aigburth Road to buy him a lead.

Geoffrey was not too happy with his new companion. 'It ate my dinner,' he complained. 'Chicken tikka sandwiches.

I only turned my back for half a second to answer the phone and they'd gone.'

'Chicken tikka?' I said. 'I pay you too well. If you'd had cheese or tuna like everyone else, he'd have left them alone.'

Roly stood on his back legs and licked my face. His breath smelt very spicy.

'Hey, did you see in the paper about Roy Quantine, boss? He's the bloke we threw out of South Albert Road when you first bought it. Dirty bugger. No wonder someone's trashed him. We're well rid of scum like that.'

'I don't think we're quite rid of him,' I said quietly. Geoffrey caught my tone and looked up sharply. 'There's been a few things happening, Geoff, I think you ought to know about.'

I told him all the latest developments.

'Nothing too important then?' he said sarkily when I'd finished. 'Just a murder, another tenant gone AWOL and you've been arrested and been given a going-over and it's still only Monday.'

'I don't count the last bit. That was pure mistaken identity.'

Geoffrey sighed. 'It was easier last month when we just had the suicide. I don't suppose that's got anything to do with all this? And what about our friend Nathan Lloyd – is he mixed up in this too?'

'Hang on, hang on. The answer is, I don't know. But I'm prepared to believe anything right now, however preposterous.' I put Roly's new lead on. 'I've got a couple of phone calls to make, Geoff. Take him for a walk round the block, would you?'

I ignored Geoff's outraged expression, and immediately rang Jim Burroughs. He was not surprised to hear from me; he'd read about Roy Quantine in the *Daily Post*. 'What's going on, Johnny?'

'Somebody was frightened he'd tell me something. They got to him first.'

'Something to do with the cameras?'

'I suppose so. Look, have you had any joy with the other business, the suicide?'

'I don't know why you're bothering with that when there's all this other.'

'I'm being paid, that's why. I've taken the case. Besides, there may be some tie-in, I don't know. So, have you got anything for me?'

'Not yet, Johnny, but I'll get on to it. I'm back in work tomorrow.'

I put down the receiver. My second call was to be to Maria. I had to take the plunge sometime. Over the last few days, I'd been thinking seriously about what she'd said about Hilary; that if anything was going to come of the two of us, it would have done so by now.

I could never accept that. Why did things have to change? Why did a relationship always have to 'come to' something? Hilary and I had had an arrangement that had worked for twenty years. Whatever else, or whoever else, we both knew we'd always been there for one another, and I couldn't imagine ever being without her.

At the same time, I recognised there was a different part of me that needed Maria. We shared things that Hilary would have no interest in, the best example being my investigative work. We got on well and I cared a lot for her. The point was, did Maria still care for me? There was only one way to find out.

I knew I'd have to call her sometime and the longer I left it, the harder it would be, but I never got a chance because at that moment, before I could pick it up, the phone rang.

'Is that Johnny Ace?'

'Yes.'

'It's Serina Barrie, Look, I'm in terrible trouble. You've got to help me.'

She was the last person I expected to hear from! 'Where are you?' I asked.

'I don't know. I'm in a warehouse near the docks. Somewhere in Bootle, I think.' Her voice was low and it sounded desperate.

'But you don't know exactly where?'

'I've been kidnapped. I'm locked in this room.'

I was sceptical. 'And they left a telephone there?'

'I'm on my mobile. They didn't find it when they searched me.'

I didn't ask where she'd hidden it. 'Who's "they"?'

'Two men. They grabbed me when I was walking to the bus stop this morning.'

It was true that she sounded genuinely terrified, but I was still suspicious. 'Why did you leave Livingstone Drive without telling me?'

There was a pause. 'There is a reason. I'll tell you everything, Mr Ace. Look, please will you help me?'

'Why don't you ring the police? They'll be able to trace the call and find you much quicker than I could.' Thanks to the latest technology, anyone using a mobile phone can apparently be immediately traced to within a hundred yards of where they're standing. Talk about Big Brother.

Another pause. 'I can't ring the police. Look – I'll explain when you come. You will come, won't you?' And, as if to make sure I did: 'I can tell you the truth about the cameras.'

'You'll have to give me more details of how to find you. There's hundreds of old sheds and warehouses between the Pier Head and Seaforth.' Not quite true any more. Many of the unused factories, warehouses and dock buildings have been pulled down to make way for new industrial units, residential housing and even green fields. 'How do I know which one you're in?'

'There's a building opposite where I'm standing with a

sign over the door, *Pavitt & Co., Toolmakers*. I can see it from here.'

'Where are the two men now?'

'Gone out. I saw them leave in the car but I heard one say they'd be back before four. I think they're taking me somewhere else.'

I checked my watch. It was three-fifteen. 'All right. Give me half an hour.'

It was cutting it fine. I still had to locate the building. I found the address of Pavitt & Co. in the telephone directory and looked it up in the *A-Z*. It was in a little street off Regent Road. I could get there in twenty minutes, traffic permitting.

Serina Barrie was my only link to the cameras. Roy Quantine had been killed for what he knew. Why had Miss Barrie been spared? Unless she was on their side! Which meant I was walking into a trap armed with nothing more dangerous than a rolled-up copy of the Liverpool *Echo*.

In normal circumstances I would have rung the police, but after my recent experiences, they were the last people I would turn to.

I wrote a note for Geoffrey telling him where I was going, and instructing him to come and look for me if I wasn't back in an hour.

The traffic was fairly light for mid-afternoon on a Monday. I passed the Pier Head and my own flat at Waterloo Dock until I reached the street housing Pavitts the Toolmakers. I swung the car sharply for a right turn and pulled up outside their low prefabricated office.

Across the road was a huge old soot-blackened warehouse, at least five storeys high. Five stone steps led up to a pair of stout wood and glass doors guarding the main entrance. I jumped out of the car and ran across the road and into the building.

I was in a deserted hallway but a list of occupants on a wooden plaque in the hall indicated the building was not completely unoccupied. I realised I should have asked Serina what floor she was on.

I ran up the first flight of stairs. On my right, a glass-fronted door bore the inscription *Continental Insurance Brokers*. There were lights on and I could see people working in the office.

I carried on to the next floor. *Raymond Marshall, Property Agents* said the lettering on the door there. Through the frosted windows, I could see a couple of VDU screens glowing and I pressed on.

The third floor looked empty. A cardboard sign *Mr A.I. Me-idith, Ort-opae-ic Con-ult-nt* with missing letters looked like it had been up for years. I knocked on the wooden door. No answer.

Could this be where Serina Barrie was being held?

I tried the door. Locked. I peered through the letterbox. The room was dusty and empty apart from junk mail behind the door. There was no sign of life.

The stairs were narrower up to floor four and again the office here looked like the *Marie Celeste*. *John Bury, Finance Consultant and Mortgage Broker* had evidently moved away some time ago, judging by the unkempt state of the landing.

I knocked loudly although I wasn't expecting a reply. Then I tried the door, but of course it was locked. I pushed open the letterbox. At first I thought the room was empty and then I saw a stockinged leg protruding from round a corner.

The leg did not move. It was lying on the floor with a black platform shoe on its foot.

Standing back, I raised my right foot and kicked the door open, bursting the lock from the frame. I stopped to listen but nobody came running at the noise.

I moved slowly down the room, half-expecting someone to jump out at me, but the only person in the room was Serina Barrie and she wouldn't be jumping anywhere.

Neither would she be telling me anything about the cameras. First Roy Quantine, now a young girl. How had she got mixed up in all this? Whatever 'this' was.

The bullet had entered her head neatly between the eyes. She lay flat on her back, her expression in death a mixture of surprise and terror. Whoever had killed her, she hadn't been expecting it.

On the floor next to her was a gun. Without thinking, I picked it up and sniffed the barrel. Cordite. It had recently been fired.

I put the gun down beside the body and looked round the room. It was bare. No furniture, no fittings. Miss Barrie was wearing a short black skirt, a skimpy silver top and a leather jacket. I went though the pockets looking for clues but all I found was her mobile phone. I took it and placed it in the inside pocket of my leather jacket.

On her wrist was a silver watch. It gave the time as three fifty-five. Another five minutes and her captors would be back. I didn't want to stick around and face the two of them, even with a gun.

The gun. I had to get rid of it. It had my prints all over it.

I didn't hear the two men come in. They wore soft shoes and crept up behind me. They didn't attack me either. I looked up at the familiar pock-marked face.

'Well, well, Mr Ace. This time you really have done it, haven't you?' and Detective Sergeant Leary pulled out a pair of handcuffs. 'Caught almost in the act. You won't be wriggling out of this one.' He handed the cuffs to the Constable at his side. 'Lock him up, Morton.' To me: 'I'm charging you with murder.'

Before he could say any more, I shoved the Constable aside, hit Leary in the Adam's apple with my right fist and ran out of the door and down the stairs.

I had a good thirty-second start as Morton had been

knocked off-balance by Leary falling to the floor, half-conscious and choking, and seemed to have twisted his ankle in the process.

I jumped down the stairs five at a time and leapt through the front door, only to see a security man fixing a clamp to the back wheel of my car.

I turned round in horror. Morton would be down at any minute. And then I heard a blast from a horn and racing round the corner came a familiar battered blue BMW with Geoffrey at the wheel and the brown head of Roly peering out of the front passenger window.

The cavalry had arrived.

Chapter Twenty-two

I ran into the middle of the road, flagged them down and jumped into the back seat as the car drew up with a screech of tyres, allowing Geoffrey to pull away without actually stopping.

'Get us away from here,' I shouted. I looked out of the back window to see Constable Morton emerge from the warehouse and hobble towards his patrol car.

'Where to, boss?' asked Geoffrey.

'I don't know. Just lose that police car.'

He answered by taking a sudden right turn, heading back towards the city. 'Is that the law following us?' he enquired as the distant wail of a siren rent the air.

''Fraid so.'

'Then let's move.' Geoffrey put his foot down and the BMW surged forward, weaving in and out of the traffic perilously. The cars in front parted to let him by, probably thinking he was the police, an understandable mistake as he was driving with his headlights full on.

'I don't think he could have got our number,' I said, 'but just in case he did, we'd better lose the car somewhere. Tell you what, drive into one of the multi-storeys in town.'

Geoffrey chose the NCP car park at the back of the St George's Hotel. I looked through the back window as we drove up the slope. There was no sign of the police car.

'What happened, then?' enquired Geoffrey as he man-oeuvred the car into a space on the third floor and turned off the engine.

I told him. His expression changed to one of horror. 'What are you going to do? You'll have to get out of town for a start, and you won't be able to do your programme.'

'I need time to think things through.'

'Where will you go?' persisted Geoffrey. 'They'll be looking for you everywhere.'

I had no idea. Leary would have a call-out on me by now. As Geoffrey had said, I could hardly turn up at the radio station. Neither could I go home or to the office. I thought of Hilary's but everyone knew about us – that's the first place they'd look. Maria's, which would have once been my first choice, was out for obvious reasons.

'They've only got to put it out on the radio that the police are looking for you,' added Geoffrey, 'and you won't be able to go anywhere in town. You're too well-known.'

He was right. I couldn't even rely on Jim Burroughs not turning me in. After all, he was still in the Force and harbouring a wanted criminal wouldn't do his career prospects too much good. Not to mention his pension.

'Linda Roberts,' I said, suddenly.

'Who?'

'Michelle Lunt's sister. She lives in Nelson. That's far enough away. She'll put me up.'

'And who's having the mutt?' As if knowing he was being discussed, Roly turned round to lick my face affectionately.

'It's all right. I'll take him with me. He's been before.'

'Really?' Geoffrey sighed and clicked his teeth disapprovingly like Walter Brennan does in the old black and white Westerns on TV. 'Not doing a line with her as well, are you?'

'Strictly business, Geoff.'

'Oh yes? And Mick Jagger's a virgin. Anyway, no time to bother about that. How are you going to get to Nelson? They've probably tagged this car.'

'And the RAV4's been clamped. I wonder how Leary managed to fix that?'

There were a lot of things I didn't understand about this whole set-up but now wasn't the time to worry about them. The first priority was to get away.

'Train?' suggested Geoffrey. 'Lime Street Station's only across the road.'

'With the dog?'

'Oh yes. See what you mean.'

'Anyway, public transport's too risky. Does your mother still have that old Metro?'

'Yes, why?' He stopped. 'You can't want to borrow *that*!'

'Why not? The perfect inconspicuous vehicle.'

'What about my mum? How will she get around without her car?'

'She can use the RAV4 – once you get it unclamped, of course. Look, it's half-past four now, Geoff. You get a taxi to yours, pick up the Metro and bring it straight back.'

'And you'll wait here?'

'With Roly. Yes.'

'I hope she's in. She might have gone to bingo.'

'You've got a mobile, haven't you? Ring her and check.'

Geoffrey's mother was at home. She was watching snooker on television. I think snooker's a form of hypnotism they put on TV to keep old people sedated in case they consider rebelling against the tedium of their lives.

'Before you go,' I said, once he had confirmed he could pick up the car, 'leave me your mobile phone. I need to ring a couple of people.'

'I told you you were wasting your time with that bloody pager,' snarled Geoffrey, throwing the phone into my lap.

One of those I had to call was Linda, who was surprised to hear from me so soon.

'It's an emergency,' I told her. 'Any chance of a bed for the night?' Or several nights, I thought.

'How can I refuse,' she replied, 'after you put me up.'

'True. Not a word to anyone, though. I'm in a bit of trouble.'

'What's happened?'

'The police are after me.'

'Again?'

'It's a long story. I'll tell you when I see you.'

'What time will that be?'

I made a quick calculation. 'About seven to seven-thirty, depending on the traffic.'

I phoned Ken at the radio station and told him I wouldn't be able to get in. 'There's been a bit of trouble with one of my tenants,' I said. 'The police need me to sort it out. Sorry about the short notice. Can you get hold of Shady Spencer to do the show?'

Ken wasn't happy. He didn't like disruption. Luckily, it didn't happen very often but I wondered what he'd think when someone handed him the five o'clock news bulletin.

It was a good job the police didn't have Geoffrey's mobile phone number or they would have traced me by now. And I had more calls to make.

Alistair was horrified when I told him of my arrest and subsequent escape. 'As your solicitor, I must advise you to give yourself up at the nearest police station, say nothing and I'll meet you down there. I'll get you released on bail while we sort it out. It's an obvious mistake.'

'It's a fit-up, Alistair, and I wouldn't bank on bail. I'll be in touch.' I put the phone down and rang Jim Burroughs.

'Jim, it's Johnny. Now listen – I haven't got long. I've been arrested for murder.' A choking noise at the other end indicated he'd heard me correctly. 'Switch the radio on for the news, that'll give you all the details.'

'Where are you?' he asked.

'Better you don't know,' I said, remembering he was stil
a serving officer. 'That bastard Leary arrested me but it wa:
a set-up. Needless to say, Jim, I haven't killed anybody, bu
I desperately need you to find out everything you can from
your end. DS Leary's definitely suspect.'

'How will I contact you?'

'You won't. I'll ring you.'

Earlier in the afternoon, I'd missed ringing Maria b
seconds and now it was too late. The moment had passed
Going to stay with Linda, however valid the excuse an
however temporary the stay, was hardly a suitable recip
for a reunion.

Instead, I rang Hilary's and left a message on he
ansaphone. I knew she'd hear about everything soon enoug
so I just told her not to worry, I was busy sorting things ou
I loved her and would be in touch.

All of this took up barely fifteen minutes and it wa
another thirty before Geoffrey arrived in the Metro, a gre
nondescript vehicle that looked as if it would have troubl
negotiating the Pier Head Flyover never mind climbing th
Pennines.

'Looks a bit knackered to me,' I said critically as I pulle
forward the front seat and ushered Roly into the back. ']
reg, is it?'

'F.'

'Ninety thousand on the clock. Your mum go rallying
does she?'

'It had seventy-seven on when she bought it three year
ago.' He thrust a bulky package into my hand.

'What's this?' It was a Safeways carrier containing
flat cloth cap and a pair of specs.

'A disguise,' he said solemnly. 'The specs are plain glass
Might fool anyone glancing into the car.'

I put on the cap and the glasses, slipped into the driver'
seat and handed Geoffrey his mobile phone. 'Thanks fc
all this, Geoff,' I said. 'Even if I do look like someon

out of *Last of the Summer Wine*. I do appreciate it, you know.'

'Part of the job. Sure you don't want me to come with you?'

'Positive. Someone has to run the business. By the way, if the police come round, you dropped me off in town, you'd no idea I was on the run and you don't know where I am.'

'Got it, boss.'

I handed him a piece of paper. 'Linda's number if you need me. Don't give it to anyone – and I mean *anyone*.'

'Trust me.'

He waved me off down the ramp and I joined the teatime traffic on Lime Street. At first I felt as if everyone was looking at me as I drove towards Edge Lane and the motorway, but they weren't and I was soon in the middle lane of the M62 doing a comfortable sixty.

Now I was really on the run.

Chapter Twenty-three

On the way, I tried to make some sense of the situation. The way I read it, Serina Barrie had made that phone call to me to lure me to the warehouse. Whether she'd made it voluntarily because she was on their side, whoever *they* were, or not, I didn't know.

Giving her the benefit of the doubt, she may have been genuinely imprisoned, although why it was me she asked to rescue her was unfathomable. Had she no boyfriend, friend, parents?

No, I reckoned she was implicated from the start and when she spoke to me it was with the deliberate intention of leading me into a trap.

Except . . . instead of killing me, they'd killed her. She could hardly have expected that. And why had they done it? The only answer I could come up with was to frame me for her murder. But if they were going to kill anyway, why not just kill me? Or both of us?

The questions I kept coming back to were: Who were they? How was Leary involved? And did any of it tie in with Michelle Lunt's death?

My mind grew weary of thinking and I switched on the car radio in time for the six o'clock news headlines.

I was the main story. 'Police are anxious to trace radio presenter Johnny Ace in connection with the shooting in Bootle this afternoon of nineteen-year-old Liverpool University student, Serina Barrie.'

That would go down well with the station bosses,

thought. Shady Spencer could well be getting a permanent slot.

No mention was made of a possible connection with the murder of Roy Quantine.

I listened to Shady's show. He read his usual asinine poetry and played some crap records. I suppose there are people around who like non-stop Gloria Estafan or Chris De Burgh, but if I hear Steve Harley's *Come Up and See Me (Make Me Smile)* many more times on the radio, I might smash the set. It must be on every computer playlist in the world, programmed to be playing somewhere every minute of every day. Reviewing the last ten years in pop music, you'd think rock'n'roll had never been invented. It's been almost totally phased out.

Luckily, the signal faded as I drove up the M6 to the M65 interchange and I switched over to Radio Four in time for *The Archers*. Roly didn't seem so keen on *The Archers*; he was asleep on the back seat.

I was on constant alert for police cars but I saw none. Nevertheless, I felt a great relief when I pulled off the motorway at Nelson and drove through the maze of narrow streets to the little terraced house I'd left only that morning.

I couldn't believe all this had happened since then.

Linda looked genuinely pleased to see me. She wore a short black skirt over black leggings with a red top and her hair hung down over her shoulders, unrestrained by the elastic band.

'Back again,' she said cheerfully. 'The neighbours will be thinking you've moved in. The dinner's ready and I've been out for some dog food for Roly.'

A smile crossed Roly's hairy face.

'Where's your cat?'

'Emily? Probably hiding in the bathroom.'

'I'm imposing on you,' I said, and realised as I said it that this time *I'd* not brought any night-things.

'We're evens then,' she smiled, when I told her. 'I've
got an Everton T-shirt you can wear.'

We ate the meal which Linda informed me was Chicken
Forestière. 'Marks and Spencer,' she confessed, 'but I
cooked the vegetables myself.'

'It was delicious.' We'd had a litre of red wine between
us, which had taken the edge off my problems.

'Come on, let's go into the front room and you can tell
me what all this is about.'

Her cat had obviously decided it was safe to leave the
bathroom and was asleep on the couch. Linda lifted her up
whilst she sat down then placed Emily on her knee and
motioned me to sit beside them. Roly seemed to accept the
cat's senior position in the household and lay at our feet.

Before I could start my story, the phone rang and Linda
went across to answer it. I couldn't hear the caller's voice
but I guessed it was a man by the blush that came to her
cheeks. I think he was asking her out, but she was saying
she couldn't go.

'That was Peter,' she said when she returned to the
settee.

'The teacher?'

She nodded. 'I said I was busy.'

'Don't you like him?'

'Actually, he's quite nice but the Head Teacher doesn'
like the staff fraternising.'

'How stupid.' What were they frightened of? Blow-jobs
in the staff room? Groping in the gym?

'I know, but maybe she has a point. Anyway, tell me
what's been happening to you.'

'Where do I begin?' I said, and proceeded to relate the
horrific events of the day.

'You're not worried about prison, are you?' Linda asked
when I'd finished the story. 'They can't convict you if you
didn't do it, surely?'

I regretted that I was unable to share her confidence in

the British judicial system. Did the woman never watch *Rough Justice*?

'I daren't risk it,' I told her. 'I'm better off trying to find the people behind it all myself.'

'And who do you think they are?'

I shrugged. 'Not a clue, but there's been too many murders for it to be a something or nothing case.'

'This Leary was the person in charge when Shelley died, wasn't he?'

'It must have been pure chance that he happened to be on duty at the time but you're right – he *is* the only connection between your sister's death and the cameras.'

'No sign of this man she's supposed to have married?'

'Jim Burroughs is working on it.'

'He might not be so keen to work for you now that you're on the wanted list.'

I'd already considered that possibility and it disturbed me. 'In which case, it's up to me to start investigating.' I smiled. 'After all, that is what you're paying me for.'

'Look Johnny, I don't mind if you forget about Shelley with all this you've got going on.'

'No, I want to carry on.' Apart from my promise to Linda, I still felt there could possibly be a link between the two cases, but time was against me now. How long could I remain free?

'Have you got a mobile phone I could borrow?' I asked her. I wanted to ring Geoffrey and it made no sense to use Linda's normal phone. The police could quite easily find their way to Geoffrey's and check his incoming calls.

'It's me. Geoff, I need to find the address Chris Voke moved to.'

'In case you were worried,' he replied icily, 'I did eventually get home safely and unseen.'

'Sorry Geoff, I'd forgotten for a minute.'

'I got the bus. Thought it best not to risk the BMW.'

'What about the RAV4?'

'Still clamped. Jack's getting one of the men to collect it in the morning. Who did you say?'

'Chris Voke. He lived in the ground-floor flat at Livingstone Drive at the beginning of the year. Moved out suddenly because his old man was ill, or so he said. They lived somewhere in Warrington.'

'I won't ask what he's got to do with all this.'

'Good.' I gave him Linda's mobile number. 'You couldn't do it tonight, could you?' I was afraid that, by morning, the law could have taken over the office. Already it might be too late.

'It's gone nine o'clock, you know.' Geoffrey sighed. 'Oh, all right. I'll get a taxi. Give me half an hour.'

He was as good as his word. Thirty-five minutes later, he rang me from the office. 'Christ, boss. The busies have been in. You want to see the place.'

'All we can expect, I suppose. Much taken?' After my recent experiences, I wasn't being entirely sarcastic.

'They've turned it over good style, but nothing obvious appears to be missing. I got the address you wanted anyway.'

'Good man.' I wrote it down in my notebook. Chris Voke's parents lived in Burtonwood.

'I've got the phone number, too, if you want it?' he said.

'Brilliant. How did you get that?'

'The phone book,' replied Geoffrey smugly. 'Not every one's ex-directory. When are you coming back?' He sounded concerned.

'When I've found out who killed Serina Barrie. Keep your mobile with you, Geoff. I'll be in touch and thanks for everything.'

I could almost feel him blush at the other end of the phone.

Chris Voke wasn't in when I rang him on Linda's land-line phone, but his father was. He didn't sound very ill either.

explained that I wanted to know why Chris had left the flat
he'd rented from me.

'Well, I don't know whether he'd thank me for telling
you, Mr Ace,' he said, 'but the truth was, he was given
money to move.'

'What?'

'Yes. An American gentleman called at the flat one
day and offered Christopher five hundred pounds to move
out. Said his wife particularly wanted to live there. My son
had only a few weeks left at university before the end of term
so he was happy to take the cash. I believe the gentleman did
eventually move into the flat.'

'If it's the same person we're talking about, you wouldn't
know his name, I suppose?'

'As a matter of fact, I do. A real Yankee name it was,
that's why I remember it. He was called Wilbur Lunt.'

Chapter Twenty-four

Mr Voke senior knew nothing else about Wilbur Lunt. His son had taken the money and was out within a couple of days. I'd put an advert in the *Echo* and Wilbur Lunt had answered it with references so good I could hardly refuse him. Especially as he offered to furnish the place like something straight out of *Ideal Home*.

Why had he wanted to move there so badly?

I put the phone down on Mr Voke and turned to Linda. 'It seems your sister and Wilbur Lunt moved into Livingstone Drive for a particular reason.'

'Connected with her job, you mean?'

'Or his. They certainly didn't go there by chance or because they liked the look of the flat.'

'So what's your next step?'

My next step was Jim Burroughs. 'Christ,' he exclaimed when I rang him, this time on Linda's mobile, 'you're taking some chances, aren't you? You're the headlines on every bloody newsreel.'

'Are they connecting the girl's death with Quantine?'

'They are now since they've realised you are the common factor.'

'They were both dead when I found them. I was set up this afternoon. The girl phoned me saying she was being held prisoner in this warehouse. I turn up like Sir Lancelot rescuing the maiden and find her lying on the floor with a bullet through her head. I've hardly time to pick up the gun when, surprise, surprise, in walks your man Leary swinging a pair of cuffs.'

'You're saying it wasn't a coincidence that Leary turned up?'

'What do you think? It was no more a coincidence than the cameras were. What's his game, Jim? Why's he got it in for me?'

He didn't answer the question. 'According to Leary, you were standing over the body with a smoking gun in your hand.'

'It was on the floor beside her. I picked it up without thinking.'

'That was a stupid mistake.'

'You don't have to tell me but, to be honest Jim, I don't think it would have mattered. He knew what he'd come to do. But, forget all that for a minute, have you found out anything about the suicide?'

'Johnny, you're wanted for murder. There's a nation-wide hunt going on. What do you want to bother with that for?'

'I know what I'm doing, Jim.' Although whether I was doing the right thing was less certain. 'And one thing I've just found out a few minutes ago confirms something you said. Wilbur Lunt *did* pay the last tenant to move out of the flat in Livingstone Drive.'

'That fits in with my information. The word is that Michelle Roberts was trailing the Liverpool connection of this Colombian drug ring and one of the key members was living in your house.'

'Lloyd,' I said immediately.

'Would that be Nathan Sebastian Lloyd?'

'The bloke who lived on the top floor. I found heroin in his room and threw him out. I told you at the time but you said he'd only be small-time.'

'Seems like I was wrong,' admitted the policeman. 'Nathan Lloyd is on Interpol's wanted list.'

'And he's disappeared into thin air like Wilbur Lunt. Are the Drug Squad still after him?'

'I presume so. That's not our pigeon.'

'Mm. It still doesn't tell us why Michelle killed herself.'

'I have a theory about that, but I'll tell you when I see you. Look, Johnny, why don't you come back and get this mix-up sorted? You're doing yourself no favours running away like this.'

'I daren't, Jim. As long as I'm free to ask questions, I've got a fighting chance.' I knew the police would oppose bail if I turned myself in. 'Look, find out about Leary, will you? He's the person behind my arrest. See what you can do. I'll be in touch.'

I'd hardly put the phone down to Jim when Linda's mobile rang. 'It's for you,' she said, handing it to me. 'It's getting like a telephone exchange in here.'

Geoffrey was back on the line. 'Tommy McKale just rang, boss. He wants to speak to you. I didn't know whether to give him this number so I said I'd get you to call him.'

'I wonder what he wants.'

'I don't know but he said it was urgent.'

'Is he at the Masquerade?'

'No, but he left a number where you'd reach him.'

'Right.' I took it down. 'I'll ring him straight away. Thanks, Geoff.' I turned to Linda. 'Sorry about this.'

She stood up. 'I'll make some coffee.'

'Tea for me, please,' I said. 'Thanks.' I dialled the number Geoff had given me.

'Good evening, Marina Health and Leisure Club, Jillian speaking, how may I help you?' I was nonplussed. It wasn't the reply I'd been expecting.

'May I speak to Tommy McKale, please?'

'One moment, who is it speaking, please?'

'Just tell him it's Johnny.'

Two clicks later, a familiar Scouse voice came on the line. 'All right, Johnny? I'm glad I found you.'

'What's with the Marina Health and Leisure business?'

'It's Denis's old gym,' he chuckled. 'We've moved it a bit upmarket. Cashing in on the new boating fraternity in the Docks.'

'Sounds very grand. How's it doing?'

'The posh housewives love it. They've fuck all to do all day but plaster themselves with expensive potions and ponce about on the weights. I've brought in a few well-muscled young men in satin shorts to serve them expensive drinks, hired a French chef for the restaurant and we haven't looked back.'

'Christ, I remember the days when that gym was just a hangout for all the local tearaways. Wasn't there a snooker hall underneath at one time?'

'Billiards. That's going back, Johnny. When we first bought it, it was full of scalleys. They'd argue about who'd potted what ball then go upstairs to the gym and knock the shit out of one another in the ring. Mind you, we had a few good fighters as well. Denis used to train them. His lads won a few bouts at the old Stadium.'

It was Johnny Best who used to promote fights at the Liverpool Stadium; his son Pete played drums for The Beatles. There's a certain continuity about things in Liverpool.

'I remember them. So, what does Denis do in the new set-up?'

Tommy laughed. 'Keeps the riffraff out and overlooks the exercise programmes. He's our Fitness Instructor.'

And to think I'd always regarded Denis as a typical Neanderthal bruiser.

'Training the new bouncers for the club, eh?' We both laughed. 'Anyway, Geoffrey says you wanted me urgently.'

'I do.' His voice took on a serious note. 'I don't know what trouble you've got yourself into, Johnny. I've seen the news on the box and I know the law's after you, but

I heard something tonight that I didn't like the sound of. Could prove more dangerous for you than a police cell.'

'What's that?'

'There's a contract out on you.'

My stomach did a back-flip. 'A contract? On me?'

'Somebody wants you dead.'

'But who?'

'I don't know, but word has it that it's something to do with one of the big drug cartels.'

'But why me? I've had nothing to do with any drugs.'

'Just sticking to first-degree murder, eh? That's what I like – a man who knows his limitations.' Tommy McKale chuckled.

Suddenly I thought about Nathan Lloyd and realised the implications. 'Oh shit,' I said, and recounted my conversation with Jim Burroughs.

'I warned you, Johnny, when you told me you'd elbowed that geezer from your gaff. These aren't men to mess about with.'

I still couldn't believe they wanted to kill me. 'You're not having me on? Throwing the guy out of his pad hardly warrants the death penalty.'

'Deadly serious, Johnny. If I were you, I'd be very careful. This city has more than its fair share of fellas who'd be willing to carry out an execution, fifty per cent up front, the rest on completion, no questions asked, no personal involvement. You know yourself. Christ, you've only got to read the *Echo*.'

I couldn't think of a reply. My stomach was in a bad way now.

'I take it that wherever you are, you're well out of town?' Tommy continued.

'Not far enough, after what you've told me.' Australia was looking good but my passport was back in the flat and besides, the police would doubtless be guarding all exits. 'Seems everybody's after me.'

'I was coming to that. What's with this murder rap? I've never had you down for a shooting man, not even the odd pheasant.'

I explained to him about the afternoon in Bootle. 'Beautifully planned,' he commented admiringly. 'You know, some of these policemen ought to be criminals. They'd make themselves a fortune.'

'They *are* bloody criminals and not only are they skimming it big-style whilst they're in the Force, they'll have a nice fat pension to look forward to at the end of it.'

'At least they're not trying to kill you.'

'How do you make that out? It could be them who's put the contract out.'

'No. I told you, these are drug people. Do you know where he went, this Lloyd?'

'Not a clue.'

'I'll put out a few feelers, Johnny, but in the meantime, lie low.'

'At the moment I'm at—'

'I don't want to know where you are! For your sake, I hope there's a few hundred miles of water between you and Liverpool, and it might be as well to have a sex change while you're at it and put them off the scent.'

'Sorry, Tommy. I never suited mini-skirts. Look, before you go, can you ask around about a bent copper called Leary?'

'Leary?'

'Yes, a Detective Sergeant. He did me for stolen cameras before this latest thing.' A thought struck me. 'You don't know anyone called Clive Fisher, do you – a photographer?'

'Doesn't ring a bell.'

I told him about the house in Kirkdale, now supposedly occupied by Violet Parker.

'Give me the address and I'll look into it,' offered Tommy.

'That's good of you.'

'Leave it with me and keep smiling, Johnny. I trust you've got one of your ladies there to keep you company. I'll ring your oppo when I've got any news.'

Linda came in bearing a tray. 'Tea and biscuits,' she smiled and stopped. 'You look frightened. What's the matter?'

'Terrified might be a better word. Not only are the police after me for murder, but now a boatload of Colombian drug barons are hiring someone to kill me.'

'For God's sake, Johnny, what is all this about?'

'Obviously more than a couple of stolen cameras.'

She sat beside me. 'What are you going to do?'

'I don't know. Go back to the beginning, I think. You've got all your sister's things from the flat, haven't you? Did you find any diaries or address books amongst them?'

'No. A few bank statements, that's all.'

I'd already seen those. 'I'm trying to find some contact name whereby I can trace Wilbur Lunt or, come to that, anyone connected to your sister that I can talk to.'

'I'd thought of that,' said Linda. 'I spent a night going through Shelley's belongings but there was nothing.' She poured out a cup of tea and handed it to me. 'Yorkshire Parkin biscuit? They're from Nelson Market, very nice.'

They were. Roly opened his eyes when he heard crunching and Linda slipped a biscuit into his mouth. I wondered where Maria was. If she could see me now, here at Linda's, that would be it. I didn't know when I'd get the chance to ring her again.

Linda put her hand on my knee and looked up at me with those hazel eyes. 'Penny for them.'

'Sorry, I was miles away.' My eyes travelled round the cosy lounge. On an oak dresser I recognised a couple of ornaments from the flat at Livingstone Drive, a figurine lampshade and a small Wedgwood vase. 'Those were your sister's, weren't they?'

'Yes. I stuck them on there for the time being. There's more stuff dumped behind the door.' She pointed to a couple of Tesco carriers. A wire was trailing out of one of them.

I had a sudden flash of inspiration. 'Is that Shelley's telephone in that bag?'

'Yes, why?' I jumped up, startling Emily who'd moved on to the top of the couch behind me. I took the phone out of the bag and examined it.

'We're in luck!' I cried.

'What do you mean?'

'It's a call display phone. It holds the last thirty numbers which called it. Just let's hope the battery hasn't run out.' I unplugged Linda's phone from the socket in the wall, fitted Michelle's in its place and pressed the 'calls' button. A number came up on the screen.

'The moment of truth,' I said dramatically. It was like getting messages from the grave but I thought it indelicate to say that to Linda. 'At last we can find out who your sister was in touch with.' I took out my pen and notebook. 'Let's go. This could be our big break. Who knows what we'll find.'

Chapter Twenty-five

There were thirty numbers stored in Michelle and Wilbur Lunt's telephone.

I wrote them all down in my notebook. Some were recurring. I recognised only two of them, my office number and the phone in the top-floor flat at Livingstone Drive – the one Nathan Lloyd had occupied. So one of the Lunts had had contact with the drug dealer despite Lloyd denying that he knew Michelle.

'Any luck?' Linda peered over my shoulder.

'I've got about twenty numbers still to check.'

'How will you find out who they are?'

'I'll ring them, that's the quickest way.'

'I've got a reverse phone book, if that's any help. Tells you the exchange of the code you're dialling.'

'Yes, that would be helpful.' She went to fetch it from a drawer in the dresser. Roly took advantage of her absence to help himself to another Yorkshire Parkin.

'You've got an awful lot of things in that notebook,' she said, returning with the phone book. 'You'd be in a mess if you lost that. I'd have thought you'd have had a Psion or at least a Filofax.'

'Can't be doing with those electronic things. You can't see them in the sun, you've all those fiddly knobs to press and then the batteries give out. As for Filofaxes, they're too bulky. I bought this little green notebook on holiday in Nice. It has ninety-six pages and only cost eighty pence. It fits in any pocket, bends easily and lasts me a year before

it's full. I've got all my life in there, look.' I showed it to
her and she flicked through the pages.

'You're big on lists, aren't you?'

'It's my organised mind.'

'A compendium of trivia,' she commented. 'Train times,
lists of books and CDs and films, combination lock codes,
make of tyres for the RAV4, addresses, lists of flats and
tenants, minutes of meetings, computer specs, and what's
this, a music quiz?'

'It's one I did on the show. Not one listener got all the
answers right. The winner only got twenty out of forty.'

She read through the questions. 'I don't wonder. I've
never heard of half of these.'

'That's because Buddy Holly had been dead for fifteen
years before you were born.' I took the book back. 'Right,
let's check these numbers.'

I read out the codes. Most of them I knew, 0171 and
0181 were London, 0161 Manchester and, of course, 0151
Liverpool, but I was surprised to find the Lunts had had
calls from Anglesey, Llandudno and Dover, as well as
several international calls.

'That's the lot,' I announced finally. 'All thirty of them
and over a period of six days, the last ones on the day she
died. Let's see what we've got.'

There was no indication from which country any of the
seven overseas calls were made, and five times the screen
came up with the inscription 'withheld'.

'That leaves eighteen numbers, by my reckoning,' I
said.

'Three are repeated,' pointed out Linda. She counted up.
'There's just eleven numbers in all to check on. Two in
Liverpool . . .'

'Those are my office and Mr Lloyd.'

'Right. Which leaves the Anglesey, Llandudno, and
Dover ones, one in Manchester and five in London which
are the ones repeated.'

I checked the list. 'So, leaving out Liverpool, we have nine numbers to ring. No use doing it now, it's nearly eleven o'clock; we'll wait till morning. Besides, I'm shattered after everything that's happened today.'

'I bet you are. Why don't you go on up to bed?' Linda handed me the Everton T-shirt and grinned.

'What about you?'

'My couch is just as comfy as yours,' she smiled. 'Go on – off you go, and how about taking your hound with you?'

I told her good night, yawned and made for the stairs. Roly followed me and resumed his place on the floor in the corner of the bedroom where he'd spent the previous night. Emily lay on the bottom of the bed.

I must have been really exhausted because I'd been asleep for nearly nine hours when Linda woke me by drawing back the curtains and letting the sun shine into the tiny bedroom. 'Wake up, time for work.'

I struggled to a sitting position and rubbed my eyes. As if to make sure I didn't go back to sleep, Roly leapt on top of the bed and started licking my face.

'What time is it?' I croaked, pushing him away.

'Nine o'clock.' Her hair was back in a ponytail and she wore the faded denims and trainers that I'd seen her in on that first day, but this time with an Yves St Laurent designer T-shirt.

'Nelson Market,' she said, catching my gaze.

Suddenly, all the horrors of the previous day filled my mind as I realised why I was there in Linda's house. 'Has anyone been round, the police . . . ?'

'No, why should they? They won't connect you with here, Johnny. Breakfast'll be ready in ten minutes, then we must get on with the telephoning.'

'Yes, Miss.'

She threw a pillow at me. 'Are you saying I sound like a schoolteacher?'

'No, Miss,' and I ducked as a second one came hurtling across.

I had a quick shower but didn't shave. Apart from the fact that I hadn't brought my electric razor with me, I thought a beard or moustache might go some of the way to concealing my identity. I also had no change of clothes to put on, so it was back with yesterday's shirt and jeans.

Linda had cooked bacon and eggs with soldiers and had started hers by the time I got downstairs.

I poured us each a cup of tea from the brown earthenware pot, doubtless another treasure from Nelson Market, and picked up the morning paper which was lying on the kitchen table.

'You're on the bottom of page one,' Linda informed me. 'Saddam Hussein beat you to the main story.'

I put it down again. I didn't feel like reading it now. It was bad enough to know that the whole country's police force plus a bunch of Colombian gangsters were after me, without having it confirmed in print.

I finished the meal and made my way into the lounge. 'In other circumstances, I'd have enjoyed that,' I said. 'But now I start work as your investigator.'

I wasn't sure what I'd find when I rang the nine numbers I'd written down. I suppose I hoped that one of the people I spoke to could give me information about Michelle Lunt's life or some clue as to who Wilbur Lunt really was, and where I could start looking for him.

The first number I dialled from the list was an 0161 – Manchester. It rang out a couple of times before a man answered. 'Yeah?'

'Is that . . .' I repeated the number.

'Who do ya want?' West Indian, I thought, but probably Manchester born, judging by the flat vowels.

'Who am I speaking to?'

A silence, then, 'Who do you want to speak to?'

'Mr Lunt asked me to ring, from Liverpool.'

'Hang on.' Muffled voices in the background then the phone was passed to someone else.

'Yo' got some stuff for us, man?' A deeper voice, same accent.

'How much do you want?'

'The five hundred grand's worth he promised.'

'Give me the address, I'll make sure you get it.'

More silence. 'Same as before,' he said, at last. 'Better hurry, man, or we'll go elsewhere.' And he broke the connection.

'Sounds like the Manchester one is a dealer,' I told Linda who was coming in from the kitchen, an apron round her waist. 'He's waiting for a consignment from our Wilbur.'

'So Wilbur is involved in the drugs set-up.'

'Seems like it. I wonder who he was acting for?'

'Try the next number.'

I dialled the Dover number. 'Good morning, Highland Shipping, how may I help you?' said a robotic voice. Why do receptionists sound like daleks nowadays?

'Could I speak with someone who deals with Wilbur or Michelle Lunt's orders?'

'Just a moment. Where are you based?'

'Liverpool.'

'Just a moment,' again. 'I'll put you through.'

'Northern. How may I help you?'

'Do you deal with consignments for Mr and Mrs Lunt in Liverpool?'

'What company?'

I hesitated. I'd no answer to that. 'I'm sorry, I don't have a company name.'

'Lunt, you say? Just a minute.' She returned after three minutes during which time I'd heard the same excerpt from *Greensleeves* five times. 'We have a record of just one delivery to that name in Liverpool, to a Livingstone Drive?'

'That's it.'

'Yes, just one item, from Eastern Europe. We delivered on July thirteenth. Are you expecting any others?'

'No, just checking, that's all. What have you got listed for contents?'

'Books.'

'Oh.' I was surprised. I thanked her and moved on to the next number, which was in Anglesey, but there was no reply. 'Must be a private number,' I muttered to Linda who had now set up an ironing board in the middle of the room and was working her way through a pile of washing. 'Nobody in during office hours.'

'Who?'

'The Anglesey one. The Dover one was a shipping company who'd delivered a box of books to your sister.'

'Funny. I never found any in the flat.'

'That's what I thought. I wonder what the box really contained?'

'Try Llandudno.'

'Could be another private home line,' I said. 'Why don't you speak and pretend you're your sister. Say you're returning their call and remember to speak posh.'

I dialled 01492 and the number. A cultured voice answered almost immediately, a lady. I thrust the phone into Linda's hands.

'Hello, this is Michelle Lunt. You rang me, I believe.' She did it perfectly, no trace of East Lancashire in her voice but it obviously didn't fool the person at the other end. Linda put her hand over the receiver and looked at me in panic. 'She knows it's not Shelley,' she hissed. 'She asked who I was.'

'Say you're her sister and find out who she is.'

'Hello. I'm sorry. I meant I was ringing *for* Shelley. This is her sister, Linda.'

I went into the kitchen to get a drink of water. There was no garden behind the terraced house, just a small yard but Linda had filled it with tubs of flowers and there was a small cast-iron patio set in the corner, a table and two chairs, against a wall covered with sweet peas on a frame.

Emily was sunning herself on the patio table.

I went back in the lounge as Linda was finishing her call.

'I don't know why you're paying me a fee for this,' I said. 'You're doing all the work.'

'Nonsense, listen.' She sounded quite eager. 'That woman was called Ruth Simpkin and she was a friend of Shelley's. Apparently, they used to work together at one time for this PR company and they stayed in touch. She rang Shelley the day before she died but there was no reply. It's a pity she didn't have an ansaphone, though I suppose if she had, the police would have taken it away for evidence.'

Or destroyed the tape. I thought. 'Was she shocked to hear Shelley was dead?'

'Horrified. She'd no idea. Shelley was supposed to be going to see her later that week.'

'Oh?'

'She'd posted a small package that she wanted Ruth to hold on to for safekeeping. Perhaps it was these books.'

Suddenly I was excited. Could this be the first break? 'Has she still got it?'

'Yes. I said we'd go over and pick it up later today. Was that all right?'

I put my arms round her and hugged her. 'You're wonderful. Let's try some more numbers. There's the five London ones left.'

'I'll be getting on with my ironing.'

I started to dial the first number but stopped halfway through because I recognised it. It was the number Wilbur Lunt had given me for Citibank, the one on the headed notepaper for the branch that didn't exist.

Leary had told me he'd left a message on an ansaphone at that number but somebody must have been on the other end on this occasion. Ansaphones don't make calls. I finished dialling, waited, and this time I got a ringing tone. It rang out just four times, then: *'This is Citibank. Currently all our operators are engaged. Please try again later or leave a message after the tone.'*

I replaced the handset before the bleep and checked the date the call from that number was received. There were two calls, one on the day Michelle died and the other two days before.

So the Citibank connection was in operation then but, when I tried it six days later, it was unobtainable. Now it was back again. I wondered what the significance was of that. Was Wilbur Lunt using his Citibank alibi somewhere else?

The next two numbers I tried turned out to be travel agents. 'Sorry, wrong number,' I said on both occasions. There might come a time when I would need to examine Wilbur Lunt's journey plans, but it could wait for the moment.

'How are you getting on?' said Linda, draping a newly pressed skirt over the back of a chair.

'One was the Citibank number that Citibank denied knowledge of.'

'And was it them?'

'The ansaphone said it was, but I think it was lying.'

'What about the others?'

'Travel agents. I've left them alone for the time being because I wanted to get on with the last two.'

The next number I dialled had appeared six times on the call display screen. Whoever they were, they'd phoned the Lunts every day over the six-day period, always about the same time, late morning. It could have been someone reporting in.

As it turned out, that wasn't a bad guess except it was the other way round. 'Room 401,' was the reply when I dialled the number.

I thought I must have misheard. Room 401? Sounded like

a hotel room except the calls would normally go through Reception. 'I'm sorry, could you repeat that?'

'Room 401,' again. Could a company be called that? 'Who do you want to speak to?'

'I'm not sure. What exactly do you do? Are you a company?'

'Who is this calling, please?'

'Somebody from your office has rung me so I'm returning the call. They didn't leave a name but my name is Ace.'

'What is your telephone number?'

I gave her the Livingstone Drive number but pointed out I was speaking from a different location. 'I'm afraid I don't recognise your number,' I explained. 'What would the call be in connection with?'

There was a pause before she answered. Probably she was checking out the number that I'd given her. 'Could you confirm your address please.'

I gave her the Livingstone Drive address and postcode and there was another silence then, 'Are you living in this property, Mr Ace?'

'I own the property,' I told her.

'But you don't live there?'

'No, but . . .'

'We have another name listed for that number.'

'Probably Mr and Mrs Lunt.'

She now sounded confused. 'Er, no.'

'Or Michelle Roberts,' I said quickly.

'Just a moment, please.' She put me on hold and, after a few moments, a man's voice came on the line. 'Mr Ace? My name is Swallow.' He sounded older, perhaps late fifties, and he had a commanding manner that suggested he wouldn't stand for any nonsense. 'Would you be so kind as to acquaint me with the nature of your relationship with Michelle Roberts?'

'Certainly, Mr Swallow. I was her landlord. Perhaps you, in turn, might tell me the organisation you represent.'

'We are a government department. Ms Roberts worked for us.'

'You're the Drug Squad, you mean?'

'I'm sorry, Mr Ace, our work is of a confidential nature.'

'I only want to know one thing, Mr Swallow, and that is, does Wilbur Lunt work for you and where might I find him?'

'I'm afraid that name means nothing to me,'

'But he was living in my house at Livingstone Drive with Michelle Roberts. They were there as man and wife.'

There was a long pause. For a second, I thought he'd hung up but I'd obviously just caught him by surprise. 'If we should need to contact you, Mr Ace, shall you be at the number you are calling from?' And he repeated Linda's Nelson number.

I realised I should have used the mobile. How stupid! If there was any connection between his department and the police they could be on their way as we spoke.

'No.' I gave him my home and office numbers.

'Thank you. We shall possibly be in touch.'

'Shit a sodding brick!' I said to Linda.

'What's the matter?'

'That was the Drug Squad your Shelley worked for, and he's got this number. If they connect my name with the newspaper stories, they'll be able to trace the address, I'm sure of it.'

'What shall we do?'

The 'we' exploded in my ear like an Exocet missile. Suddenly I realised the danger I had plunged Linda into. What were the penalties for harbouring a wanted criminal – if the police got to me first? Or if the drugs people caught up with me here, they would surely show Linda no mercy. Her life was on the line, the same as mine.

'I need to go to Llandudno – fast,' I told her, wondering if she would be OK on her own here.

'No problem. The car's outside. Let me switch the iron off and give me two minutes to get a couple of things.' She ran upstairs.

'I think I should go alone,' I called out. 'It could be dangerous.'

'You'll need me with you to get petrol and things, in case you're recognised. Besides, I want to meet Shelley's friend. She may give me an idea of what sort of person she'd become.'

I couldn't argue with that; it was possibly for the best.

'Walk, Roly,' I shouted. He jumped up and bounced across the room excitedly.

'Don't build his hopes up.' Linda came down the stairs, struggling into a denim jacket. 'He won't be stretching his legs far on the back seat of the car. Ride, Roly.' He picked up his lead in his mouth and brought it over to me.

'Put him in the car,' instructed Linda, throwing me the keys. 'I'll bring a bowl and some water for him.' She was giving Emily a final stroke and locking the windows as she spoke.

The Fiesta was parked outside and we were on the M65 within five minutes after I'd put the phone down. Linda was at the wheel. I wore the glasses and flat cap that Geoffrey had given me.

'I've still got one more number to ring,' I said, taking out my notebook. I was sitting in the front passenger seat. The urgency of the occasion must have stimulated Linda because she was doing at least fifty, staring intently through the windscreen like a vet inspecting an animal for fleas.

'Use my mobile. It's in my jacket pocket.'

'On second thoughts, I think I'll wait till we get to a Services.' I didn't think I'd hear much over the roar of the little car's engine. Years of playing the drums haven't done a lot for my hearing.

By the time we'd reached the M6 without hearing a

police siren, I began to relax. 'I don't think they can be after us,' I said.

Linda kept her foot down. Her speed had crept up to fifty-five but we were still in the slow lane and being overtaken by everything in sight. 'Are we stopping for lunch?' she asked.

'It's only half-past eleven. Keep going another half-hour, eh?'

'OK. There's a Little Chef by Queensferry, why don't we go there?'

'We could do.' I feel that all these places like Little Chef and Hungry Hippo, or whatever they're called, have driven the old-fashioned, good value transport caffs into oblivion. On the other hand, girls like Linda probably wouldn't have eaten in transport caffs anyway.

We reached the Welsh border via the M6 and M56, without incident. When we crossed the M53, I thought of Hilary, a few miles up the road in Heswall. She'd be worried sick about me when she read the paper. I'd have to ring her.

It was half-past twelve when Linda pulled up in the Little Chef car park. I arched my back. 'These cars are too small for us six-footers,' I grumbled.

I borrowed her mobile phone and rang Geoffrey's mobile number. 'It's me,' I said unnecessarily. 'Can you talk?'

'Thank God it's you, boss.' I could hear the relief in his voice. 'We've had the busies in again all morning. They've only been gone half an hour. Wanted to know where you might be, went through all your papers and they've been round to all the houses.'

'This'll give the tenants something to gossip about,' I said. 'What about the radio station? Have you heard from them?'

'No, but I'd say you'll be lucky to still have a job. The papers are full of it.'

'Running away won't have helped, I don't suppose.'

'Helped?' squeaked Geoffrey. 'You're in pigswill up to your ears. I'd rather pleat sawdust than have to defend you.'

'Don't tell my barrister that.' Somehow, the handling stolen goods charge seemed to have paled into insignificance, but I knew the two were connected. The hard part was to prove it.

'Nobody else been in touch?'

'Yes, both your girlfriends.'

'Both?'

'Yes. Hilary *and* Maria. Maria rang last night after she'd heard about it on the radio. Hilary read it in the *Post* this morning. I told them you were safe and not to worry.'

I felt so pleased that Maria had bothered to ring. It meant she still thought something about me; it would be easier for me now to contact her. When, that is, I'd solved the case.

'You didn't tell them where I was?'

'Don't be silly. I take it you're still with er . . .'

'My client, yes.' I quickly changed the subject. 'Geoff, was Detective Sergeant Leary with the police when they came? A fellow with a face like the surface of a volcano.'

'That's the one. Pitted.'

'He's the one that's out to get me.'

'Seems to be doing his job well.'

'What did it say in the *Post*, Geoff?'

'It was all about Miss Barrie, but it mentioned how a girl had already committed suicide in one of your flats and that you'd found a dying man in the Gents at the Stirling at the weekend.'

'Implying they were all somehow down to me?'

'Something like that. Oh, and they said you were already waiting trial for handling stolen goods.'

'Nothing about seducing Meg Ryan?'

'What?'

'Never mind.'

'Listen, is there anything I can get you, boss?'

'Not at the moment, thanks. I've changed vehicles now. Your mother's Metro is outside Linda's, it's quite safe. If you need me, ring me on this number, it's Linda's mobile, but don't write the number down just in case. And ring me from your mobile, not from the office or at yours.'

My next call was to Alistair. Needless to say, he was apoplectic about my flight. 'Will they make this murder charge stick?'

'You tell me, you're the solicitor. She was dead when I walked in. I picked up the gun—'

'That was foolish.'

'You don't have to tell me. Seconds later, Leary walks in on cue.' I put on my Spike Milligan Eccles voice. '"I'm arresting you on a charge of beating this woman to death with a copy of a Steve Harley record".'

Alistair was old enough to remember *The Goon Show* but he didn't laugh. 'This isn't funny, Johnny, it's not a game. This could finish your career.'

'Which one?'

'All of them.'

'Don't worry, Alistair. I'm not running away to escape. I'm going to get to the bottom of this. I said I wanted to be an investigator – well, now's my chance, but you can get your friend Brendan to start preparing my defence, just in case.'

'Let's go and have something to eat,' said Linda, as I switched Alistair off. 'I'm starving. It's all the excitement.'

'Just one more,' I told her, taking out my notebook. 'I'll try that last London number.'

I keyed in the digits carefully and waited. After a couple of clicks, the number rang out twice before someone answered. I almost dropped the phone as I recognised the deep voice and the New York accent.

It said, 'Wilbur Lunt.'

Chapter Twenty-six

'Wilbur Lunt?' I repeated the name in astonishment. Linda's eyebrows shot up.

'Yes. Who is that?'

'Mr Lunt, this is Johnny Ace – your ex-landlord in Liverpool.'

A pause. 'I see. How did you get this number?'

'It was on the call display telephone in your flat.'

'That was pretty smart of you, Mr Ace. What is it you want with me?'

'I'd like to see you, face to face. I think we have a few things to discuss.'

'I don't think so.'

'The police could well be interested in this number, especially as they are not too convinced that your wife's death was suicide.' I don't know why I said that, other than I needed to think of something to frighten him, to give him a reason to see me. 'Not that Michelle Roberts was your wife, of course. Then there's the matter of the packages from the Highland Shipping Company.'

'All right, Mr Ace, you've convinced me. Where do you want to meet? I would have thought the options were limited in your case.' So he'd read the papers.

'I think it would be in both our interests if we were quite alone. You're in London, so shall we say outside H&M's at Oxford Circus, tomorrow at noon?' An area which would be difficult for the police to cordon if he tipped them off, and crowded enough to offer me a means of escape if necessary.

'I shall be there.' The line went dead.

'Phew.' I was sweating. I turned to Linda. 'You heard all that?'

'Meeting him could be dangerous, Johnny. If you really think he killed Shelley . . .'

'He'd hardly try anything in the middle of Oxford Street.' But then I remembered the case of Markov and the poisoned umbrella that was in all the papers a few years ago.

'But he might put the police on to you.'

'I'm relying on his curiosity. He'll want to know what I've got on him. Besides, he's got nothing to lose. He knows I couldn't be in league with the law to trap him, not in my position.'

We went into the Little Chef for lunch, being careful to leave the car windows open for Roly. There's hardly anywhere you can take a dog in with you these days. Even most pubs ban them. I can remember when an old man could sit in his local in the snug with a half of mild, a spittoon within hacking distance and a spaniel at his feet. Not any more. I blame Europe. All these new regulations.

The Little Chef was half-full but nobody gave me a second glance, even though I noticed my picture on the front of the *Daily Express* in the newspaper rack. I wondered how long my beard would take to grow.

'Are we going straight to London or stopping in Llandudno tonight?' asked Linda, as we ploughed our way through the Chicken Kiev.

I'd thought about catching a train to London and leaving Linda to drive home, but it made sense to stay away from public transport.

'Probably we'd be better driving down this evening to avoid the traffic. I know a little hotel we can stay at where we can park the car.'

'I've not brought anything to wear.'

'Neither have I. We seem to make a habit of this, don't we? Still, it's a good excuse to add to our wardrobes.'

'Will they sell Everton T-shirts in Llandudno?'

'I should hope so.'

'Remind me to ring Nicola to feed Emily.'

We finished the meal and walked back to the Fiesta. I'd brought some chicken out for Roly. I wasn't sure whether he'd like the garlic but he wolfed it down without stopping to taste it before polishing off a bowl of water.

'I'll take him for a walk round the block,' said Linda, putting his lead on. 'He'll be bursting.'

We eventually reached Llandudno. Being August, the resort was crowded. Linda drove along the Promenade, past the superbly maintained sweeping terrace of Victorian hotels, right up to the pier, then turned left, back into the town centre. 'Do you know where this road is we're looking for?'

'No. Stop and we'll ask someone.' Sod's Law says that the person you ask for directions is inevitably a stranger to the district who probably doesn't even speak English. It took us four failed attempts before the fifth person, an old lady in a fur coat and hat in the summer heat, pointed out that we should, in fact, be in Rhos on Sea, a few miles down the road.

Rhos on Sea reminded me of England in the 1950s, a sort of Enid Blyton never-never land of bow-windowed, red-bricked suburban semis with neat privet hedges and wooden garden gates.

Ruth Simpkin lived in one of them. She was in her early fifties, a smartly dressed woman with a friendly manner. She wore a light grey Jaeger suit with a white blouse and sensible grey shoes, and her hair was short and gently waved. Ruth was the sort of woman one would find in a coach party touring 'Morse's Oxford'.

She sat us on pink Queen Anne chairs in her front room and offered us a cup of tea, which we both declined. 'A

sherry, maybe?' We settled for that and she served us from
an ornate inlaid drinks cabinet.

'Would your dog like a drink?' Roly was sitting
decorously at my feet, his breath smelling heavily of
garlic.

'That's kind of you,' smiled Linda.

'So long as he doesn't attack Penny and Tuppence, my
Yorkshire Terriers. They're shut in the kitchen.' She needn't
have worried. Roly treated them with total contempt and
drank thirstily from a silver water bowl, completely ignoring
the smaller dogs.

Mrs Simpkin returned to the lounge and pulled up a
matching chair. 'So you are Michelle's little sister. She
once mentioned she had a sister, although she rarely spoke
about her family.'

Linda looked sad. 'We've talked on the phone over the
years, but I haven't seen her since I was sixteen.'

'You must have been devastated when you heard she'd
died, especially in that way?'

A tear formed in Linda's eye and she didn't reply.

'When did you work with her?' I asked.

'About three years ago. We were both with this public
relations outfit in Knightsbridge, very upper crust. I was on
the admin side but Michelle, being young and attractive and
very outgoing, did mostly promotion work. She was very
good at it, too.'

'Did you know any of her friends?'

'She didn't really mix too much with the other girls.
Most of them were rather empty-headed – bimbos rather
than brainboxes. Michelle was very bright. Wasted in the
work, really.'

'Where did she go to when she left?' asked Linda.

'Another PR firm. I'd already left by then. I got married,
as a matter of fact, and my husband was in business in
Llandudno so I moved up here.'

'Did Michelle have any boyfriends?'

'Nobody special. That is, of course, until she met
Wilbur.'

'You've heard of Wilbur?' I exclaimed.

'Of course. He was the love of her life.'

'Did you meet him?'

'No. By then I was already living up here in Wales but
she wrote and told me all about him. She was a great
letter-writer, was Michelle, and very efficient.'

I knew that already. Only somebody very organised
would have written and despatched all those contingency
letters to the solicitor in Liverpool. 'You said you had a
package.' I was anxious to get down to business.

Ruth Simpkin looked hard at my unshaven appearance before turning enquiringly to Linda, as if seeking
approval.

'I'm sorry, I should have introduced you. Johnny knew
Shelley in Liverpool. He's been helping me with the funeral
and everything.'

I nodded approvingly at Linda's tact. She'd been careful
not to put the woman on her guard by mentioning investigations, nor had she given my full name just in case Ruth
Simpkin recognised it from the newspapers.

'Michelle and Wilbur were living in my flat as Mr and
Mrs Lunt,' I said, 'although we've since found out that
they weren't actually married.'

'I shouldn't think they would be,' said Mrs Simpkin
surprisingly, 'in view of the fact that Wilbur Lunt already
had a wife.'

'*Wife?*' echoed Linda and I in unison.

'In America. Of course, he'd promised Michelle he
was going to leave her and maybe he would have done
so, one day – but he definitely had a wife and three
children back in Philadelphia so he couldn't have married
Michelle.'

'She told you this?'

'Yes.'

'When?'

'Oh, ages ago. She wrote to me from America, just after he'd met Wilbur – it must have been coming up to the Christmas before last. She was mad about him.'

'How very odd,' I murmured.

'Why is it odd?'

'Because Wilbur Lunt told me he'd met Michelle in London last August when she was working in PR. She'd gone over to Connecticut to meet his family and they'd got married. They lived in Manhattan for a time until his job brought him back to Britain this year. He was supposed to be with Citibank.'

Ruth Simpkin frowned. 'That's nonsense. Michelle met him in New York. She'd been over there for a couple of years and she knew quite well that he had a family, but she was hoping to marry him when his divorce came through.'

'You knew she was back in England – didn't you see her at all?'

'I knew she was back because we got one of those cards giving her new address – just *her* name on it, mind you, not Wilbur's, and no phone number. I wrote to her but didn't receive a reply. That was in June. The next I heard was when I received this letter three weeks ago, warning me that a Special Delivery package addressed to her was on its way and that she'd be coming up to collect it. I thought it was very strange. This time there was a phone number so I rang her back but there was no answer.'

'What day was that, when you rang her?' I wished I had made a note of the times and dates on the call display screen.

'Let me see, it was on a Thursday which would make . . .' she ticked the dates off on her fingers '. . . July the sixteenth.'

'The day she died. Which means she must have posted the package before that. Please may we see it?'

Ruth Simpkin rose to her feet and walked over to a mahogany Davenport, from which she took out a bulky Jiffy bag. 'Here you are. It is unopened. Would you like some scissors?'

The label was addressed to Michelle Lunt and the envelope was sealed with green packing tape.

'Yes, please.'

Linda looked worried as I slit open the top of the bubble wrap envelope, as if she was frightened about what was inside. I was hoping it might contain letters or documents revealing more about Michelle's life. Ruth Simpkin looked on in mere curiosity.

None of us expected a plastic bag containing what had to be half a million pounds' worth of pure heroin.

'Oh my God,' cried Linda.

'Is that what I think it is?' asked Ruth Simpkin, going pale.

'Heroin,' I said. I didn't know if there was really half a million pounds' worth, but I was sure the street value wouldn't have been far off this sum, once it had been doctored. 'Whatever was she doing with this?'

'And why send it to *me*?' Our hostess looked quite indignant. 'I hope you don't think I'm implicated in some form of addiction.'

'I'm sure you're not, or you wouldn't have shown it to us,' I reassured her. 'The fact is, Michelle wasn't working for a public relations firm any more. She was with some government department and assigned to the Drug Squad as some sort of undercover agent.'

Mrs Simpkin accepted the news with remarkable equanimity. 'Really? Well, it doesn't surprise me. She used to say she'd always wanted to be a barrister and, as that hadn't happened, she sometimes wished she'd joined the police instead. I think she found PR work rather trivial.'

'Did she ever tell you who Wilbur worked for?'

'No, I don't believe she ever mentioned it. Why? Was he with the Drug Squad too?'

'We don't know. Either that or he was involved in some nefarious activity and Michelle was tracking him.'

'I don't believe that. After all, she wrote to me saying she was crazy about him. Why would she do that?'

I couldn't think of a reason.

'How would she get hold of this stuff in the first place?' asked Linda, looking at the parcel in front of us.

'Possibly the result of some drugs haul. I don't know, I can only speculate, but it looks dodgy to me. Why hasn't it gone straight to her superiors, whoever they were?'

'You don't think Shelley was involved in drug smuggling, do you?'

'Don't jump to conclusions,' I said guardedly. I didn't want to shatter any illusions she had about her sister but the prognosis was not looking good. I knew one thing. If Michelle *had* been double-crossing her employers and they had found out, her 'suicide' looked even more suspicious.

'What are you going to do with it?' asked Mrs Simpkin.

'I'm not sure yet, but I'll take it away with me if that's all right with you?'

The woman looked relieved. 'It certainly is. I don't want it in my house a moment longer than necessary.' She shuddered. 'To think it's been here all this time. Imagine if the police had raided us.'

I knew all about visits from the police but I thought it unlikely that Mrs Simpkin would suffer one. On the other hand, I'd hardly expected a dawn raid myself.

We stayed a few more minutes. Linda asked Mrs Simpkin about her sister and they exchanged reminiscences together whilst I tried to figure out some connection between the heroin, the cameras and Serina Barrie's murder, but I was in the dark.

'Time to go,' I said, at last. I promised to let Mrs
Simpkin know the outcome of the investigation and we
took our leave.

I put the bag of heroin, fastened safely back inside the
envelope, under the front passenger seat of the Fiesta. Roly
resumed his place on the back seat as Linda and I climbed
into the front for our long journey to London.

Before we set off, I rang the hotel, The Four Stars in
Sussex Gardens near Paddington Station, and it was as
well that I did as they only had two single rooms left. I
said we wouldn't arrive till midnight.

'Will it take that long?' asked Linda.

'We'll want to stop for something to eat on the way and
there's the toiletries and clothes to buy.'

'Let's hope they keep the rooms for us.'

'They will. I gave your name, though. I daren't use
mine.'

We drove back into Llandudno and I stayed in the car
while Linda went off to the shops. I couldn't risk being
recognised in the streets.

While she was away I rang Geoffrey and Jim Burroughs
from Linda's mobile, but there was little news. Geoff had
recovered the RAV4, which was now parked in its rightful
place at Waterloo Dock. Jim had been able to find out
nothing new but seemed seriously concerned at my refusal
to hand myself over to the police.

'It'll go against you at your trial,' he warned.

I told him a trial wasn't on my list of options.

I also rang Hilary but got her ansaphone. I left a message
saying I was fine and would be in touch as soon as I'd got
the matter sorted. I knew I didn't need to tell Hilary I was
innocent.

I didn't feel it was the time to ring Maria, although I
would have welcomed her insight into the case. Linda's
perspective was coloured by her personal involvement.

Linda returned with new underwear for both of us, tights

socks, a couple of T-shirts and two sponge bags full of grooming paraphernalia.

'I bought a couple of Melton Mowbrays from Marks' to eat on the way,' she said, 'in case we get peckish.' She also produced a couple of cartons of freshly squeezed orange juice. 'Do you want to drive, only I'm not used to London traffic?'

I picked up the A5 at Betws-y-Coed and stayed on it until the M54 at Telford, then joined the M6 and M40. We stopped at the Cherwell Valley services for something to eat and arrived in Central London six hours later. I parked the Fiesta on the service road right outside the front of our hotel.

'What are you doing with the . . . parcel?' Linda couldn't bring herself to say heroin.

'I'll leave it in the car.'

'What if it's stolen?'

'Then some thief will have a lucky day. Come on, Roly.' He leapt out of the car and I put his lead on. He'd enjoyed another meal of leftover chicken on the motorway. I could see him turning his nose up at tins of dog meat in the future.

'You look dead beat,' Linda said sympathetically.

I groaned. 'I feel ten times worse. I could sleep for a week.'

We checked in. The porter didn't seem too happy about our canine companion, but a five-pound note allayed his disquiet and within five minutes we were sitting companionably on the single bed in Linda's room, supping a last cup of tea, made with the kettle and tea bags supplied, with Roly on the floor beside us.

'What's going to happen tomorrow?' she asked.

'You can take Roly for a walk in Hyde Park. I'm going to meet Wilbur Lunt. I'll see you back at the hotel, all being well, at one o'clock.'

'Can't I come with you?'

'Better you don't. Who knows what might happen?'
Her sister was already dead. 'Remember, you're the client
you're paying me for this.'

'I suppose so.' She hesitated. 'You know, Johnny, it'
an awful thing to say but sometimes I wish I'd neve
learnt of Shelley's death. After all, I never saw her, ou
lives were totally separate yet she's turned *my* life upsid
down.' She sighed. 'Roll on September, when I'll be bac
in the classroom with my kids.'

'Your monsters, you mean.'

She smiled. 'My monsters, yes. This is like a bad dream
isn't it?'

'Yup – it's a nightmare all right.' It was only four day
ago that the police had burst in on Hilary and me in m
flat. Since then there had been two murders, and now
was on the run from the police. I racked my tired brai
again. What possible connection could there be betwee
stolen cameras, Wilbur Lunt and a bag of heroin?

Perhaps, very soon, I was going to find out.

Chapter Twenty-seven

I didn't wake until nine o'clock, but the eight hours' sleep had done wonders for me. I felt refreshed and ready to face whatever the day might throw at me. Judging by recent events, that could be a lot.

I knocked on Linda's door to wake her and while she got dressed, I took Roly round the block. I bought a paper from a shop in Edgware Road that sold mainly Arabic publications. Happily, the Serina Barrie murder had been relegated to a small paragraph on the inside pages.

Apart from a young couple with rucksacks and French accents, we were the only people in the dining room for breakfast. Obviously the other guests were early risers. An Irish lady brought out a fried breakfast for Linda and cereal and brown toast for me.

I wore the new Umbro T-shirt Linda had got for me in Llandudno, with my jeans and trainers. Outside it was already quite warm and the sun was shining brightly.

I checked with Geoffrey but there had been no new developments, except that Maria had rung again. I was glad about this. I didn't know how much to read into it, but I felt better knowing she had been in touch.

Linda was reluctant to let me go alone to meet Wilbur Lunt, but I explained I'd learn more on my own. I didn't know what to expect when I came face to face with him, except that I would need to be on my guard. If he was a criminal who felt I was in his way, he could have his own men there ready to take care of me. If he was

connected with the law, he could have the police waiting.

I had a strategy worked out, but whether he'd go along
with it I wasn't sure.

I left the hotel at ten-fifteen and took a number 15 bus
from Edgware Road towards Oxford Circus. I didn't get
off until the first stop in Regent Street, which allowed me
time to search the pavement for Wilbur Lunt as the bus
stopped at the traffic lights close to H&M's.

There was no sign of him.

I walked back from the bus stop, crossed over into Oxford
Street and stood in a doorway, where I had a good view
across the road. Every step I took, I half-expected someone
to walk out in front of me and claim a million-pound reward
from the *Sun*.

At one minute to eleven I saw Wilbur Lunt walking
from the direction of Selfridges towards our appointed
meeting place. He seemed to be alone but I wasn't taking
any chances. I hailed a cab and asked the driver to hang
on while I collected my passenger. I then darted through
the traffic across the road to Wilbur.

'Mr Ace. On time, too.' He looked fitter than when I'd
last seen him. He was wearing a smart navy suit with a deep
blue shirt. His tie boasted a repeated pattern in matching
blues, of wolves howling at the moon. He looked every
inch a merchant banker. In my jeans and T-shirt I felt
scruffy and at a disadvantage.

'Follow me,' I said. 'It's all right, I'm not going to kidnap
you,' I added as he looked wary. 'I have a taxi waiting.'

I took his arm but he pulled away. 'Where are you
taking me?'

'Somewhere quiet but public. Just to make sure we're
quite alone.' If he had somebody trailing us on foot, this
would be when he'd object.

But: 'Suits me,' he shrugged. 'I hope this won't take
long, by the way. I have an appointment at twelve and

they are expecting me.' The inference being that if he didn't make the meeting, someone would come looking for him. Perhaps he was carrying a tracking device but I couldn't see myself searching him.

I said no more but ushered Wilbur into the taxi. 'St James's Park,' I told the driver.

'How did the inquest go?' Lunt asked as we drove past Hamleys towards Piccadilly Circus.

'Suicide. They read out your letter.'

'Good.'

'You were described as Michelle's partner but it transpires you're already married with a family, I believe?'

'That's correct. Does that offend you in some way?'

'As a landlord, you mean?'

'No, not necessarily as a landlord. Just generally.'

Who was I to moralise, with my track record? Indeed, who better than I to sympathise with his dilemma.

'Not at all. I was merely curious as to whether a wedding was ever on your agenda?'

He answered coldly. 'Michelle and I were to be married in September when my divorce came through. Contrary to what you may believe, we were very much in love. My marriage had been over for some time – in fact, I haven't seen my wife and family for several months.' His voice broke slightly. 'She's living with somebody else now; I don't want to go into details.'

It confirmed everything that Ruth Simpkin had told us, yet I still had my doubts, not least of which was why, if they were so ecstatic together, did Michelle Roberts kill herself?

'Forgive me for being sceptical,' I said, 'but all I have ever heard from you has been a load of lies, both when you took the flat and after Michelle died.'

He sighed. 'Regrettably, the cover story I gave you when I took the flat was necessary to protect our safety. We were both involved in dangerous investigation work. The roles of the rich merchant banker with his trophy wife suited our purposes admirably.'

'You mean your prospective landlord might not have wanted spies or undercover police in his property?'

'That too,' he conceded with a smile.

The taxi proceeded slowly through the congestion at Piccadilly Circus in the direction of Trafalgar Square.

'But why carry on with the lies after she died?'

'To safeguard sabotaging the operation. I couldn't do anything to save Michelle, so the obvious thing to do was to slip quietly away.'

'You went back to the States when Michelle died, but now you're here in London again. Is this permanent?'

'Nothing is ever permanent in my job.'

'So you're still on the case, as it were?' Silence. I continued, 'Are you living alone now?'

'Yes. I have a studio apartment in Kensington.' He looked me in the eye. 'You should know that Michelle and I were very close. We found ourselves in a unique position, able to be together in the same foreign country because of our jobs. Of course, I was attracted to her when I first met her.'

'Was that in England or New York?'

'New York. I was on a business trip from Philadelphia. Michelle was already working there.' He looked almost sheepish. 'Yes, I know that isn't what I told you before, but we had to stick to the same story for everyone.'

'You can drop us here,' I told the taxi driver as we came up to the Duke of York's column. We alighted from the vehicle and started walking in the direction of the lake.

'Were you and Michelle involved in the same undercover work then,' I asked, 'because you certainly weren't working for Citibank. I checked with them.'

'Oddly enough, I *was* employed by Citibank – indirectly,' declared Lunt, 'although only the people at the highest echelon of the bank would know it.'

'I don't understand.'

'I work for an American investigation company specialising in financial fraud which includes, among other things, counterfeiting. Last year, the banks became aware of a new organisation, probably based in one of the emerging East European countries, that was printing and passing forged banknotes in various currencies, including dollars. My company was called in by the heads of a group of these banks to bring the perpetrators to justice.'

'So you're nothing to do with drugs?'

'I'm afraid not. That was Michelle's side of things, but by a lucky coincidence, both our cases involved the city of Liverpool.'

'Why did you choose that particular flat to live in – my flat?'

'I could have lived anywhere, but Michelle was given information from her superiors that one of the tenants in that building was a key member of the outfit she was targeting, so it was crucial for her to be on the spot.'

'These were heroin dealers?'

'Amongst other substances.'

'And the tenant in question would be Nathan Lloyd, I presume?'

'The very same. He lived on the top floor.'

'And you made sure there was a vacancy in the house by persuading the existing tenant to leave?'

'Mr Voke was very satisfied with his settlement.' Lunt paused. 'Now answer *me* a question, Mr Ace. Why do you say Michelle's death may not have been suicide?'

'To make you curious enough to meet me,' I confessed. 'Nothing more. I've no evidence that suggests it was anything other than suicide, except her sister is convinced she wasn't the type to kill herself.'

'She had a sister?'

'Yes, and it's her sister who has hired me to find out the truth behind Michelle's death. You see, I too am an investigator, albeit a one-man band. A private eye, if you like.'

'I thought you were a DJ as well as being a landlord. You had a radio show.'

'That's a hobby and my houses are merely an investment.'

'How versatile.' He laughed heartily. 'So we're all gumshoes now. Well, well, well.'

I returned to my questions. 'Why did you tell me all that rubbish about meeting Michelle's mother?'

'I didn't want to risk jeopardising my own operation by sticking around for the police to ask me too many questions. It was too late to do anything for Michelle. In fact, although I knew she came from Colne, I thought all of Michelle's family were dead. I just made up the story about her mother so that you'd feel you'd have somebody to deal with, and I could make a discreet exit.'

'I see.'

'Look, Mr Ace, contrary to what you may think, I was very fond of Michelle and her death came as a terrible shock to me.' He ran his fingers through his thick grey hair. 'That last morning when I left the flat . . .'

'On your way to Vienna?'

'That's right. Well, she was laughing and happy. We'd been out the night before for a meal and had had a particularly good time.'

'Yet twenty-four hours later, she had killed herself?'

'Don't ask me why. It may sound silly to you, but I almost wish she had been murdered. As it is, I'm tormented by the thought that in some way I might have done something that pushed her into it, but I've searched my conscience time and again, and I don't know what it could be.'

It was a convincing performance. Even I, cynical as I am, was moved by it. Yet there was nothing I could say to reassure him, other than to tell him that the note she'd left had said nothing specific, only that she couldn't carry on any longer.

He was looking for answers that would assuage his guilt but they weren't answers I could give.

'You don't think her death could be somehow connected with her investigations?' I asked.

'I don't know, but it's possible, I guess. You see, that morning she had a meeting arranged with a colleague of Lloyd's, to buy some drugs from him. It was to be a sort of trial run to give her credibility.'

'And did the meeting take place?'

'I don't know. All I do know is that by the afternoon, she was dead. Any connection between the two events would only make sense if she'd been murdered – and Michelle committed suicide. I just can't understand it.'

I thought about what Jim Burroughs had said, that he had a theory about Michelle's death. I needed to ask him what that theory was.

'One other strange thing,' remarked Wilbur. 'No drugs were ever found in the flat.' He looked hard at me as he said this, and I thought of the package in the Fiesta.

For some unknown reason – instinct, probably – I decided not to mention the matter to Wilbur Lunt. 'Should they have been?'

'Not really, except that if she did go ahead with the meeting, what did she do with the drugs she bought?'

'Probably she never went, for whatever reason.'

'I guess not.'

There was something here, I thought, that didn't ring true. Michelle had died on a Thursday; that package of heroin had been posted to Ruth Simpkin on the *Tuesday* – two days before this supposed meeting. Did this mean there was *another* package? And if so, where was it? And where had the first one come from?

I moved on to another tack. 'One of the tenants upstairs said he hadn't seen your car all week. Why was that?'

Lunt smiled. 'Let me guess. Mountbatten?'

'It was, as a matter of fact.'

'I thought so. He liked to keep an eye on me. My Mercedes was in for repair, and as I knew I was going to be out of the country later in the week, I didn't bother with a replacement car and took taxis instead. Obviously, Mountbatten concentrated his vigil on my car rather than me.'

'What was that telephone number you gave me that was supposed to be Citibank?'

'My office number in London. Mostly just an ansaphone to take messages.'

'And an address to enable you to write your own references?' He looked sheepish and didn't answer. 'I thought as much,' I said.

We reached the lake and stood watching a young couple feeding the ducks. I'd warmed somewhat to the American, now that I'd heard his explanations. Possibly it was because I identified with his relationship problems or perhaps because we were both in the same profession.

It didn't get me any nearer to finding out why Michelle had died.

'Tell me about your own trouble,' said Wilbur Lunt. 'From what I've read, it looks pretty serious to me.'

'It is. Basically I've been framed for theft and murder and I don't know why.'

'Are these charges connected with Michelle?'

'I honestly don't know. At one time I thought so but now I'm not sure. The only common link is this Nathan Lloyd. I threw him out of the flat when I found heroin in his room.'

I told him about the cameras and the murders.

'Have you upset anyone in the police?'

'Not that I know of, except . . . the officer who arrested me was the same one who dealt with Michelle's suicide.'

'I spoke to him on the phone. What was his name? Creary? Geary?'

'Leary. What did he say to you?'

'Very little. He seemed anxious to get the case cleared up as quickly as possible, which suited me as I didn't want my department involved.'

'Are you still chasing the forgers?'

'Of course, or rather, the people passing the notes. They'll lead us back to the printing works. That parcel you mentioned . . .' I'd forgotten about the parcel '. . . from Highland Shipping, contained a batch of forged English ten-pound notes sent to me for inspection.'

'Right.'

'The batch was of particular interest to me because I'd been given a fake note just like the ones it contained just a week before.'

'Really?'

'Yes. In your house, as a matter of fact.'

'Livingstone Drive?'

'That's right. By your friend, Mr Mountbatten.'

'*Badger?*' I was completely gobsmacked.

'I thought his name was Neville,' Lunt commented.

'Before he acquired the dreadlocks, he had silver streaks put in his hair for a bet so everyone called him Badger and the name stuck. But you can't think *he's* involved.' I looked at the American and shook my head. 'He's lived in that flat for years.'

'What does he do for a living?'

'As far as I know, he's still at university. He's doing a PhD on some obscure English poet called Matthew Prior.'

'For a student, he seems to have a very extravagant lifestyle. He drives an S-reg Porsche and wears Armani suits. Where do you think his money comes from?'

'I believe he has an independent income,' I said lamely. All sorts of rumours abounded regarding Badger's wealth. He seemed to be on speaking terms with a lot of high-ranking Liverpudlian underworld figures and could be relied on to obtain any unusual items on request, no questions asked.

Wilbur Lunt was not impressed. 'That covers a multitude of sins.'

'You seriously think he could be part of the gang?'

'Why not?'

'Anybody could pick up a dud note in change and pass it on. It doesn't mean anything.'

'Maybe. Maybe not.' He didn't sound convinced.

'How did he come to give it you?'

Wilbur Lunt smiled. 'He sold me some raffle tickets. I gave him a twenty and the ten-pound note was my change. Anyway, Mountbatten isn't my problem now; someone else can worry about him. I'm operating down here.'

'On the same case?'

'Yes, but the London part of the operation. These people have contacts in major cities all over Europe.'

'Including Manchester?'

He stopped walking for a moment. 'Why do you mention Manchester? Any specific reason?'

'You'd had a call from a Manchester number so I rang them back. They seemed to be expecting a consignment from you – five hundred grand's worth of stuff, so they said. I took it they were referring to drugs.'

He hesitated for a moment. 'No. Currency notes, that would be. Like I said, it was an undercover operation and it's still ongoing so I can't say any more. But to get back to your situation, had you ever met Leary before the night Michelle died?'

'No, never.'

'So, you think the chances are that something about Michelle's investigation is behind it all?'

'Yes – but I don't know what, exactly. All I do know, which you've just confirmed, is that Nathan Lloyd was the man she was watching and I evicted him from the flat.'

'He could be a dangerous enemy.'

I recalled Tommy McKale's warning and told Wilbur Lunt about the contract supposedly out on me.

'What you must realise, Johnny – may I call you that? – is that this is no tinpot local firm that Michelle was chasing. These people are part of an international organisation that is as well structured as any legitimate multi-national company. I'd take the warning seriously.'

'If that's the case, how does an ordinary copper like Leary get involved – if, of course, he is mixed up in this?'

'He's probably only a peripheral figure in the grand scheme of things, but of course, with his position, he has influence in that area. As to *how* he gets involved, that's easy – an eye closed here, a small backhander there, and before you know it, there's no turning back. It's a slippery slope, as the old saying goes. The wonder is, there's any straight policemen.'

'If there were,' I said bitterly, 'they'd be in museums.'

Wilbur looked at his watch. 'I must go, I shall be late for my appointment. I'm glad, after all, that we had our little talk. I hope you feel our meeting has been beneficial.'

I said it had and we turned and walked together down The Mall, back towards Trafalgar Square.

'I can't say my guilt at Michelle's death has lessened in any way,' he continued, 'but I am glad to have set the record straight with yourself.'

'She knew you were married when she met you, if that's what you mean,' I said. 'You didn't deceive her about that, so you can't blame yourself in any way.'

He sighed. 'I suppose you're right, though it doesn't seem to make it any easier for me. You're not married, are you?'

I find it difficult to explain to people my own situation. It always comes out sounding as though I'm keeping a harem. 'No,' I said shortly. 'I'm not.'

We walked on until a vacant taxi came along. 'You don't mind if I take it, do you?' said Wilbur Lunt politely. 'Only

I can't afford to be late. You have my number if you need to get in touch again.' He opened the back door of the cab. 'Good luck, Johnny.'

'Thanks, Wilbur,' I replied and we shook hands. I felt a certain empathy talking to him; he was quite a likeable person and yet, something rankled about his role in the affair.

I watched his taxi disappear into the mass of vehicles swarming round Nelson's Column and hailed one for myself. 'Sussex Gardens, The Four Stars Hotel,' I told the driver.

Linda was sitting reading the *Evening Standard* in her room. Roly lay on the bed, fast asleep. He looked wet and very bedraggled.

'He's shattered,' she giggled. 'I let him off the lead in Hyde Park and he went berserk. There was a man with a briefcase sitting eating his lunch on a bench and Roly pinched all his sandwiches. The man was furious.'

'Did he eat them all?'

'Every one.'

'Good. It'll save money on Chappie.'

'And then he chased every bird in sight and ended up in a lake.'

'The Serpentine,' I murmured. Roly opened one eye, smiled, and went back to sleep. 'That explains the damp patches on the bed.'

'How did you get on?' she said. 'I've been worried about you.'

'Wilbur Lunt was very pleasant, and everything Ruth Simpkin told us about him turned out to be pretty much true.'

'He was married then?'

'Yes, but his divorce is coming through in a few weeks, just like Ruth said. I also discovered that Wilbur works for a law-enforcement agency in America, a different outfit from Michelle's and that their work wasn't the reason they were together. The fact that they were both detectives was a coincidence. He was after forged money, she was chasing drug dealers. Two people in one place on different assignments who lived together simply because they were lovers.'

It sounded so romantic. Romeo and Juliet. Abelard and Heloise. Wilbur and Michelle.

'What are you going to do now? The police will still be after you.'

'I don't know.'

I borrowed Linda's mobile and rang the office. There was no reply, only the ansaphone. I didn't leave a message. That was odd. Geoffrey should have been there. I rang his home.

'Oh, Mr Ace, I'm so glad you rang.' His mother was sobbing. 'Our Geoffrey's been taken to the police station. They came for him this morning. Said he's helping with their enquiries, whatever that means.'

I tried to calm her. 'Don't worry, Mrs Molloy. Obviously there's been some mistake. I'll sort it out.'

I rang Alistair who promised to find where Geoffrey was being held and go along to represent him. 'Don't worry,' he said, echoing my words. 'I'll get him out, they've nothing on him.' His voice suddenly became alarmed. 'Have they?'

'Of course not.' Aiding and abetting my escape and illegally releasing a clamped vehicle, did they come under 'perverting the course of justice'? I didn't know. I wasn't a lawyer.

'Johnny, where are you? You're not doing yourself any good running away like—'

I pressed the button to cut the call and took out my green notebook. 'I'm going to ring those travel agents again.'

'The ones on Shelley's phone?'

'Yes.' I wanted to confirm that Wilbur Lunt had been going to Vienna on the day Michelle died. I'd no reason to doubt it and I could see no significance in it if it was untrue, other than he'd told me another useless lie. But it was a loose end that I could tie up.

The first travel agent had no record of a Mr Lunt travelling on the date mentioned. It was possible, they said, that he'd made enquiries about flights and they'd rung him back with the times, but nothing had been booked.

I struck paydirt with the second agent. A Wilbur Lunt had booked and paid for a one-way flight on the evening of 16 July, the same night that Michelle Roberts was hanging from the ceiling in Livingstone Drive.

But the flight was not to Vienna. It was to Philadelphia.

Chapter Twenty-eight

'He was flying to Philadelphia?' Linda looked at me in astonishment. 'I don't understand.'

Neither did I, but I knew something wasn't right here. Wilbur Lunt declared he'd not seen his wife and family for months; his divorce was going through – indeed, his wife was already living with someone else. Or so he said.

So why did he fly to Philadelphia on the very day Michelle killed herself? And why lie and say he was in Vienna?

I checked the list of Michelle's incoming calls again and realised there was still one number that I hadn't contacted, the one in Anglesey.

I dialled it now and this time there was a reply.

'Paulette Cope.' It was a cultured voice, deep for a woman, and I put her age at late forties.

'Hello. I'm ringing concerning Michelle Roberts.'

'Oh yes?' She sounded suspicious.

'On behalf of her sister. I don't know if you knew, but Miss Roberts is dead.'

'I had been informed.'

I wondered who had informed her. She hadn't been at the funeral and Ruth Simpkin had not mentioned her name.

'We're just trying to trace people who knew her.'

'How did you get my number?'

'It came up on her call display phone.'

'I see. What is it you wish to know?'

'What was your relationship with Miss Roberts?'

'You are a friend of her sister, you say?'

'She's here now – would you like to speak to her?'

'Not for the moment. In answer to your question, Michelle and I were colleagues.'

'You're with the Drug Squad?'

'That's a melodramatic title for our department, but yes.'

'Mr Swallow is your boss?'

'You've spoken to him?'

'Only briefly.'

'I don't like talking on the telephone,' she said. 'Why don't you both come to see me?' I was wary. If Swallow had told her who I was, she could have the police waiting for me when we arrived. 'I'm in Anglesey, as you probably realise.' She gave me the address. 'It's just outside Holyhead. I shall expect you both tomorrow at eleven.'

She was a lady used to giving commands.

'Back to Wales, is it?' said Linda, who had watched me write down Paulette Cope's address.

'I guess so.'

She took my arm. 'Come on then, I'll drive this time. You look tired.'

'No, I'm fine.' I didn't fancy creeping along with Linda behind the wheel. 'I tell you what though, I am hungry. We've not had lunch yet. Let's get something to eat before we set off.'

I looked across at the brown hairy animal snoring on the bed. 'What about Roly?'

'Leave him here. He's out for the count, and he's eaten enough to last a week.'

I settled up our bill and asked for a couple of hours' extension on Linda's room so we could leave our luggage and Roly there for the time being.

Then we walked across to the Mahal in Edgware Road and had an excellent curry, after which I felt much better.

I remembered the last Indian meal I'd eaten, the takeaway at Hilary's. It seemed a lifetime ago and I wondered when I'd ever be there again.

It was past three o'clock when we finally collected Roly and our belongings and returned to the Fiesta. It wasn't the car I'd have chosen for the six-hour drive, and by the time we were making our way across the Menai Straits, it was already going dark.

We'd made several brief stops for Roly including a snack at a Burger King along the way. The young fella had taken a liking to their Whoppers.

'I hope there's a decent B and B here,' said Linda as we drove into the deserted town centre of Holyhead.

'I can't see a Holyhead Thistle anywhere,' I said, 'nor anything resembling the Dorchester.' I parked the Fiesta in what looked like the main street. 'Come on, let's stretch our legs and have a look round.'

We put Roly on his lead and set off. Eventually we found a small hotel called the Holborn which looked clean, had vacancies and would accept Roly under sufferance and a returnable deposit. Linda was given a room on the ground floor whilst I was put in a tiny attic with a skylight.

'I should have brought my telescope,' I said conversationally to the proprietor, looking through the cracked pane of glass at the stars, but he uttered no response. Obviously not an astronomer.

'What do you make of it all?' asked Linda as we regrouped in the Residents' Lounge. There were dark patches beneath her hazel eyes and she looked weary.

'I honestly don't know.' And I didn't. I'd been convinced of Wilbur Lunt's sincerity when I was with him. His account fitted in with Ruth Simpkin's version of events, yet now I'd found him out in another lie.

Another thing niggling at the back of my mind was the package of heroin. Why had Michelle sent it to Ruth Simpkin – and where had it come from in the first place?

Roly yawned noisily. He obviously felt it was past his bedtime. Or perhaps he was missing the excitement of the streets of Kirkdale.

'As long as this Paulette Cope hasn't called out Scotland Yard to arrest me, we could find out something tomorrow,' I added.

And at that, we called it a night. Linda went off to her quarters while Roly and I trudged back up the narrow stairs to the top of the house.

After an enormous breakfast, the three of us set off for Paulette Cope's house. We found it to be a little cottage situated a couple of miles outside Holyhead, set a hundred yards off the main road, backing on to the fields and approached via a rough cart-track.

Overgrown climbing flowers covered the walls, partly obscuring the front door, and attached to the side of the cottage was a small aviary made of wire netting in which lots of small birds whistled and chattered as they flew around from perch to perch. Roly immediately lunged in their direction but I held tight to his bad.

'Reminds me of Alfred Hitchcock,' remarked Linda, as I took hold of the brass knocker and banged it loudly against the door.

'Blood in the shower job, you mean?'

'No, silly. *The Birds* not *Psycho*.'

I was more concerned about the Welsh version of the Mounties waiting for us but I needn't have worried; Paulette Cope had not alerted the police.

The door opened and a woman of startling appearance stood on the threshold. She had straggly ginger hair tied up in a bun with grips but escaping in places and hanging past her cheeks. She wore gold pince-nez and a mustard-brown suit, the skirt finishing just below the knee to reveal thick lisle stockings. She was well past sixty; the firm contralto voice had made her sound younger on the phone.

'Mr Ace, I believe?'

I was impressed. When I'd telephoned, I hadn't given my name. I looked past her apprehensively but I could see no army of police waiting to jump out and arrest me. 'And you must be Shelley's sister?' she continued. 'Do come in.'

I had to duck through the low doorway as the three of us were led into an oak-beamed living room. The latticed windows were tiny so, despite the morning sunshine, the room light was switched on.

'Have a seat.' She gestured to two chintz-covered armchairs whilst she herself sat on a leather swivel chair in front of an oak roll-top desk. Roly settled himself meekly at my feet. I think he was a little intimidated by our hostess.

'So, what is the nature of your investigation?' she began.

'Doubtless you know, I am a private enquiry agent?' I responded, and she nodded. 'Well, Linda here has hired me to look into the circumstances of her sister's death.'

'I thought that was established at the inquest. Michelle Roberts committed suicide.'

'Yes, but I want to know why,' broke in Linda.

'And whether it was really suicide,' I added.

'Ah,' said Paulette Cope. 'So you have your doubts?'

'There's a few things about the affair that I find perplexing,' I admitted, 'but before we go into that, would you tell us who you are?'

She had been employed, she said, in Mr Swallow's department until her retirement some years ago. Her husband, whom she referred to as 'The Brigadier', had been much older than she and had long since passed on. Now she worked for her old employers on an ad-hoc basis, usually as a go-between or adviser to operatives out in the field. She had been assigned to look after Michelle Roberts when she came to England, and had kept in regular touch with her.

'When did you last hear from her?'

'She hadn't faxed any reports for some days, which was

unusual, but she rang here the day before she died. She left
a message on my machine, but when I phoned her back
there was no reply.'

'What was the message?'

'Only that she'd called.'

'What did you know about Wilbur Lunt?'

'That Shelley was madly in love with him and that
they planned to get married later in the year. I was very
happy for her. He was in a similar profession, as you
probably know.'

'Forgery, I believe.'

'The department were not keen on her association with
Wilbur, however.'

'Why was that?'

'They never like personal relationships. They believe,
probably correctly, that they interfere with the agent's
duties. Shelley had always been a first-rate operator, her
work came before everything, and they wanted it to continue
that way.'

'Did you ever actually meet Shelley?' asked Linda
shyly.

'Once – she came up here to the cottage. Your sister
was a lovely girl, my dear. Vivacious. She reminded me
of our own daughter.'

'Not the sort to take her own life?' I said.

'Not at all. That's why I am concerned. Everything about
her death has been rushed through and hushed up. The
department didn't want to draw attention to its presence
in the area and, for some reason, the Merseyside Police
wanted an equally speedy conclusion.'

Her words made me feel we had an ally. Thank God!
'I think I know why,' I said, and told Mrs Cope the brief
details of my own predicament.

'As I see it,' she observed when I'd brought her up to
date, 'your only remaining living witness is the young man
who sold you the cameras.'

'I've got a friend trying to find him as we speak.' In view of what she said, I hoped Tommy McKale would get to Clive Fisher's son in time.

She looked at me earnestly. 'You don't know what happened to Shelley's Detail Book, do you?'

'I'm sorry?'

'All operatives have a Detail Book in which they record details of their progress. They are always instructed to conceal it very carefully, usually under floorboards or in roof spaces. Shelley's was a yellow and black Filofax. She called it The Bee.'

I looked at Linda and she shook her head. 'No, we've not come across it.'

'I can't imagine the police would find it either. They wouldn't know of its existence. Perhaps you should take another look in her room.'

'But surely your people would have come to pick it up?'

'Not necessarily. Shelley would have kept them up to date on a daily basis and they wouldn't want to risk arousing suspicion by nosing around the premises. After all, it would be unlikely that any future occupant would go round lifting up the floorboards.'

'You think it might tell us something?'

'It's certainly your most likely source of information.'

We stayed another ten minutes and listened to Mrs Cope's life story. She had been in Government Intelligence at Cheltenham during the Cold War era. Her only child, a daughter, had been killed at twenty in a car accident.

'Do let me know what happens,' she said as she walked with us to the car. 'And good luck.'

I drove a few miles down the A5 until I came to a lay-by. 'I want to phone someone to look for that book,' I told Linda. I couldn't risk going to Livingstone Drive myself, and Geoffrey was in police custody. Who else could I ask? It would be too dangerous for Hilary, and

for Maria – even assuming she was speaking to me again.
And I couldn't expect Jim Burroughs to risk his pension.

There was only one man I could trust to help me.

Tommy McKale.

Chapter Twenty-nine

'I take it you're phoning from New Zealand.' The distinctive Scouse voice sounded very welcome at the other end of the line.

'I might just as well be, although New Brighton would be nearer the mark. Any word on the contract?'

'Nothing new. As far as I know, it's still on.' I guessed that it was Leary who'd organised that. He would have told the drug gang that I was out to jeopardise their operation, thus doubling his chances of getting me one way or another.

'Look, I need someone to do some breaking and entering.'

'You've come to the right man. I'll get Big Alec Clapham on the job.'

'Actually, there is no breaking in as such, but—'

'Don't worry, Big Alec won't mind. He'll do anything as long as it's not sheep-shagging or felching. He's never been keen on hamsters.'

'I thought it was gerbils they used.'

'I don't believe it matters. Either way, they've both got very sharp teeth.'

I told Tommy about the hidden black and yellow 'Bee' Filofax in Michelle's old flat. 'The new tenant's an accountant so he's out during the daytime.' I started to tell him where in my office the keys to Livingstone Drive were kept but he cut me short.

'Big Alec won't need no keys.'

'How will he get in?'

'This boy'll get in through the roof, a slate at a time, if necessary.' I didn't argue.

'I need it quickly, Tommy. Is that a problem?'

'He'll be there within the hour. How will I get it to you?'

'I'll think about that when and if he can find it. If the information in it is what I anticipate, this is the one thing that could save me.' What I hoped was that Michelle Roberts had found that Leary was in all this up to his neck and that she had documented the evidence. 'You'll be well paid, Tommy.' And I didn't mean by Linda. If he got me out of this mess, I'd really owe him.

'The least of my concerns, my friend. It'll give me great satisfaction to put one of those bastards away. They come in the Masquerade, demanding free drinks, harassing my girls, just because they're coppers, and I can do fuck all in case they object to my licence.'

'By the way,' I said, 'has Badger been in the club lately?'

'He was in over the weekend, why?'

'Tip him off, will you? There's been talk of forged notes and someone's been marking Badger's card.'

'I'll tell him.'

'I don't want him put away before he's paid the rent.'

I wasn't sure how much of what Wilbur had said about Badger was true, but it didn't do any harm to warn him.

'Quite right. And make sure he pays you in coins to be on the safe side.' His voice took on a new note of solicitude. 'Are you managing OK, Johnny?'

'So far so good.'

'I don't like that fellow they've got doing your show. Sounds a poncy bastard.' Shady Spencer wouldn't like to hear that. He fancies himself as a bit of a ladies' man. 'Always spouting bloody poetry.'

'I'll try and get back in one piece then.'

'Before you go, I've got a bit of interesting information for you.'

'What's that?' Good news was something I was short of.

'The house in Kirkdale that you asked me about?'

'Yes?' My voice betrayed my excitement.

'Your Mrs Parker has a grandson by the name of Barry Aspin who lodges with her from time to time.'

'He's not called Fisher then?' My last living witness, as Paulette Cope had described him.

'Not to my knowledge. Big Alec went round the night before last and had a quiet word with him.'

'Oh dear. How is he?'

'Alec? He's fine. The lad has a broken arm though and a few scratches but he's willing to stand up in court and say he sold you the cameras.'

I wondered what the alternative would have been for him.

'How do I reach you?' he demanded. I gave him Linda's mobile number. I knew it would be safe with him. 'Don't worry, son. You'll be hearing from me soon.'

Linda had picked up the gist of what had happened from my side of the conversation.

'Do you think this Mr McKale will find Shelley's diary or whatever it is?'

'If anybody will, it'll be Tommy.'

'Do we go back home now then?' she queried.

'I suppose so.' My options were limited and dwindling all the time. Once you'd been accused of a crime, there was no such thing as being innocent any more. That was something you had to prove, despite the law saying otherwise. Worse still, even when you were found not guilty, some clever bastard would murmur 'no smoke without fire' and make a mockery of it all.

'I'll just let Roly stretch his legs.' She took the lead and went round to the rear door of the car. Our canine friend was curled up on the back seat and didn't seem keen to take the trip.

'I think that walk in Hyde Park's knackered him for the week,' I commented, turning round in the driver's seat to watch. 'That envelope is still there, isn't it?'

She looked under the seat. 'Yes.'

Something about that package was nagging at the back of my mind. Why had Michelle sent this parcel of drugs to Ruth Simpkin in Llandudno, the one friend she knew she could trust? Who was she afraid would find it? And then, it hit me with the force of a sledgehammer.

Would Michelle Roberts have sent that parcel and promised to pick it up later if she was planning to kill herself?

'How do you think all this is going to end, Johnny?' asked Linda when she returned a few minutes later, dragging Roly behind her.

I didn't answer at first. We were looking at it from two different viewpoints. Linda's chief interest was to find out the truth about her sister, what game she had been playing and the reason why she committed suicide.

My chief concern had to be to prove my innocence regarding the cameras and the murders, and my best chance of doing this was to find the real culprits. I just hoped that by doing so, Michelle Lunt's role in the affair would be revealed.

Either way, the first step was the Filofax.

'Happily, I hope. I don't fancy a ten-year stretch in Walton. Look, let's have a bite to eat, eh?'

We stopped off at a pub in Llanfair. I let Linda go to the bar to order the food and drinks whilst I sat in a corner hiding behind Geoffrey's specs and my third day's growth of beard.

At Bangor, we stopped to fill up with petrol and pick up a *Daily Post*. The Serina Barrie murder was still big news locally, although it had been relegated to page

seven and eight; I was relieved to see that the picture
they used of me didn't look anything like the face I saw
in the driving mirror.

We reached Nelson by teatime. Geoffrey's mother's
Metro was still outside Linda's front door.

Roly seemed glad to be back and drank two bowls full
of water the minute he got in the house.

I switched on the TV but the best it could offer was
Pet Rescue. Someone wanted a good home for four sheep.
No good for Big Alec, I thought, remembering Tommy
McKale's comments.

How long would I have to wait before Tommy rang?

I went upstairs to take a shower and when I came down,
Linda was emerging from the kitchen carrying two plates
of garlic prawns and chips. 'I thought we might as well
eat while we're waiting,' she said. 'And don't look at me
like that. I know I'm getting podgy round the middle.'

'Nonsense,' I lied.

We ate the meal and she settled down for an evening
of soap viewing. I was fidgety. I was beginning to feel
more imprisoned than if I'd been in Walton when Linda's
mobile phone rang and saved me from *EastEnders*.

I took it into the kitchen to avoid competing with the
television. 'That was quick,' I said.

'We don't waste time,' said Tommy McKale. 'Do you
want the bad news or the good news first?'

I hate it when people play silly games. It's all the quiz
shows on TV that do it. Everybody wants to be Dale
Winton. But it's easier to play along than argue.

'The bad,' I said.

'There's been another murder, Johnny boy.' His voice
took on a grave tone. 'Barry Aspin's dead.'

It took a moment for the name to sink in.

'The lad who sold me the cameras? Fisher's son?'
Although I realised now there never was a Clive Fisher,
photographer.

'That's the one.'

'The lad who was going to give evidence? But you only told me about him this afternoon!'

'Hit and run accident early this morning on his way home from some club in town. They must have heard we'd been leaning on him and they were waiting for him.'

'Poor bastard.' These people were ruthless.

'At least he won't have to worry about his broken arm not mending right.' Compassion didn't seem to be a word in Tommy McKale's vocabulary. 'But it's you who's the poor bastard, Johnny. Now you've nobody to testify. Your witnesses don't last long in this world do they?'

I didn't need reminding. 'What's the good news?'

'Big Alec's found your book.'

'Already? That's brilliant.'

'He doesn't mess about but he had an awful job finding it. Had half the frigging floor up.'

'I hope he didn't leave any traces.' I didn't want my tenant fetching the police in.

'Don't worry, Johnny. The place would be good as new when Alec left, rest assured.'

'When can I pick it up?'

'How about tomorrow morning, seeing that you tell me you're not a million miles away? Come to the gym – you can lie low there for a while. I've got decent quarters round the back.'

'That's brilliant, Tommy.' I couldn't wait to get back to the Pool. I was restless stuck out here on the edge of the moors. I felt disorientated away from Liverpool and my network of contacts and friends. My territory.

Linda was still glued to the box so I gave Jim Burroughs a ring. 'Any news?' I asked him. There wasn't. I listened patiently to his usual lecture about giving myself up, jumping in when he at last paused to draw breath. 'Jim what did you mean the other day when you said you had a theory about Michelle Roberts' death?'

'Rohypnol,' he answered promptly.

'That's what they call the date drug, isn't it?'

'Correct. It's not beyond the bounds of possibility that someone could have popped a roofie in the girl's drink then suggested she slip a noose around her neck. The drug destroys willpower, you see.'

'Oh, come on, Jim, I can't accept that. Nobody's going to be persuaded to kill themselves!'

'Depends on their state of mind. If they're depressed already, someone comes along with more bad news then hands them a rope and tells them all their troubles could soon be over. You get my drift?'

'I suppose it's possible,' I admitted.

'Just an idea I had.'

'Nothing on Leary?'

'If he's bent, he's covered his tracks well.'

'What do you know about a Barry Aspin, killed in a hit and run the night before last?'

'Nothing, why?'

'He's the young lad who sold me the cameras.'

'I thought that was someone called Fisher.'

'It was Aspin and someone wasted him just like they did Quantine and Serina Barrie. Everyone who had anything to do with those cameras is dead.' Except, I suddenly thought, the old lady who lived in Kirkdale, Aspin's aunt, Violet Parker. Maybe I should go and see her.

I must have been telepathic because, soon after I'd finished talking to Jim Burroughs, Geoffrey rang. After Alistair's intervention, he'd been released from police custody without charges.

'I've an urgent message for you from some woman called Mrs Parker. Sounded old.'

'What did she want?'

'To see you about her nephew's death. Says she has

information for you to clear your name. You want t
be careful, Johnny; coming back to Liverpool could b
dangerous. The law could be waiting for you.'

Did I have an alternative? 'It's already fixed, Geoff,'
told him. 'I'm coming back in the morning. I'm stayin
at Tommy McKale's gym.'

'The posh new Leisure Centre, you mean.'

'That's the one.'

'Does this mean my mum'll get her Metro back a
last? She's been paying out a fortune in taxis going t
the bingo.'

'I'll reimburse her,' I promised, 'and she'll have it bac
tomorrow sometime. Did the old lady leave a number?'

'She did.'

'Give it me tomorrow.'

Linda wasn't keen to let me go. 'You must be crazy
she declared, as *EastEnders* gave way to *Brookside*. 'You'
either get killed or arrested.'

'No, I won't.' I picked up the dog's lead. 'I'm going t
take Roly round the block. I need some fresh air after a
the driving.'

I was feeling claustrophobic cooped up in the little hous
and I wanted to talk privately to Hilary and Maria, which
couldn't do with Linda around. There was a phone box o
the corner just two blocks away but progress was slow a
Roly wanted to stop at every lamppost and gateway.

I was lucky. It was Hilary's night off and she wa
at home.

'Oh Johnny, darling, I'm so relieved to hear from yo
Are you all right? Where are you?'

I told her I was just outside of Manchester and I wa
fine. I didn't mention Linda.

'I'm hoping to come home within a couple of days,'
said. 'With a bit of luck we could go out on Sunday night

'What about the police and all the trouble? It's bee
awful, Johnny. You've even been on *Crimewatch*.'

I could think of worse shows to be on, *Blind Date* for starters.

'It's all going to get sorted now,' I assured her. 'I've missed you,' I said.

'I've missed you too. Can't we meet somewhere secretly? I just want to hold you close to me.'

I wanted it too but there was one hell of a lot of tidying up to do first, and I couldn't forget that there was still a contract out on me. I promised to ring her again as soon as I could.

I then rang Maria's. A male voice answered the phone. It took me by surprise. This was something I hadn't contemplated, that she had already found a new boyfriend.

'Hello, can I help you? Hello. Is anyone there?'

I nearly put the phone down in my confusion. 'Er, is Maria in, please?'

'Who is it?'

'Johnny.'

'Just a minute.'

I suddenly thought: What if it's the police? Though why they should be at Maria's I didn't know. I was becoming panicky. Days on the run were getting to me. I touched the flat cap I was wearing and rubbed the beginnings of my beard. What was happening to me?

'Johnny?' Maria's voice came through loud and clear.

'Maria. I've been wanting to ring you for days.'

'Are you all right? Where are you?'

'Who was that who answered the phone?'

'Oh, that was Robin.' Her son. 'He's home from university for a few days. It's vacation time.'

'Of course.' I felt a surge of relief.

'Johnny, I'm sorry about what happened before, when you came round. You were telling the truth, weren't you? She was a client.'

'Yes, she was. Nothing happened between us, Maria.' Which was true. 'You don't know how much I wish you were with me to help me with this case,' I said. 'It's got quite out of hand.'

'I know you haven't killed anyone or stolen anything,' said Maria, 'but how come the police think you have?'

'I've been framed. By the police, or rather, by one policeman. But I think I'm on the verge of solving it.'

'Can I come and meet you anywhere?'

I didn't think a reunion would be a good idea at the moment. 'Not yet, but with a bit of luck, this will all be over by next week. I'll ring you and we can go out and celebrate.'

'I'm so sorry I haven't been there to help you.' She sounded contrite.

'I understand,' I replied stoically. In my mind, I could almost see Tommy McKale shaking his head in disbelief and murmuring, 'The jammy bastard's got away with it again.'

I felt a great relief that I was in touch with Hilary and Maria again. I needed them both. They'd come to complement each other in my life. One of them alone didn't work for me, and I couldn't bear to even think of a future where I didn't have either of them.

I knew, of course, I had no right to demand their loyalty. If I couldn't make a commitment, why should I expect them to do so?

In my own way, I did my best to give them both all they wanted from me in terms of kindness and affection and generosity, and I suppose I hoped that that was enough. So far it had been. I just wished it would stay that way, that what I had to offer them was enough to make them want to keep me in their lives for ever.

Maria and I said our farewells. It occurred to me that I hadn't told her about Roly, but that could wait. It would be a nice surprise for her when we got together again.

Progress back to Linda's was halting, Roly retracing every step along the way, but we passed nobody, for which was grateful. I stopped outside her door and looked towards the motorway. Tomorrow I'd be back on Merseyside. I took hold of the brass knocker and tried to bang it gently without waking the whole street. Linda came to the door in a short Snoopy night-dress.

'You've been a long time,' she said. 'I was worried. I thought you'd been captured.'

'You make me sound like a prisoner of war,' I said. 'Blame Roly.' I remembered what Hilary had said about Pepper. 'Marking out his territory.'

'I'll boil you some hot milk,' volunteered Linda. 'You can take it up with you.'

I'd rather have had a Scrumpy Jack but I let her get on with it. I thought Linda would make somebody a good grandmother. Obviously her vocation in life was to look after a man, which was fine as long as the man wasn't me. Forget the Ovaltine; what I wanted was a few nights of lust and passion with Hilary.

'I don't know how you keep going,' Linda went on. 'I'm dead beat. Do you realise, yesterday we were in London, we woke up in Anglesey this morning and we've hardly stopped since. I never usually travel beyond Burnley from month to month.'

I said nothing. If we'd been back in the Pool, I'd have been on my way to the Masquerade Club now.

'You will take care won't you, Johnny?' she went on. 'I feel guilty for getting you into this mess.'

'I think I'd have been in it anyway, one way or another.' I took her in my arms, smiled into those hazel eyes and gently kissed her. 'You've been very kind to me, Linda, letting me hide out here in your house and everything.'

'Nonsense. You're working on my case.'

'I suppose so, but I do appreciate it and can I ask you one more favour?'

'Go on.'

'Look after Roly for a few days for me. He might be

in the way if there's trouble.' And I had the feeling there
was going to be a lot of trouble. 'I'll fetch him when it's
all over and I bring you my report.'

Linda seemed quite happy with that. She gave me some
Yorkshire Parkins to go with the milk and I threw one to
Roly. He wagged his stump in appreciation and trotted
after me up the stairs.

I slept well after all the travelling but I was still up at
first light. I couldn't wait to get back to Liverpool. Once I
got to see Violet Parker, and once I had read Michelle's
diaries, I felt sure I'd be on the brink of solving the case.
But I also knew I could be walking into a trap. The trick
was to stay alive to see it through.

Chapter Thirty

I left Linda's for Liverpool at nine-thirty, giving the rush-hour traffic time to dissipate. I promised to ring her as soon as I had any news. She was still the client.

I'd transferred Ruth Simpkin's envelope from the Fiesta to the Metro and then put my foot down on the gas. It was eleven o'clock when I reached Liverpool and pulled up outside the Marina Health and Leisure Centre.

A group of women in sports gear were standing chatting outside the door. If they noticed me at all, they probably mistook me for a labourer with my stubble and flat cap. Two of them, in cream leggings, had such big bottoms they looked like cheeses.

I put the drugs envelope under my jacket and went into Reception. 'Tommy McKale,' I told the girl. 'He's expecting me.' She directed me to a waiting area and, two minutes later, Tommy came down.

'Christ, you look rough. Come with me.' I followed him through a corridor to the back of the Leisure Centre, and out into a small courtyard, behind which was a brick outbuilding. 'The office quarters,' he explained.

'It's a bit posh for Toxteth, isn't it?'

'Do you mind,' he objected. 'We're not Toxteth any more. Docklands, if you please.'

A brown Jaguar XJ8 rolled up the driveway. 'That's good timing,' said Tommy. 'Here's Big Alec now.'

I observed the registration plate: it was a brand new

car. Breaking and entering was obviously a profitable occupation.

When he stepped out of the car, I was surprised to find that Alec was a couple of inches shorter than me, but he more than made up for it in girth. He must have carried eighteen stone of hard muscle. His skin looked like leather one eye was half-closed, and a long scar crossed his cheek from below the eye to his chin. A man, I thought, who would never be popular at Postman's Knock.

Tommy introduced us. 'Alec, Johnny Ace.' We shook hands and I winced, my arm feeling like it had been pulled through one of those Victorian cast-iron clothe mangles.

He nodded to me and turned to Tommy McKale. 'Have you got a drink, Tommy? My mouth's as dry as a camel' arse.'

'Yeah, come in both of you.'

Big Alec opened the door of the Jag and brought out a paper bag, which he handed to me.

'These are what you want, pal.'

I peered inside the bag. There was the yellow and black Filofax, The Bee, and with it, another book, a thin leather diary. 'What's this?' I asked him.

'Dunno. It was lying there with the other.'

I opened it and saw daily entries written in tiny spidery writing. I couldn't believe my luck. It was Michelle' private diary! This could hold the solution to the mystery which could mean the end of my problems.

I followed Big Alec into the office building and Tommy rang through to the bar. 'Cider for you, Johnny?' I nodded 'And a lager for you, Alec?'

'Make it two,' demanded Alec gruffly. 'Them bottles is only halves.'

'What's your next step, Johnny?' asked Tommy.

I told him about Violet Parker's phone call to Geoffrey 'She wants to meet me to give me information. Presumably now that they've murdered her grandson, she wants to get back at them.'

'I'd be careful here,' warned Tommy McKale. 'Sounds like a trap to me. You're being set up. If she wanted to grass on them, all she had to do was phone the busies.'

'People like her don't grass.'

'Bollocks. They'd shit in their own grandmother's mouth if they thought there was anything in it for them. Criminals don't have codes of honour any more, Johnny. That's for fucking fairytales.'

'So what do I do?'

'You don't ring her, for a start. Forewarned is forearmed, as Machiavelli used to say. You ought to read him, Johnny. A very good businessman. No, you just turn up on the doorstep, force your way in and she talks. And you take me and Alec with you for backup just in case she has company.'

'Sounds OK to me. When do you want to go?'

'No time like the present. The way things have been going, the old bat could be dead by teatime.'

'What about the diaries?'

'I'll put them in the safe. Plenty of time to read them later.'

'Could you put this in as well?' I handed him the parcel of heroin. 'But don't ask what's in it.'

'Never seen it,' replied Tommy, taking it from me and putting it safely with the diaries.

'Let's go then,' I said.

'Hang on, what about my fucking drink?' snarled Big Alec.

We waited for the drinks to arrive, took all of a minute to pour them down our throats, then they piled into Big Alec's XJ8 and I followed in the Metro, heading towards Kirkdale.

There was no sign of any movement in the house as I stepped out and knocked on the front door. The other two

stayed in the car, parked further up the street, watching.
I knocked again and this time I heard a shuffling noise
and the door was slowly opened a couple of inches. In the
gloom I could make out the features of Parrot Woman. I
quickly put my foot in the doorway, in case she decided
to shut me out.

'You wanted to see me.'

'Ace, is it? You were supposed to ring.'

I knew then that her intention had been to lure me to
the house just as Tommy had predicted. 'Give you time to
have your pals waiting for me?' I said.

'You killed my grandson, you bastard,' she spat at me.
This time she hadn't unhooked the chain but I slammed
my shoulder against the door and forced my way past her
into the dark front room. Behind me, Tommy and Big Alec
were getting out of the car to join me.

She ran across the room after me, waving her stick and
screaming. 'Get out, I'll call the police.'

I sat on a wooden dining chair and faced her. 'Is that
what they told you – that I killed Barry? Well, they're
lying. *They* killed your grandson, not me.'

She stopped. 'Why would they kill him?'

'To make sure he didn't talk. They've killed everybody.
You're the only one left alive who knows anything about
the cameras.'

The old woman sat down, exhausted by the shouting.
Tommy and Big Alec entered and shut the front door
behind them.

'Now,' I continued, 'I want to know exactly who's who
in this pantomime. Roy Quantine first set me up for the
cameras. What was he to you?'

Big Alec moved across the room and stood to one side of
the old lady. With his face, he didn't need to do any more.

Violet Parker glared at me and her protruding nose
seemed to assume Pinocchio-like proportions. 'Roy was
my nephew, wasn't he – my sister's lad.'

'Not a long-living family, are you? First your nephew, then your grandson, both dead within a week of one another. I hope you're well insured.'

'You killed them, you bastard.' She reared up again and Big Alec took a threatening step forward. She shrank back in her chair. Tommy McKale stood silently by the door watching.

I didn't bother denying it again. 'Let's get it straight. Quantine tells me about the cameras and your Barry is here to sell them to me, right? What I want to know is, who gave the orders to them?'

She looked round at the three of us. 'Attacking an old woman, you could get life for this. I've only got to scream.'

'Scream all you like, missus,' said Big Alec. 'It'll be the last sound you make.'

She peered at him through her cataracts. 'You're the one what was here the other night. Broke our Barry's arm.'

Big Alec was short on chivalry. 'And I'll break your neck next,' he said. 'Now talk. Who's giving the orders?'

She started to whimper. 'It were our John.'

'Your John?'

'My brother's lad.'

'Another nephew,' I said. 'Crime must run in the family.'

She emitted a croaking laugh. 'Hardly in our John's case.'

'What do you mean?'

'Our John's a copper, ain't he?'

'What?'

'In the CID.'

'What's his name?' I asked but I already knew the answer.

'John Leary.'

Why? That was all I wanted to know. 'Why me?'

'You were interfering with something he was doing at

that house of yours near Sefton Park, that's all I know.
He wanted you out of the way. Roy tips you the wink
about the cameras, Barry sells them to you and John picks
you up.'

'Where did Serina Barrie fit in?'

'Is that the girl what lived in your house?'

'Yes. The one who was murdered.'

'I think she was John's girlfriend.'

'Oh, come on.' I couldn't swallow that. He was twenty
years older than her and an ugly sod with his pock-marked
face. Serina Barrie had been very attractive.

'I don't know what she was.'

'Someone shot her and it wasn't me.'

'Try proving it.' The old lady snorted and cackled
again and only an urgent shake of my head prevented
Big Alec from hastening her departure into the next
world.

'Who else is involved beside your nephew?' Leary
hadn't killed Quantine. And then I remembered the man
who looked like Al Pacino. 'There's a dark-haired man
looks Italian, about forty-five.'

She started to laugh again but it developed into a cough.
From her apron pocket, she dragged a grimy handkerchief
and expectorated a wad of green phlegm. Tommy McKale
closed his eyes in disgust.

'That'll be his pal, Larry.'

'He's not in the police too, is he?'

'No, Larry's a businessman.'

'I think I know that bloke,' broke in Big Alec. 'Larry
Vicenzio. Runs a bent shipping business, import and export.
He lives in a bloody great house in Blundelsands near the
station, along from where they've built them new Gothic
flats. Not a man to be messed with.'

'What do you know about Nathan Lloyd?' I asked the
old woman.

'He lived at your house too, didn't he? He was in business

with our John.' She waved her stick. 'You won't get away
with this. You killed my boys.'

'I didn't kill anyone,' I repeated. I tried to think what
my next move should be. The way it looked at the moment,
Leary was involved in the drug ring somehow with Lloyd,
perhaps importing the stuff through Larry Vicenzio's import
company. Larry seemed favourite for the murders. Serina
Barrie I wasn't sure about.

The question was, what to do next.

I looked around for a phone. 'I'm going to ring Jim
Burroughs,' I told Tommy. 'I think we could do with the
law in on this.'

'Careful,' warned Tommy. 'Can you trust any of them?'

'I think I can trust Jim,' I said, and dialled his work
number. It rang for an age before he answered.

'Jim, it's Johnny Ace. Listen carefully.' I told him
everything that we had heard from Violet Parker.

'Christ, Johnny. You don't half stir things up,' he said
when I'd finished. 'This is going to cause ructions at
headquarters, believe me.'

'I'm frightened there might be people involved higher
up in the Force than Leary, Jim. Be careful who you
talk to.'

'Leave it to me – I'm going right to the top with this. I
never liked that Leary, smarmy bastard that he is. Where
are you now?'

'In Kirkdale at the old lady's house. Mrs Parker.' I gave
him the address and telephone number.

'Wait there. I'll let you know what's happening.'

'Well?' asked Tommy McKale.

'He's sorting it. Wants us to wait here.'

Mrs Parker sat silently in her chair. She'd heard me
talking to Jim Burroughs. Could she have had the first
doubts about my involvement in the killings? I didn't have
time to ponder on it because there suddenly came a sharp
knock on the front door.

Tommy, Big Alec and I looked at one another. It was too soon for the police to get here. 'In the kitchen,' ordered Tommy.

The three of us ran into the small kitchen as the knock sounded again. We watched from the door as the old lady rose to answer but, before she could get to her feet, the door was pushed open. I looked into the mirror on the side wall and gasped at the reflection of the man coming into the room. The newcomer was Larry Vicenzio.

'Hello, Grandma – no, don't get up.' He moved swiftly across the room and stood behind her chair. In his hand he had a scarf which he brought over Violet Parker's head and pulled tight round her throat. She gave a strangled cry and her lips turned blue as she fought for breath.

Vicenzio jerked the scarf viciously and pulled tighter, but before her death throes could begin, Big Alec roared across the room with startling speed. With one hand, he grasped Vicenzio by the hair, bent him backwards and smashed the side of his other hand into the base of Vicenzio's nose, sending the bone upwards into his brain. Vicenzio's arms twitched and the scarf fluttered from his grasp to the floor.

Mrs Parker lay slumped unconscious in the chair.

'Shit, what a fuck-up,' said Tommy McKale, walking back into the room.

I peered down at the lifeless form of Larry Vicenzio flat on his back on the carpet. 'Is he dead?'

Big Alec didn't bother to look. 'Hard to tell with a blow like that. Sometimes they live, sometimes they don't.'

'We'd better call an ambulance,' I said. 'For the old lady,' I added. I didn't think that Tommy or Big Alec would have troubled the emergency services for Vicenzio.

'Let's hope she lasts out till the boys in blue get here,' said Tommy McKale, peering at Violet Parker's grey skin. 'She's your last witness.'

'Can you do the kiss of life?'

'On that old crone? You must be joking. I'd rather do
on Vince.'

I felt the old lady's pulse. 'She's still alive, but it's very
weak. See if there's any brandy anywhere.' I felt that a
ourse with the St John Ambulance Brigade might be
seful if I ever did set up in office as an investigator. My
nowledge of first aid was limited to a vague notion of a
t Bernard trundling up a snowy Swiss mountain with a
arrel round its neck.

Tommy rummaged in the kitchen and found some whisky
a a cupboard. 'There's just a bit in here,' he said.

'That'll do me.' Big Alec grabbed the bottle from him
nd took two full swigs before handing me the dregs.

I lifted the bottle to Mrs Parker's lips but the remaining
rops dribbled down her chin on to her shawl and she made
o movement. She still didn't have her teeth in and her face
oked shrunken.

'Tell her Everton have won,' grinned Tommy McKale.
The shock will either wake her or kill her.'

We were saved such extreme measures by the wail of a
ren as the ambulance arrived.

'What's been going on here, then?' asked the first
aramedic, as his colleague ran back to the vehicle for
arious items of life-saving medical equipment.

'Game of Ludo,' said Tommy solemnly. 'Got a bit out
' hand.'

'Have the police been informed?'

'They're on their way,' I said.

By the time they came, both Violet Parker and Larry
icenzio had been rushed to nearby Walton Hospital. I had
job persuading Big Alec to stick around, understandable
the circumstances, given that Vicenzio looked decidedly
ady for the mortuary toe-tag.

'You tell them,' he said. 'It was self-defence. He was
rottling the old bat and he turned on me when I tried to
op him.'

'You saved the old lady's life,' I pointed out to him
being careful not to add she was favourite to occupy th
next drawer in the morgue. 'They'll probably award yo
the George Cross.'

Two police cars drew up outside. Detective Inspector Jim
Burroughs was first through the door, closely followed b
a chubby man with a smooth pink skin and thin lips. Jim
didn't waste time on preliminaries.

'This is Chief Superintendent Gibbon.'

'I'm afraid there's been some trouble here,' I said. 'Afte
I phoned you, a man broke into the house and tried t
strangle Mrs Parker. My friend here,' I gestured toward
Big Alec, 'bravely managed to restrain him and we ran
for an ambulance to take the old lady to Walton.'

'Where's the attacker now?' asked the Chief Superir
tendent.

'Er, he went to hospital too.'

Jim Burroughs groaned.

Gibbon peered at Big Alec. 'Don't I know you?'

'He used to be on *Coronation Street*,' I said quickly.

The Chief Superintendent turned his attention to me. 'Fc
the moment, I shall ignore the fact that you are wanted fc
murder among other things,' he told me sternly. 'If wh.
you told the Detective Inspector here is true, this is a vei
serious matter and your evidence will be of vital importanc
to the prosecution case.'

Tommy McKale spoke for the first time. 'He'll nee
round-the-clock protection. All his witnesses have bee
murdered and there's a contract out on him.'

The Chief Superintendent carried on. 'I'm going
arrange for twenty-four-hour security on those two peop
in hospital. Meanwhile, I need you three gentlemen to con
to the station and make a statement.'

We followed him out of the house and were driven to tl
police station in two cars. I sat in the back of the secor
one, next to Jim Burroughs.

'If Violet Parker dies,' I said, worrying about the outcome, 'I'll have no evidence to support my story.'

'Unless the other guy talks.'

'Vicenzio? I can't see him talking. Besides, he didn't look so good either when they took him away in the ambulance.'

Burroughs sighed. 'Are you sure you're not on a backhander from the Crematorium?'

I was very concerned. After evading the police for a week, I was now in their clutches. Leary could yet blag his way out of any charges if it was his word against mine. I was still the one holding the gun beside Serina Barrie's body, and the one who had found Quantine in the Stirling toilets. Not to mention the cameras.

I broke out in a cold sweat wondering if I should make a run for it again. Without a witness, I had no proof of anything.

And then I remembered the diaries.

Chapter Thirty-one

I spent three arduous hours in an airless room dictating my statement to a muscular young policewoman with low typing skills.

I documented how I had come by the stolen cameras and stated that I believed Detective Sergeant Leary had deliberately orchestrated the false charge in order to prevent me from carrying on with my investigation into Michelle Lunt's death – an investigation which might have uncovered Leary's own dealings with Nathan Lloyd, a known drug dealer.

I pointed out that Roy Quantine, Barry Aspin and Serina Barrie had all been murdered to prevent them talking, and that the only witness to the masquerade who was still alive – just – was Violet Parker.

For the time being, I disclosed nothing about the Lunt or the diaries. I wanted to sort out that particular puzzle for myself.

'So what's your theory behind all this?' asked Chief Superintendent Gibbon when he had read carefully through my statement. We were in his office an hour later, opposite sides of a big mahogany desk. Jim Burroughs sat alongside him and the door was guarded by a uniformed Sergeant.

'It all started,' I explained, 'with the suicide of Michelle Lunt, who was working as an undercover agent targeting the drugs cartel of which Nathan Lloyd, a tenant of mine, was the Merseyside connection. Detective Sergeant Leary was nvolved in some way with Lloyd.

'I was hired as a private investigator by the dead woman's ister to find out why she should kill herself. Leary wanted ɔ get me off the case in case I found any evidence against im so he concocted this charge of handling stolen goods ɔ either distract me or discredit me.'

'Wait a minute,' interrupted the Chief Superintendent. This is more than handling stolen goods. You have been harged with murder. If, as you insist, you are not guilty, Ir Ace, then to whom do you attribute these killings?'

'I'm sure Quantine was killed by Vicenzio. He saw me ı the Stirling Club that night and realised that Leary's cheme to discredit me hadn't worked. I was still pursuing ıe investigation. He witnessed me talking to Quantine, was ʇightened Quantine would open his mouth so he panicked, ɔllowed him to the Gents, cut his throat and was out of ıe club within seconds, before the alarm was raised.'

'What about the shooting of Serina Barrie?'

'I don't know why she was killed. Vicenzio probably ˙red the shot but I'm sure Leary organised it because he ˙as waiting to arrest me when I arrived at the warehouse. ˙Vhy he wanted her dead, I've no idea.'

'I can tell you one thing you may not know, Mr Ace. ˙erina Barrie was an addict.'

'No!' I was genuinely surprised. That explained, though, ˙hy she'd dropped out of university.

'So, going along with your hypothesis for the moment, ˙etective Sergeant Leary might have been her supplier, in ˙hich case he would be in a position to demand favours ˙f her.'

'Like posing for the pictures, you mean?'

'And informing you about the cameras.'

'Which Quantine had already stolen.' I had never been ˙le to accept Serina Barrie and Roy Quantine as acquaint-˙ɑces. She'd probably never met him. 'So, I repeat, why ˙ould Leary want Serina Barrie killed?'

'Perhaps she became frightened when Quantine wa
killed and wanted to pull out. Maybe she tried to blackmai
Leary. Either way, they must have seen her as a weak link.
I thought it was probably them who'd persuaded her t
leave her flat.

'So they decided to kill two birds with one stone an
hit on this plan to get rid of her and fit me up on a murde
charge?'

'Something like that. Pretty stupid of you to pick up th
gun, though. Played right into their hands.'

I didn't need him to tell me that. 'When Serina rang m
from that warehouse,' I said, 'she knew she was leadin
me into a trap.'

'But what she wouldn't have known was that she wa
the bait, poor kid.'

I wasn't so sure about the poor kid bit but I let it pas

'Vicenzio must have killed her immediately after sh
made the call to me and arranged for Leary to arrest m
as soon as I entered the building. What about the Constabl
with Leary? Could he have been in on it?'

'Morton? I don't think so. He'd not worked with Lear
before – he's new to plainclothes work. No, I'm incline
to believe he was duped like the rest of us.'

I didn't miss the significance of the 'rest of us' bit. It sug
gested the police were going along with my story at las

'Barry Aspin's "accident" would be down to Vicenzi
again,' I said. 'He probably found out that the boy ha
been got at and might have been prepared to talk.'
avoided going into details about Big Alec and the youth
broken arm.

'Do you think Sergeant Leary was involved in that killir
as well?' asked Jim Burroughs, who had been listenir
intently to all this.

'No. I can't really see Leary approving of his ow
family being murdered. After all, he and Quantine we
cousins and Barry Aspin would be a second cousin.

guess that by this time, matters were being taken out of his hands.'

'I'd go along with that,' agreed Chief Superintendent Gibbon.

'All you need now,' I said, 'is Leary's confession. He must realise he's out of his depth with these people.'

'I've checked on the computer,' said Gibbon. 'Lloyd is wanted by Interpol and Vicenzio is known as a hired killer throughout Europe.'

'There's also Mrs Parker,' I pointed out. 'She'll be able to confirm what I have told you when she comes round, or the part she knows at any rate. She certainly knows Barry sold me the cameras at her house.'

'What about Vicenzio?'

'I don't think he'd have been in on the initial plot. He's the hired muscle, probably Lloyd's right-hand man.'

'But when he found out that half Leary's relations had been dragged into the affair, he wasted no time in getting rid of them to make sure they wouldn't talk.'

'And Leary was powerless by now to do anything about it. He was in too deep.' I looked Chief Superintendent Gibbon in the eye. 'So am I still under arrest?'

'Not at the moment but I don't want you disappearing again. I shall require you to hand in your passport.'

'No problem.' I had too much unfinished business here to think of fleeing the country.

Chief Superintendent Gibbon had something else on his mind. 'How did Tommy McKale and Alec Clapham come to be with you today?'

'Mrs Parker sent a message asking to see me. I thought I might be walking into a trap like with Serina Barrie so I took them with me for protection.'

'Hm. You certainly picked a couple of dubious characters.'

I gave him an innocent look. 'I didn't know they'd ever been in trouble with the law. Tommy McKale owns various

business enterprises across the city and is a respected
member of the Masonic Lodge, like many of your senior
officers, I believe.'

Gibbon tightened his lips.

'And has Mr Clapham got a record?'

'Nothing proven, shall we say.'

'There you are then.'

'There's plenty we suspect him of – GBH, extortion,
aggravated burglary . . .'

'But as you say, Chief Superintendent, nothing proven.
Innocent until found guilty.' I made a mental note, though,
not to cross Big Alec, if I hadn't known already. 'And,
remember, there's still a contract out on me. If you're
not supplying me with a bodyguard, I'll need my own
minders.'

I was about to suggest he devoted his energies to picking
up Lloyd when a Constable came in with a piece of paper,
which he handed to Gibbon.

'Well, well,' he said, reading it. 'That's a blow for your
friend Mr Clapham. Larry Vicenzio died of his injuries in
Walton Hospital half an hour ago. This time we could have
Mr Clapham for murder.'

'Come off it,' I said. 'Both Mr McKale and I will testify
that he acted in self-defence after bravely saving Mrs Parker
from being strangled by Vicenzio. You haven't a hope with
that one.'

'Pity. Worth a try though,' mused Gibbon philosoph-
ically.

'What about the old lady? No news on her?'

'Not mentioned. As soon as she recovers consciousness,
we'll take a statement and see if it confirms your story.'

'And Detective Sergeant Leary? What are you going to
do about him?'

'I think you can safely leave that to us, Mr Ace. We
shall be carrying out a thorough internal investigation.'

But it never came to that. Just as Detective Chie

Superintendent Gibbon and Detective Inspector Burroughs rose to their feet to signify the interview was over, the door opened again and a policewoman rushed in.

'It's Detective Sergeant Leary, sir. They've found him hanging in one of the cells. He's dead.'

Chapter Thirty-two

Leary had left a note admitting everything. It was a long one as suicide notes go. Six pages. He must have been up all night composing it.

Oddly enough, his story was much as Wilbur Lunt had described it, almost as if he'd known Leary.

He apologised to his wife and children for going off the rails. It had all started when he'd turned a blind eye to a couple of minor transactions eighteen months ago, then he'd accepted a small amount of money from Lloyd to pay a medical bill. His wife's cervical smear test had proved positive and, because of the long NHS waiting list, she'd had the cone biopsy done privately.

From then on it was all downhill. By the time I came on the scene, he was well and truly implicated and his attempt to get rid of me became ever more cumbersome.

Serina Barrie was mentioned in passing. He'd originally tempted her with cocaine in a vain attempt to seduce her, but it ended up with her threatening to expose him to the police authorities if he didn't continue to supply her with regular amounts. He didn't regret her demise. However, when members of his own family were killed, against his wishes, he was filled with remorse.

'Lets me off the hook nicely,' I told Jim Burroughs, who'd shown me the letter against all regulations. 'I won't be hypocritical and pretend I'm not glad the pock-faced bastard's dead. He's caused me enough grief.'

'Lucky for you he wrote it,' Jim replied soberly. 'Gibbon

never told you, but we got word from the hospital that the old lady isn't likely to pull through. Pneumonia's set in.'

We'd been for a big lunch at the new Crown Plaza Hotel by the Pier Head. Free of his wife Rosemary's scrutiny, Jim had partaken of his maximum driving allowance of two pints of Newcastle Brown and we were now parked outside Mrs Parker's house in Kirkdale. Jim had given me a lift back there to pick up the Metro. I was pleased to see that Geoffrey's mother's car was still intact. Big Alec's Jag had long since been removed.

'I wonder who'll get that place,' I said, glancing towards the terraced house. It wasn't dissimilar to Linda Roberts' home in Nelson.

'Why?'

'No reason, only half her family's been wiped out in this caper so perhaps it'll come on the market. It'd make a handy let, with all those nurses working up the road at Walton. I must remember to look out for it at the auctions.'

'No wonder you're so bloody rich,' Jim snorted. 'Always an eye for the main chance. And this lot's ended nicely for you, hasn't it?'

'Wait a couple of days, Jim, before we go out and celebrate. The job isn't over yet. Still a few loose ends to tie up.'

There was the mystery of Wilbur Lunt's trip to Philadelphia. Why had he lied and said he was in Vienna? And I had to find Nathan Lloyd before his hit-men found me. I was sure Vicenzio wouldn't be his only minder.

I thanked Jim then drove the Metro to my office where Geoffrey was very relieved to find both Mrs Molloy's vehicle and myself safe and sound.

'Good to see you back, boss,' he said with obvious sincerity. 'You're in the clear now then?'

I assured him I was. 'Do me a favour, Geoff. Run me up to my place to pick up the RAV4.'

'Sure thing, boss.'

We walked down to where his old BMW was parked.
'You got it back, then,' I said, as I climbed into the front
seat. I recalled my last ride in the vehicle, fleeing from
Leary and Morton through the streets of Bootle.

'Three days' parking I had to pay for.'

'Put it on your expenses.'

'Is everything boxed off now?'

'Almost.'

All except one important thing, I thought. The package in
Tommy McKale's safe. Somebody somewhere was missing
half a million pounds' worth of heroin and, sooner or later,
they would come looking for it.

He drove along Aigburth Road towards the city when I
remembered the diaries. They were also stowed away at
Tommy McKale's office.

'Can you make a small detour, Geoff? The Marina Health
and Leisure Centre.'

'McKale's old gym, you mean.' Geoff swung the BMW
round. 'I might have known he'd be involved some
where.'

'I couldn't have managed without him.' I told Geoffrey
about the day's events as we went along.

Tommy McKale was at Reception when I walked in
He greeted me heartily. 'You're a free man again, then?'

'And you and Big Alec as well, I take it?'

'No problem. I gave the Super the old Masonic hand
shake. Big Alec was his Grand Master last year.'

Saints preserve us, I thought.

'I suppose you've come for the books?'

'Certainly have, Tommy. I'm relying on them to wrap
this thing up.'

'I'll get them for you. Do you want the other as well?'

The heroin was the last thing I wanted. 'I'll leave that
for now if it's all right with you.'

Fifteen minutes later, Geoffrey and I were in the parking
lot at Waterloo Dock. The RAV4, black and gleaming

stood in its customary place. 'Glad to be back home, are you?' Geoff beamed.

'Certainly am.' I gathered up Michelle Lunt's diaries. 'I'll be in touch, Geoff. I take it everything's running all right in the flats?' It was. Giles at Livingstone Drive didn't appear to have noticed that his flat had been burgled.

'Shirley at Princes Avenue was asking about you again.'

'Tell her I'm away in South America, mountain climbing. I'm not due back till Christmas.' I didn't feel I could cope with any more woman trouble at the moment.

Geoffrey smiled. 'I'll tell her.'

'Thanks for everything, Geoff.' I walked inside and up to my flat. A pile of letters greeted me on the doormat, but most of them looked to be junk mail. I picked them all up and threw them on to my desk. They could wait until later.

I walked from room to room, getting the feel of the place; marking out my territory. I'd been away just five nights and I was glad to be home and free.

At some stage, I knew I should ring the radio station and inform them I was now available to do my programme again. That is, if they still wanted me after all the publicity. I reckoned it could wait another day.

I opened a bottle of Scrumpy Jack from the fridge and put a Larry Williams CD on the hi-fi for background noise. It seemed an appropriate choice of music. The man who sang *Bony Moronie* was ostensibly shot dead by the LA police, who objected to his thriving drugs and prostitution rackets.

I settled on to the settee and turned to the first page of Michelle Lunt's black and yellow Filofax, The Bee. I don't know what I expected to find but I hoped it would shed some light on her death.

The pages consisted of a series of typewritten sheets – copies, I imagined, of reports sent back to her Head Office, probably to Mr Swallow, and going back to when she first arrived at Livingstone Drive with Wilbur Lunt.

They didn't reveal much. From what I gathered, after a quick readthrough, she'd been part of a pretty straightforward operation. Lloyd had already been identified as a leading player on the Liverpool drug scene, which was the reason why Michelle had moved into Livingstone Drive, as Wilbur Lunt had told me.

Her task had been to gain Lloyd's confidence and infiltrate the gang by posing as a prospective purchaser. Once accepted, she was to set up a deal with them and, at the moment of transaction, let the cavalry move in and catch the villains bang to rights, swag in hand, just like in all good Gene Hackman movies.

So what had gone wrong?

Michelle Roberts had been playing a very dangerous game. If Lloyd and the gang had suspected her for even one moment, she was dead.

And she *was* dead. But by her own hand.

I checked the pages for July tenth to the sixteenth, the last week of her life, and found something very strange. The pages were blank. There was no mention of any appointment arranged with Lloyd for the morning of 16 July, as claimed by Wilbur Lunt. Nor had she recorded sending the package to Ruth Simpkin, nor receiving the heroin in the first place. Where had it come from?

One thing was certain. Somebody, somewhere, was missing that package of heroin, currently lying in Tommy McKale's safe, and it was a pretty safe bet they were going to come looking for it. You don't give up on half a million pounds that easily. The question was, would they come looking to me?

There was nothing more to be gleaned from the Filofax so I picked up Michelle's personal diary and turned to that same week in July.

This time I could hardly believe what I was reading. It was all in there. The diary told an astounding story of love, betrayals, the details of the drug deals and, ultimately, the story of Michelle Lunt's *murder*.

Chapter Thirty-three

Mon, 13 July. I had no need to worry. The money arrived today from Highland Shipping just as Wilbur said it would. Nobody could tell in a million years that the notes are forged. Certainly Nathan Lloyd won't know. Everything is set for the swap tomorrow. Wilbur's contacts in Manchester rang and he's arranged the sale of the heroin for Thursday afternoon. Wilbur's been moody again today, maybe the strain is getting to him, but it won't be long now before we're away. I love him so much.

I turned to the entry for Tuesday, 14 July.

Everything went perfectly with Nathan Lloyd. He and his two companions counted the money and never suspected a thing. They handed over the package quite happily. So now we have the heroin and on Thursday, Wilbur will exchange it for REAL *money and at night we set off for Vienna and our new life together.*

I struggled to make sense of this. Michelle was obviously so besotted with Wilbur Lunt that she'd allowed him to persuade her to dupe the drug cartel with the counterfeit notes. Then she'd double-crossed her bosses and planned to abscond with Wilbur and the proceeds of the heroin sale.

So how had she ended up dead? I read on and it all became horribly clear.

Wed, 15 July. I don't believe it. The most dreadful thing ever. This explains all Wilbur's strange moods of late. He told me today that he's going back to Courtney and the children!!!! He said he'd never wanted to marry me and he's leaving tomorrow for ever. I can't believe he could be so cruel. I fear he's been using me all this time just to get hold of the drugs and he's going to keep all of the money and there's nothing I can do. I can't tell the office that I've bought the heroin without their knowledge, and he knows it. I've burnt my boats.

But she obviously realised there was something she could do, because a later entry for the day read . . .

Wilbur went out this afternoon. While he was gone I took the plastic bag of heroin out of the Jiffy bag and replaced it with one filled with sugar. Then I posted the heroin to the only friend I can trust, Ruth Simpkin in Rhos on Sea. When Wilbur has left, I can collect it and perhaps I can sell it myself and use the money to start a new life abroad. I'd love to be there when the Manchester people find Wilbur is trying to take half a million pounds from them for a packet of Tate and Lyle. Perhaps they'll shoot him and it will serve him right. He's going there on his way to the airport. He's booked his flight to Philadelphia tomorrow – he showed me his ticket. I can't believe it has ended like this after I've loved him so and I thought he loved me. I've given up my career and my life for him and it's too late for me to turn back now. I feel desolate, totally desolate, but I must go on.

But she hadn't gone on. There was no entry for the next day because, on 16 July, Michelle Roberts had died at the end of a rope in my flat in Livingstone Drive.

Why?

I tried to imagine the possible scenarios. Lunt must have been frightened that Michelle could break down and confess all to her bosses, who would then go after him. Conversely, eager for revenge, she might tell Lloyd that Lunt had paid him with forged notes, whereupon the drug cartel would be on his trail.

From Wilbur Lunt's point of view, Michelle was a distinct liability and would be better out of the way. And why risk committing cold-blooded murder when you could arrange a foolproof suicide?

Jim Burroughs's theory could well be right. The pathologist had stated that Michelle had died in the afternoon when Wilbur was supposed to have flown off to Vienna. But nobody, to my knowledge, had ever questioned Wilbur's assertion that he had left the flat in the morning.

What if he had stayed until after lunch, slipped her the roofies then helped her hang herself?

My thoughts were interrupted by the ringing of the telephone. I picked up the receiver. 'Johnny Ace.' In the background I could hear street noises but nobody spoke. Then the call was cut.

Somebody was checking that I was in.

I thought of Lloyd and his hit-men. Already after me for interfering in their operation, they might now think that I had the heroin as well.

I ran into the bedroom and from beneath the bed I fetched a small baton similar to those used by the police. Within half an hour, the entryphone buzzed. I didn't answer it but I knew the caller would easily gain access.

In theory, entryphones are a security asset. If nobody's in the flat to release the catch, the caller can't get through the communal front door.

In practice, the caller rings all the flat bells until one of the residents answers. He then says 'Royal Mail' or 'Interflora' and the door is opened for him.

Videophones aren't much better, except that the caller

has to go to the expense and inconvenience of purchasing a uniform – but who is going to deny access to a smiling stranger with a peaked cap and a bunch of flowers in his hand?

And a sub-machine gun under his coat.

My caller didn't have the sub-machine gun. Just a small automatic pistol.

I had made up the bed to look as if I was asleep in it, then I'd hidden in the bathroom behind the door, which I left ajar.

I heard my visitor knock gently on my front door, then he inserted a strip of plastic beside the Yale lock and slowly edged the door open. I hadn't bothered with the mortise lock. No sense in making things difficult for him. I wanted to see what he looked like.

He crept through the door, shut it behind him and moved round the lounge. His footsteps padded through the corridor. He stopped in turn outside the kitchen and study then walked on. He was within inches of me at the other side of the bathroom door but he carried on to the open door of the bedroom.

The two shots that rang out startled me. I hadn't bargained for such swift and final action. Had I really been lying in that bed, I'd have been next in line for the Crematorium. That was probably why I hit him harder than I otherwise might have done. The baton caught him just below the temple and he was out for a good ten minutes.

I turned him over to look at his face. It was Nathan Lloyd himself.

By the time he came round, I had handcuffed his hands behind his back. Useful things to have, handcuffs. Hilary and I have used them a fair bit in the past. Luckily, these weren't cheap Soho sex toys but the real things.

I had also tied his ankles firmly together with a piece of old microphone wire, left over from The Cruzads days. The gun, I kept. I never knew when it might come in useful.

As I sat waiting for him to recover consciousness, a germ of an idea came into my mind. If it worked, I could be rid of Lloyd and Lunt and clear Michelle's name in one stroke.

'I suppose you know you've been double-crossed,' I told him when he finally came to. He winced – a quantity of blood was matting in his hair. 'Those were forged notes that Michelle Lunt gave you.'

I could tell by his expression, a mixture of rage and horror, that this was news to him.

'You were set up,' I went on, 'by Wilbur Lunt. And he's done a runner with your heroin. He killed the girl first, of course.'

I waited whilst Lloyd took this in. I think he was having a bit of trouble coming to grips with it all, so soon after his injury. Concussion can play strange tricks.

'I can get the heroin back for you,' I said.

He struggled a bit before answering. 'What's in it for you?'

I had to be careful here. If I said nothing, only justice, he'd suspect something. These people only thought in terms of money. 'A hundred grand,' I said. 'Take it or leave it.'

He didn't argue. He knew there was half a million pounds' worth of dope out there he might never see again, and I guessed his chums in the drug cartel would not be too pleased to learn he'd parted with it for a bundle of fake notes. Colombians were not noted for their mercy. I was giving him the chance to save his skin or face serious retribution.

Cheap at twice the price.

'Be at Violet Parker's house at six o'clock tomorrow night. I'll be there with the package. Have the money with you and make sure the notes are real. If anything happens to me before then, you'll never find the heroin. Right?'

He nodded.

I knew, of course, that he'd bring his henchmen with him, with every intention of killing me as soon as they got their hands on the heroin.

Only, I didn't intend to be there myself.

I released his bonds and sent him on his way, telling him I was keeping his gun to defray the cost of replacing the duvet.

I then set in motion the second part of my Grand Scheme.

I dialled the London number at which I had reached Wilbur Lunt. I was banking on the fact that he no longer regarded me as a threat after our little chat in the park, and hoped he had not bothered to change it.

I was in luck. There was that deep American accent. 'Wilbur Lunt.'

'Wilbur, it's Johnny Ace here,' I boomed cheerily. 'How are you?'

He sounded slightly wary. 'Fine. How are *you*, Johnny? Sorted your problem out?'

'Yes, I'm back in Liverpool and in the clear now. That bent copper Leary confessed all and topped himself.'

'All?' I could see he was struggling to work out if his name could have crept into the confession. Evidently not, because he answered more cheerfully: 'That's good news.'

'And I have more good news. For you.'

'Me?'

'Yes. We found a parcel hidden under the floorboards of your old flat. The electrician was checking some wires and he came across it. It had Michelle's writing on the front so I thought you ought to have it.'

This time he could hardly keep the eager anticipation from his voice. 'Do you know what's in it?'

'No, it's well sealed. Feels soft, though – maybe jewellery wrapped in cotton wool. Anyway, I thought I'd let you know.'

I waited, knowing he was considering the implications of my story.

When I'd rung Wilbur's contact in Manchester earlier in the week, he was still expecting a delivery so my guess was that, at the last minute, Wilbur had discovered that someone had substituted sugar for heroin and not kept the appointment.

I could imagine his rage on that Thursday, arriving in Manchester, with his flight to Philadelphia booked, and realising he'd been had. He would know Michelle had had something to do with it, but it was too late to ask her. He'd left her at the flat, hanging at the end of a rope.

The odds were, the heroin was hidden somewhere in the flat but he daren't go back and look.

Unless . . . that might be why he was back in London, trying to find that parcel. I remembered how he'd insisted on taking a photo of the house when I met him that first time at Livingstone Drive. Perhaps he'd already sent someone up there with the photo as a guide. Maybe Giles had had other 'burglaries'.

No wonder Leary had wanted the case closed quickly, knowing half a million pounds' worth of heroin could have been in there. If murder had been suspected and his colleagues had searched the room and found the drug, the balloon would have gone up.

'When can I pick it up?' Wilbur Lunt sounded almost too eager.

I gave him Violet Parker's address in Kirkdale. 'It's my girlfriend's house but I'm going there after the match. Can you make it at six o'clock?'

He said he'd be there. He could hardly keep the delight out of his voice. I could imagine him racing off to his nearest travel agent and booking the next available plane on Saturday night, back to Philadelphia and Courtney.

But I had a strong suspicion he'd never make the flight.

Chapter Thirty-four

My third, and final call that night was to Paulette Cope. I had thought about ringing Mr Swallow direct but I'd met Paulette so I felt it would be easier to talk to her and leave her to organise things with her department.

She was amazed at my story. How Michelle had realised Wilbur Lunt had become involved with the drugs gang that she was investigating, and how she had managed to rescue a valuable quantity of heroin from their clutches, despite their constant surveillance, before she was cruelly murdered by the man she thought had loved her.

I was almost in tears at the end of my narrative. If only Verdi had been alive, he could have made it into a wonderful opera.

'Where is the heroin now?' asked Paulette.

'Locked away in a safe place, ready for your collection.' I gave her the address of the Marina Health and Leisure Centre. The Manchester Connection would never get their 'stuff' now.

I told her that the protagonists in the affair were meeting at six o'clock at this address in Kirkdale, Liverpool and perhaps she could arrange a team of officers to arrest them.

I gave her all the details and left her to it.

I was quite exhausted after all this. I ran a hot bath full of Hilary's oils and relaxed under the bubbles for an hour. I had my first shave in days and felt a million years younger.

Then I microwaved a Marks & Spencer readymade meal,

opened a bottle of wine, stuck Mozart's *Jupiter Symphony* on the hi-fi, very relaxing, and I was almost asleep before any of them were finished. By ten I was in bed.

The next morning, I had more phone calls to make. I rang Jim Burroughs and told him about my plan. 'I don't want you to say anything to your lot,' I said. 'Let Michelle's people deal with this. It's their show, and if things pan out like I intend, it could get messy.'

'You're taking some chance there,' he said. 'I haven't heard a word of what you've just told me, OK?'

I rang my boss at the radio station and managed to convince him I hadn't turned into another Ronnie Kray.

'Shady's been doing very well with your show,' he said. 'He reads some nice poetry. The listeners like it.'

'Bollocks,' I said. 'He gets his auntie in Garston to ring in. Nobody else listens.'

'And he plays singers people have heard of, like Andy Williams and Steve Harley.'

'Middle of the road pap,' I snorted. 'I'll be back on Monday. The ratings don't lie.'

I got hold of Maria to find she was about to leave for a two-day break. 'I was hoping I might see you this weekend,' I said, once I'd explained that all my troubles had been sorted and I was back in harness again.

'Oh Johnny, I'm so sorry. I've promised to take Robin down to London for the weekend. We've been given tickets for *Miss Saigon* tonight.'

There wasn't much I could say. We arranged to go out on Wednesday evening for a meal and I said I'd pick her up at eight. At least we were back together again, and hopefully the Linda incident would be forgotten.

I rang Hilary. She'd just come in from a night-shift and was about to go to bed. 'I'm on duty again tonight,' she said. 'If only you'd told me but it's too late to swap now.'

She promised to come round the following evening and

stay the night. 'I hope you're feeling refreshed,' she said coyly.

With another seven hours to wait before the 'Kirkdale Siege', I decided to drive up to Nelson to bring Roly home and also acquaint Linda with the outcome of the case.

I rang her to make sure she'd be in, but when I arrived at Nelson, there was a man with her in the house.

'Oh Johnny, this is Peter,' she said. A slight, balding man with bushy eyebrows and a friendly smile stood up from the settee and shook my hand. He looked about forty and wore cavalry twill trousers, two decades after they had gone out of fashion.

'Pleased to meet you,' he said. 'I've heard a lot about you.'

Peter looked perfect for Linda. Safe and reliable. Roly, I noticed, kept his distance. He was a dog who preferred a bit of excitement. He'd get that with me, sure enough.

We left Peter watching the racing on Channel Four and Linda and I went into the kitchen, where I told her all that had happened since I'd left her house the previous morning.

Well. Nearly all.

I saw no point in telling her that her sister had pulled off a half-a-million-pound scam right under the noses of a gang of ruthless international drug dealers and the Home Office, or whatever department it was she ultimately worked for. Why ruin her illusions?

But I did break it to her that Wilbur Lunt had murdered her sister. I think people feel less disturbed about murder. Suicide always implies some neglect on the part of loved ones.

'Wilbur was running out on her,' I explained grimly. 'Going back to his family in Philadelphia. He was involved in some fiddle and was frightened she'd report him so he killed her.'

'Poor Shelley.' She started to sob so I squeezed her

shoulder then went back to join Peter in the lounge. I felt she needed a few minutes to grieve on her own. Peter and I exchanged pleasantries about the weather, holidays and the forthcoming football season. He was a Burnley fan. I felt he fitted in well in this picture of domesticity.

Linda eventually came back into the room, wiping her eyes on a tea towel. 'She did well, our Shelley, didn't she, managing to rescue the heroin from those people? And then she gets killed.' Her voice was still trembly.

'She was a hero,' I said.

'You've been so good to me, Johnny, and you've done brilliantly solving the case. Tell me how much I owe you and I'll settle up with you now.'

'Nonsense, you've already paid me quite enough. I should pay *you* for helping *me*.'

She tried to insist but I was adamant and eventually she gave in.

'To think that less than a month ago, I hadn't heard from our Shelley for years and now all this has happened.'

'At least she's at peace now.' It sounded trite but what else do people say in those circumstances?

'She deserved better than that Wilbur.'

I couldn't argue with that. Thinking about Wilbur reminded me that I had to get back to Liverpool. Paulette Cope was phoning me at seven to let me know how the arrests had gone.

I was hoping there wouldn't be any.

I said goodbye to Peter, and Linda walked with us to the RAV4. ''Bye, Roly,' she said, patting his rough brown coat. 'Come and see me again.' He licked her face.

I gestured towards the house. 'Peter's very nice,' I said. 'You want to stick with him.'

She gave a contented smile. 'Thanks for everything, Johnny. It didn't start out the happiest of occasions but I've really enjoyed our, what shall I call it, adventure?'

As good a word as any, I thought.

'And I'm really sorry about your girlfriend.' She tried to look it, but her hazel eyes smiled mischievously.

'I'm seeing Maria next week. I think it might be all right.'

She threw her arms around me and kissed me noisily. 'Don't forget me,' she said.

'Invite me to the wedding,' I replied, and climbed into the car.

At six o'clock, I was back in the flat, pacing up and down and wondering what was happening at Violet Parker's house. Had everyone turned up? Had it all gone according to plan – *my* plan?

I was soon to find out.

Paulette Cope phoned promptly at seven. 'It all went terribly wrong,' she told me immediately. 'Our people managed to open the front door of the house as you suggested, and were all in place surrounding the house well before six o'clock.'

A minute or two after the hour struck, two sets of men had arrived, almost simultaneously. There were six of them altogether, and they had hardly entered the house before shooting broke out.

'By the time our chaps could reach them,' said Paulette, 'five of the men were dead.'

I smiled with relief. My plan had worked admirably. I'd predicted that Lunt and Lloyd would each have brought a couple of minders, which would account for the total number who showed up.

I'd also banked on a gun battle when Lunt and Lloyd faced each other and I hadn't been wrong.

'Who's the lucky survivor?' I asked.

'You might guess,' she said, grimly. 'Wilbur Lunt.'

Epilogue

I ascertained where Lunt had been taken and, after thanking Paulette for her assistance, I drove over to Walton Hospital, Roly in the back of the car, and blagged my way into the Intensive Care Ward.

'He has internal injuries and he's lost a lot of blood,' said the sister, leading me down the corridor. 'He shouldn't really be having visitors but, I suppose, as you're family . . .'

I noticed a couple of plainclothes men by the door as we swept inside the ward. She warned me not to stay with him too long. I didn't intend to.

Wilbur Lunt looked very different from the smart businessman I had first encountered at Livingstone Drive and again just three days ago in London.

He was wired up to various bags and bottles, tubes were inserted into various orifices and he didn't look a good bet for a telegram from the Queen.

'They think I'm your brother,' I told him when he asked in a rasping whisper, how I'd got in. I think he was afraid I was going to disconnect his life-support machine and the idea did occur to me although, by the state of him, I didn't think I'd need to.

'You might as well tell me everything,' I said. 'You're going to croak any minute.' Don't sugar the pill, Johnny. 'Just tell me. Why did you kill Michelle?'

Wilbur didn't argue. I think he'd already realised he was on his way out and maybe he was glad to have someone to confess to.

'Simple. She threatened to tell my wife of our affair. I couldn't let that happen.'

So it wasn't fear of retribution from Lloyd and the mob, nor was it to stop Michelle confessing to the police. Michelle Lunt had been murdered because Wilbur Lunt did not want to risk losing his wife and family.

In the end, it wasn't down to money at all. Just love. Unfortunately for Michelle Lunt, she'd loved the wrong man.

Wilbur continued, his voice getting weaker by the second. 'I pretended to make it up with her, told her I'd stay and slipped a couple of Rohypnol tablets into her drink.' So Tim Burroughs had been spot on.

'Then we started to make love. We often played games when we had sex. Michelle was very adventurous in that direction. We'd tie one another up, that sort of thing. Sometimes, we pretended to strangle each other.

'It was easy for me to fix the rope and suggest to Michelle that she put her head in the noose. I let her do it all herself. Then I asked her to tighten it. That was when I told her I wasn't staying with her after all, and the best thing she could do was kill herself. I threatened her – said I'd inform her superiors that she'd kept the heroin. She would be disgraced, end up in prison, and wasn't it simply better to end it all? And she did. Like a good little girl.'

And, as he said these words, Wilbur Lunt smiled. I was sickened and felt like thumping him, until I suddenly noticed that his smile was like a rictus. It had frozen on his face.

Maybe it hadn't been the thought of Michelle swinging at the end of a rope that had amused him. Maybe he'd seen angels coming to greet him. Whatever. Wilbur Lunt certainly wouldn't be smiling again.

Machines started bleeping and nurses came racing in. I edged quietly away. Poor Courtney, I thought illogically. And the kids. He'll never come to them now. But Courtney

was probably well rid of him. He'd have shit on her too in
the end.

I called in on Jim Burroughs on the way home and filled
him in on the final details.

'Christ, you pulled some stroke there,' he said. 'Taking
a chance, weren't you, that both lots would show up?'

'No, it was odds on they would, Jim. It's amazing how
naked greed can cloud a person's judgement.'

'I see you've still got that animal with you.' He eyed
Roly warily. My dog was gnawing peacefully on one of
Jim's slippers.

'I think he's adopted me.'

Jim returned to the subject of what I now thought of as
the 'Kirkdale Massacre'. 'All dead, you say?'

'Yes. Great, isn't it? No contract out on me any more.
I can walk the streets with equanimity – and think of the
taxpayers' money I've saved. How much does it cost to
keep the buggers in prison these days? I know it's more
than the Ritz.'

'Your view of justice is more like the Wild West,'
grumbled Jim.

'What's happening with the job?' I asked him. 'Are you
staying or what?'

'Still not made my mind up.'

'I told you I was thinking about setting up in the investigations business – properly, with an office in town and
all that, didn't I? How would you like to be a partner?'

'I could be interested,' he said, noncommittally.

'You'd be allowed to play in The Chocolate Lavatory
on your nights off.'

'Now you're tempting me.'

'Have a muse,' I said. 'I'll call in next week and we'll
talk about it then.'

I drove back home, parked the car and climbed out.
Somehow, I didn't feel like going up to my empty flat.
This, of course, was the downside of having two girlfriends.

If I had the freedom to do whatever I wanted, then they each must expect similar rights and there would be times I might want to see them and neither would be available.

So here we were, it was a Saturday night and I should have been out enjoying myself. I'd lots to celebrate. Instead, the case was over, I'd got my freedom again and I was all on my own.

Er . . . not quite on my own.

Roly jumped out of the back seat and stood beside me, wagging his stump eagerly. In his mouth he held his lead.

I smiled. 'Fancy a walk do you, son?' He barked and I took it to mean yes. I clipped his lead on and we walked up towards the Pier Head and right along until we came to the Albert Dock.

We stopped beside the rails looking out to the river, across to Birkenhead. On the skyline was the outline of Bidston Mill.

Only three weeks had passed since Michelle Lunt's body was found hanging in Livingstone Drive, but it felt like a year.

I resolved to ring Ruth Simpkin and put her in the picture, probably with the same story I had fed to Linda. She had, after all, been Michelle's best friend.

I also owed Tommy McKale. Without him and Big Alec, I'd never have found Michelle's books. The whole investigation had turned on that discovery. Knowing that Tommy wouldn't accept money, I'd think of something decent to buy him. Perhaps an antique or a painting at one of the auctions.

Talking of which, I wondered if I'd get Violet Parker's Kirkdale house. That would hold a certain piquancy, I felt.

Drops of rain started to fall and a chilly wind was blowing across the brown waters of the Mersey. Typical August weather.

In a week's time, the football season was starting and I'd be back at Goodison Park in my usual seat.

'Come on, Roly,' I said, patting him on his rough brown coat. 'Time to go home. We'll get a bag of chips on the way, eh?' He turned round to look up at me.

And he smiled.

Murmuring the Judges

Quintin Jardine

In Edinburgh's old Parliament House, an armed robbery trial is about to take a macabre turn. While the lawyers tussle over the evidence, the judge suddenly collapses in mortal agony – the victim of an apparent heart attack.

For Deputy Chief Constable Bob Skinner, with his life finally back on track after the near-collapse of his marriage, the last thing he needs is to be faced with the most baffling case of his career. But as the wave of brutal robberies continues, it emerges that Lord Archergait's death may have been murder – and he's not the only judge whose life is in danger.

With a gang of ruthless killers still at large, it's down to Skinner to piece together a puzzle of sinister complexity.

'Deplorably readable' *Guardian*

'Captures Edinburgh beautifully' *Edinburgh Evening News*

'Remarkably assured' *New York Times*

0 7472 5962 3

HEADLINE

Night Mares

Manda Scott

Dr Nina Crawford – driven, dedicated, a survivor – runs Glasgow University's prestigious veterinary hospital. But she's losing her grip – on her operating theatre, on her surgeon's skills, and on her mind. Horses are dying of the highly infectious *E. Coli*, and nothing she can do can control it. Now she is spiralling into the depths that led her, years before, to attempt suicide.

Kellen Stewart is Nina's friend and therapist and when her horse needs emergency surgery she is suddenly part of Nina's tragic dilemma. And soon it becomes clear that it's not only horses' lives that are being threatened . . .

'Even more accomplished than the acclaimed *Hen's Teeth*' *Sunday Telegraph*

'Gripping and topical' *Good Housekeeping*

'A familiar landscape warps into terror . . . something epic in this struggle between horse and human . . . Horses, sex and death create [a] potent cocktail' Helen Dunmore, *The Times*

0 7472 5880 5

HEADLINE